the RED RIBBON

PEPPER BASHAM

BARBOUR BOOKS
An Imprint of Barbour Publishing, Inc.

Published by Barbour Books, an imprint of Barbour Publishing, Inc., 1810 Barbour Drive, Uhrichsville, Ohio 44683, www.barbourbooks.com

Our mission is to inspire the world with the life-changing message of the Bible.

ecpa Member of the
Evangelical Christian
Publishers Association

Printed in the United States of America.

PRAISE FOR THE RED RIBBON

"The tragic history of a little-known small-town is honored and infused with hope in *The Red Ribbon*. Pepper Basham's inviting storytelling will challenge the way readers view mountain culture, clans, feuds, sparkin', and kisses."

–Beth Erin, Faithfully Bookish

"Pepper Basham brings characters to life like few authors I know. She drew me in, made me care about her story and the characters living on the page."

–Mary Connealy, author of the bestselling *Woman of Sunlight*

"Every book from Pepper Basham gets better and better, and this gripping tale drew me in from the first page. Basham brings the Appalachian Mountains to life with authentic turns of phrase, heart-thumping danger, and a romance so sweet you may just swoon."

–Misty M. Beller, *USA Today* bestselling author of the Hearts of Montana Series

"It wouldn't be a Basham book without a perfect mix of heart fluttering kisses and Appalachian shenanigans, and *The Red Ribbon* delivers on both. With a clever and gutsy heroine, an industrious and devoted hero, a heap of scoundrels, and a mess of quirky characters, *The Red Ribbon* unravels the true story of the Hillsville Courthouse Massacre and will keep readers racing through the pages until they reach the thrilling conclusion."

–Lynn H. Blackburn, award-winning, bestselling author of the Dive Team Investigations series

"With red ribbons, Pepper Basham offers readers a gift of strong characters, vivid setting, and a plot that will engage. Step back to the turn of the century in Appalachia, when feuds were real and long-standing. Work with the heroine to bridge the divide between the factions while trying to stay alive and wrestle with her past. Reach for the future alongside her. . .and learn with her that kissing can be mighty fun. This book is filled with heart, hope, and history. Highly recommended to readers who love their historical romance with a layer of suspense."

–Cara Putman, bestselling and award-winning author

Dedication

To the folks in my hometown of Carroll County, Virginia
For the many told and untold stories we will never know

Cast of Characters

Ava Burcham - orphaned at twelve when her father was murdered and her mother and brother died shortly after. Best friends with Jeremiah Sutphin.

Jeremiah Sutphin - carpenter and school friend of Ava Burcham, though Jeremiah has a bit more than "friend" on the mind when it comes to Ava.

Granny Burcham - Ava's grandmother and only living relative. Though a recluse, she's a voice of wisdom and humor.

Mr. & Mrs. Temple - the couple who took Ava in after her family died. Mrs. Temple taught Ava how to sew, and Ava works at the Temples' Alteration shop in Fancy Gap.

Abraham & Tucker Burcham - Ava's deceased father and brother.

Ellis & Jennie Sutphin - Ellis is Jeremiah's cousin and close friend. Jennie is Ellis's wife.

The Allens & their crew

Floyd Allen - patriarch of the Allen family and known for his quick temper. A local businessman and farmer, Floyd also held various law offices during his lifetime.

Sid Allen - Floyd's brother, and shopkeeper of a popular mercantile in Fancy Gap. Sid was also said to have had a temper, but not one as infamous as his older brother.

Wesley & Sidna Edwards - Floyd and Sid's nephews by their sister, Alverta. When Alverta's husband died prematurely, Floyd became a father figure to the boys. Sidna was named after his uncle.

Garland Allen - local preacher, brother of Floyd and Sid Allen.

Claude Allen - son of Floyd Allen.

Victor Allen - son of Floyd Allen.

The Courthouse Clan

Sheriff Lew Webb - high sheriff of Carroll County who took office in January 1912 after being a deputy for many years.

Sheriff Blankenship - resigning sheriff, left office in December 1911.

Dexter Goad - county clerk of Carroll County and known rival of the Allens due to political differences and some unfriendly history.

William Foster - Commonwealth attorney for Carroll County and another perceived rival of the Allens.

Casper Norris - deputy of Carroll County and acquaintance of Jeremiah.

Pink Samuels - deputy of Carroll County and one of the main lawmen involved in the Allens' story.

Peter Easter - referred to as "Easter" in the story, was "deputized" to help Pink Samuels bring the Edwards boys from North Carolina to Hillsville for trial.

Judge Thornton Massie - respected judge of Carroll County and the region around it. He wanted to ensure justice and do so peacefully.

William Baldwin - lead of the Baldwin-Felts Detective Agency.

Sheriff Bud Easter - replaced Sheriff Webb after the courthouse shooting.

Others

Keen Gentry - local whose reputation isn't the best.

Mooney Childers, Luther, and Martin - "coworkers" of Keen Gentry

Zeb Daniels - one of the Daniel clan—a local group known to be dangerous moonshiners. Zeb is also working with Keen Gentry.

Tom Hall - local hotel owner in Hillsville, Virginia.

Joe Creed - local boy and former schoolmate of Jeremiah and Ava. His mama is Elmira and his sister is Sadie.

Elmer Williams - older local man and friend to Jeremiah.

Judge Bolen - Floyd Allen's lawyer and friend.

Doc Nuckolls - local doctor, pharmacist, and coroner.

Maude Iroler - local girl and former girlfriend of Wesley Edwards.

Rebekah McCraw - local girl and girlfriend to Will Thomas (Wesley Edwards kissing her started the whole mess).

Will Thomas - local boy and rival to Wesley & Sidna Edwards, especially when Wesley kisses Will's girlfriend.
Elsie Combs (and the Combs family, Callie Mae, Laura Alice, Ezra & Rosie) - friends to Ava.

Chapter One

If you're gonna court trouble,
you're bound to find a marriage of misery.
Granny Burcham

December 1911

The coming dusk cast gray shadows across the box-shaped build-ings of Main Street, Hillsville, as Ava Burcham kept a vigilant watch toward Beaver Dam Road. The chill of the December evening slipped beneath the collar of her coat, inciting a shiver, but she shook it off. With a noiseless advance, she slid a few steps farther down the street toward the north of town, weaving in and out of shadows cast by the hodgepodge of rectangular buildings.

For three months, whenever she'd come to town, she'd kept watch on the events that took place at this particular corner. She'd finally narrowed down the peculiar events to a specific day. Thursdays. A young boy carrying a crate would run up to a clump of bushes, pause a moment at the edge, and then run off in the opposite direction, his crate much less cumbersome than before.

Clutching the strap of her ever-present satchel, Ava slid behind a tree as a dark figure appeared on horseback from Beaver Dam Road. She'd never gotten this close to the rider before, but he'd come every single time about an hour after the boy's drop-off. If Ava guessed right, it was an exchange for liquor, likely the illegal sort, from the way they were behaving. She tugged her coat closer around her shoulders. With one good look at the man on horseback, enough to identify him, she could turn him into the law, but they weren't likely to believe her with-out more to go on than vague accusations.

Especially from the likes of her.

The man slid from his horse and approached the bushes. Ava moved a little closer, carefully keeping to the shadows. His gait looked

9

familiar and there was something about the way he wore his fedora, low, nearly covering his eyes. If he turned toward the fading sunlight just a bit, she'd glimpse his face.

The fewer illegal moonshiners in Carroll County, the better.

Just as the man turned from his crouched position by the bush, someone bumped into her, nearly toppling her to the ground. With a quick pivot, she faced a young man not much taller than herself.

A dark handkerchief hid half his face, and the low tilt of his derby concealed the shade of his hair, but a slight hint of blond curled at his collar.

He held the strap of Ava's satchel in one hand and attempted to pull it plumb off her shoulders, the strap jerking her neck.

"Let go, and there won't be no trouble."

She jerked back, loosening his grip on her satchel and sending him a little off-balance. "It ain't yours to take."

He froze, blinking a few times at her refusal, as if he wasn't quite sure what to do next, so she cast a glance toward the rider. He and his horse were disappearing into the woods. Shoot fire! She'd missed the whole exchange.

She turned her full fury on the rascal who not only wanted to steal her satchel but blew her opportunity.

"Give me your money, and I'll let you go without any harm," her assailant demanded, his voice hitching up into a higher pitch.

Was this thief even old enough to shave? "I don't have any money for you to take." She smacked at his hand on her satchel strap hard enough to sting her own fingers. "So you might as well let loose and go on."

The young man proved stronger than she'd calculated, because with another twist he pulled the satchel off her shoulder, nearly decapitating her. Without a pause, he set off at a run up the street, his hand digging into her bag.

Oh no he didn't!

She chased after him, kicking at her skirts, her voice in full working order. "Thief! Thief!"

With a glance back as he turned beside the hotel, the thief's hat flew off, revealing a pale face and blond, spindly curls.

"Joe Creed!"

As if called by a mother's reprimand, the boy slid to a stop. He turned, slowly, pulling a fistful of ribbons from her satchel, half of them red, since most gals seemed to prefer more dainty colors. "What—"

"Your mama would be horrified if she knew you're the one who's been goin' around stealing women's bags all over town."

"You ain't got nothin' in here but ribbons and lace." He sent a look of absolute disgust down at the colorful array streaming between his fingers.

"Lucky me, I'd say." Ava drew up to his side, trying to catch her breath. "I'm a seamstress, not an heiress, Joe Creed." She jerked the satchel out of his hands. "And what on earth are you doin' thievin'? This ain't like you."

His chin tilted upward with the usual combination of mountain pride and youthful arrogance. Clearly not leavin' much room for intelligence at the moment.

He refused to answer.

"You just wait until your mama finds out about—"

Before she could finish her sentence, Joe pulled a pistol from inside his jacket and pointed it toward her. "My mama ain't got nothin' to do with this. And I want your money, Ava. I know you got some." The face of her old schoolmate hardened as he turned the gun toward her. Some dark mood fell over his expression, dulling his eyes, drawing his mouth tight. She knew that look. Had lived with it for a good portion of her childhood. But at least Joe's eyes held a little bit of sense. Something Ava's mama rarely had.

Well, she'd attempt to appeal to the sense. "Joe, why don't you come with me to Mr. Temple and see if he has some extra—"

"Speakin' of the Temples..." His gaze trailed down to her bag. "I've heard tell from my mama what money you make sewin' at their shop. One of the best sewin' gals I'm told." He slid a step closer, one golden brow raised in challenge. "I bet you ain't come all the way up to town without some of it on you, so, if you don't want trouble, you'll hand it over."

"Have you been the one all this time?" Maybe a little distraction could get him to lower that revolver. "The thief goin' around stealing womenfolk's belongings?" Ava pinched her fingers around her satchel strap to keep them from quivering. "Why on earth would you do somethin' like that, Joe?"

"Best that you don't know all the reasons." He grabbed her wrist and yanked her toward him with more force than she'd expected. "I won't ask again, Ava." The youthful lilt of his voice dropped to a warning growl. "I got places to be, and your money's gonna help me get there. Now."

"Whatever you've got yourself into, this ain't the way to solve it." Ava pulled against his hold, glancing behind her toward the street, a sliver of fear branching like ice through her chest. Maybe, if someone had heard her yell, they'd come looking. She just needed a little more time. "If you really need help, I know there are folks—"

"There ain't no folks to help. Not now. I got to get the money on my own and fast." He waved the gun as he spoke, his lack of care with the weapon sending a tremor up Ava's spine. Desperation and inexperience weren't good company. "There ain't no other way."

"Put down the gun, Joe, and I'll give you the money." Ava moved her hands to the satchel, fingering the secret pocket she'd sewn into the side to hold her cash. " 'Cause if anyone sees you pointing that gun at me, you'll get into a heap more trouble than just thievery."

"Won't matter if I don't set things right."

Ava's fumbling paused, and she searched his face. "Are you beholden to somebody?"

"Stop talkin' and get the money."

"Who is it? The Hawkses? The Allens? Daniels?" Was he part of the liquor run? Had he gotten caught up in it like so many others in these parts? "Maybe you can talk to the law and—"

His laugh took a dark turn. "Ain't you lived in this place long enough to know most of the law is connected with one of them families?" He leveled the revolver on her again. "Stop talkin' and get me that money so we can both get on with our business."

A sliver of fire rose through her chest in rebellion against his threat. "I'll give it to you when you lower that gun, else you'll have to either shoot me or try to take my satchel back one-handed." She narrowed her eyes at him in hopes of hiding her fear. "And, if you recollect, Joe

Creed, I don't hit like a girl."

His brows shot north, her reference to an unexpected brawl with a school bully reflecting in his eyes. She attempted to keep her breathing steady. A sudden vision bled past the memory of the school brawl—Mama in the same position as Joe, gun outstretched, eyes wild, just before pulling the trigger. Ava's shoulder twinged, as if she felt the bullet graze over her skin once again.

Oh, how she wished Tucker hadn't taken that death shot for her.

After a stare which lasted for nigh eternity, Joe released a sigh and began lowering the pistol. "Fine. Now get to it."

Ava tugged five dollars from her secret pocket, payment for two shirtwaists and a skirt she'd mended. Five whole dollars.

"Joe Creed. You put that gun down, boy."

A gravelly voice boomed through the dusk from the direction of Main Street. Joe jerked from the unexpected intrusion, firing his pistol. Ava froze, and something like ice trailed beneath her skin toward her heart as she waited for the sting of the bullet to strike. Joe's bottom lip dropped and he stared at her as if he was waiting for the same thing.

She turned to see sheriff-elect Lewis Webb marching toward them, his gray brows drawn together. "See, that's the trouble with guns, boy. Half those that got 'em don't know how to use 'em."

Joe's hand trembled as he looked from his gun to Ava and back to the sheriff. Then, with a shake of his head, he dropped the gun and set off at a sprint down the road.

Ava released her stilled breath on a quiver.

"Well, blast it all." Sheriff Webb came to a stop beside Ava, his height almost matching her own. With a narrow-eyed look in her direction, he called behind him, "Go on and get 'im, Casp. We've been after some hard evidence for a few weeks now, and I reckon Miss Burcham's gone and found us some."

"You got it, Sheriff." Newly appointed Deputy Casper Norris ran around the other side of Ava and pulled his revolver from his belt holster.

"For heaven's sake, put your gun away, Casper." He rolled his eyes heavenward. "That boy's more scared mouse than hungry mountain lion."

Casper, nearly ten years Ava's senior, sent the sheriff a wrinkled frown before stashing his revolver back in the holster and dashing off in Joe's direction.

There wasn't a holster in sight on the sheriff, but Ava had heard he rarely carried a gun. Folks said he preferred talking through disputes, if possible, and since he'd been a deputy for years and years before being elected sheriff, the notion must have worked for him more than not.

"Now, as for you, young lady. . ."

Ava turned her gaze slowly from Casper's retreating form to Sheriff Webb, whose kind smile usually greeted her on the streets of Hillsville. Not this day. A frown crinkled beneath his graying moustache. "How many times have I told you that it ain't befittin' a lady to walk around town by herself after dark?"

Ava looked up at the starry sky, the faintest hint of pink still visible from the fading sunset.

"Don't you dare say it ain't dark yet." He interrupted her thoughts before she could even voice them. "You know exactly what I mean. What does this make, Miss Burcham? The third time in as many months?"

Plus a few more. . .but he hadn't caught her for those. "Sheriff, I know there's an exchange of something illegal going on over near—"

"I know, Miss Burcham. I know." He rested his hands on his hips, his sturdy frame and swath of thick hair giving him a more youthful appearance than his sixty-some years. "You've mentioned it to me on several occasions since I was elected, and I have my boys investigatin' your claims as they're hired and *trained* to do." One of his bushy brows rose to send his point home.

After nearly having her satchel stolen, being shot, *and* losing the chance to figure out who the man was on the horse, Ava stifled the uncustomary desire to burst into tears. Though she couldn't quite stop her nose from tingling a warning. "But I can help. They won't suspect me of trying to uncover blockade whiskey."

"Ava." He ran a palm over his beard, releasing a rush of air from his nose. "We can't stop illegal moonshinin'. Too many people rely on it as a way of life. Too many folks know how to keep quiet and will do so for the good of their families." His pale gaze steadied on hers. "This ain't a battle you're equipped to win, girl."

"But. . ." She shuffled a step closer to him. "If we can just stop one, then it could help dozens. Save families. Children."

"Ava." His expression softened with his voice. "Puttin' yourself in danger like this ain't gonna bring them back."

She stared up into the face of the kindhearted man, barely clinging to the tears stinging a rim around her eyes. What wouldn't she give to bring her father back? Her brother? Why had God allowed her to survive and yet taken her entire family away? Her hand went to her shoulder where a scar marked a half-moon shape and left an invisible gash upon her heart.

"I have to try."

He released a long sigh before gesturing with his chin back toward the street. "Try during daylight hours when I don't have to find someone to escort you home."

"I can get home—"

"No." He raised a palm, then took her arm and tugged her back toward the faint lights of Main Street. "I just so happened to see someone who's headin' toward Fancy Gap and can escort you all the way."

"I am perfectly capable of taking care of—"

"And you're capable of letting someone drive you the two hours it'll take for you to get to the Temples'."

They turned the corner of the Childers Hotel onto the dirt lane of Main Street, the thoroughfare ridged from a day's supply of wagon wheels and horses' hooves. A few stray lanterns from the remaining shops still lit the way past the drugstore, courthouse, and bank. The memory of Joe's gun misfiring erupted another set of shivers over her skin.

"It ain't enough that you nearly got shot, but you're cold, besides," Sheriff Webb grumbled. "It's a good thing your friend came into town late for supplies so he can see you home."

Ava's feet slowed to a stop and she closed her eyes. *Oh Lord, please don't let it be—*

"Jeremiah Sutphin!" Sheriff Webb called, guiding Ava closer to the mercantile and the familiar silhouette of her best friend as he tossed another piece of lumber in the back of his wagon.

Of all the people to find out about her little personal blockade whiskey investigation, not to mention run-in with Joe and his pistol, Jeremiah was the worst. How many times had he already tried to convince her to stop?

And she'd promised she'd try.

Twice.

Jeremiah's dark gaze traveled from Sheriff Webb's face to fasten on Ava's. His look of concern took a downward tilt into an expression that reminded Ava of Mrs. Temple's bloodhound on a grumpy day.

"Sheriff." Jeremiah raised a brow. "Ava."

"Miss Burcham is needing an escort to the Temples' this evenin'. I suspect you're headin' that way?"

The faintest twitch at Jeremiah's lips softened the disapproving frown. "I am."

Sheriff Webb turned to Ava, giving her arm a gentle squeeze. "Stop courtin' trouble, girl. Ain't you had a bellyful already?"

Her shoulders slumped from the immediate struggle between fighting against the illegal whiskey that led to her daddy's death and the sliver of sense that urged her to move on. But how could she? She carried the weight of her whole family.

He gave her a little nudge toward Jeremiah, but she turned, reaching into her satchel for her discarded dollars, before pressing them into the sheriff's palm. "You'll see Joe gets this, won't you?"

Sheriff Webb looked up from his palm with wide eyes.

"Somethin' dark has forced him into this, Sheriff. If a little bit of cash will help him out of a bind instead of leading him deeper into a mess, it's the least I can do."

Sheriff Webb rolled his eyes heavenward and heaved out another twenty-pound sigh. "Ava, the boy shot at you."

"Somebody shot at you?" Jeremiah echoed, his low-pitched voice raising uncharacteristically high.

Well, that bit of information didn't bode well for the conversation on the ride home. "Not on purpose."

Jeremiah stared at her for a few seconds, as if trying to impart some unspoken message which probably included a lecture starting with "Not again, Ava."

"I know what desperate looks like, Sheriff." She folded his fingers over the bills. "If this can help Joe at all, please give it to him."

Sheriff Webb examined the money in his hand. "You have a kind heart, just like your daddy." He cleared his throat and shoved the bills into his pocket. "And I know you mean well, Miss Burcham." His grin slanted, and he patted her on the arm. "But next time, could you mean well from the safety of Mr. and Mrs. Temple's house or your granny's front porch?"

"Because if you keep lookin' for trouble, you're bound to find it," Jeremiah murmured as he pushed the last piece of lumber into his wagon. "You always do."

She narrowed her eyes at the back of his head.

"Get on now, you two." The sheriff waved Ava toward the wagon and, if she wasn't mistaken, his lips twitched beneath his moustache like he wanted to grin. "I got a thief to tend to."

Now, why on earth would he be smiling? Ava steadied her shoulders and turned back toward the wagon, Jeremiah waiting by the wheel to help her up. A look at his somber expression solidified one notion: it was going to be a long ride home.

Chapter Two

*Women keep ya on yer toes, boy. Ain't nothin' that'll drive
you crazy, for the good or bad, like a woman.*
Granddaddy Sutphin

O f all the people to fall in love with, he had to go and pick the
half-crazy, strong-willed one, didn't he? Jeremiah Sutphin cast
another glance at Ava from his periphery as she sat beside him on the
wagon seat. Only the thinnest remnant of the sun skimmed across the
dark silhouette of the mountains in the distance, but with almost a full
moon rising, the road stretched out ahead of them in a silvery trail. He
barely even needed to light the lantern attached to his wagon, except
for the benefit of other folks.

With the pale light creating an even paler look on Ava's face, some
of Jeremiah's frustration cooled from a boil to a simmer. How many
times had he warned her about trying to fight all the injustices of the
world by herself? How many times had he gotten her out of trouble?

A shiver shook her shoulders, and he nearly growled into the
silence they'd shared for the past fifteen minutes. He seriously doubted
that tremor originated from a sudden guilty conscience, if he knew
her at all. Placing both reins in his left hand, he tugged a blanket from
behind his back, a convenience to soften his ride but also to combat
the early winter evening. He tossed the blanket onto Ava's lap and
then returned his hand to the reins and his attention to the moonlit
road.

"I ain't crazy." Her whispered words etched into the silence. "I
know what I seen."

Jeremiah sighed out the remnant of his irritation at her constant
defense of her sanity. "Putting yourself in danger ain't the smartest way
to get people to listen to you, Ava."

She pulled the blanket more tightly around her shoulders, her
walnut-colored hair glistening fairy white in the moonlight. "The only

way they'll really believe me is if I have some proof. Otherwise, they just think I'm some emotional female making up stories like my. . ."

Her voice trailed off, but Jeremiah filled in the ending. Her mother. Ava had fought living in the shadow of her mother for years. "You've gotta find another way to be heard, Ava." He shook his head and tapped the reins to move the horses along at a faster pace. "Sneaking around to catch illegal moonshiners? That ain't the way. Most of 'em have been doing this for years longer than you've been alive, and they know how to keep theirselves hidden."

"Or *who* will help them stay hidden," she murmured, her bottom lip pouting out in a frown.

Her words brewed with a coming tirade about the need for the community to stand up against lawless moonshiners, so Jeremiah racked his brain for a distraction. Something. Anything.

"You going to the shuckin' next Saturday?" Heat fled his face with the question. Sure, he'd thought about asking her for weeks, but actually saying it? Out loud? When did a man know the time to step from friend to. . . ?

"I reckon so." She looked out over the countryside, the tension in her frown lessening. "The girls will want me to bring my ribbons to fix their hair."

He squeezed the leather between his palms and cleared his throat. She'd never given him any indication of interest other than friendship. Nothing. And there wasn't one person in his life, besides his cousin Ellis, that he'd care to ask for advice on the matter. Unfortunately, Ellis was off schoolin' in North Carolina and couldn't help at all. "You're pretty popular with those ribbons."

She spared him a small smile. "I usually don't get into trouble with those, but it's not what I want to be known for." She groaned. "The girl with the ribbons."

"Those ribbons seem to mean a whole lot for the girls you give them too, though. They're all smiles and laughs after you're done. There's a lot to be said for that, I reckon."

The stiffness in her shoulders relaxed and she nudged him with her elbow. "You're good at that."

The breeze blew loose strands of her hair against her cheek and he had the strangest urge to touch an errant piece. He blinked out of his stare and returned his attention to the road. "What do you mean?"

"You always find a way to make things sound better." She fidgeted with the loose strings on the blanket, keeping her head down. "Even when I tutored you in school, you'd look for that silver linin'."

He chuckled, heat warming his cheeks all the way down his neck. "Silver linings were all I had when it came to my writin' skills. I've just never been able to put what I think into words like you can."

"You can use your words fine when you don't have to write 'em down, though."

Her smile spread over him like sunlight. "Nothin' like you can. You write better than half the people who work up those stories in the paper."

She tilted her head and studied him, her pale gaze glimmering in the lantern light like a pair of stars. *Sunlight? Stars?* Have mercy! Those words weren't fit for sayin' aloud or he'd never hear the end of it. He swallowed through the tension in his throat.

She brushed off his compliment with a shrug. "You don't have to make words sound so sweet when you can craft such beautiful things with your hands." She nodded toward the ornate wooden holder for his lantern, a design he'd brought to life from his head to his fingertips. "You've got a gift, Jeremiah. Enough to make your own business instead of workin' for the likes of Preston Dickens."

Which was exactly his plan. He'd already accepted two new building jobs of his own within the next few months. If things worked out as he hoped, he'd finish his own house by March and then. . .well, then he'd really have something to offer Ava Burcham.

"You still writing those magazine articles?"

"For fabric magazines." She wrinkled her nose with a renewed frown. "Just because I know about sewin' don't mean I want to write about it all the bloomin' time." A sigh heaved through her and she turned to face him. "I want to write about important things, Jeremiah. News. Information. Things to really make a difference and inspire people."

He turned his head to keep his grin from showing. The woman lived with so much passion it nearly flared from her like a gasoline fire.

"I know you're smilin'." Her grumble teased with humor. "I can feel it."

He chuckled, returning his gaze to hers. "I ain't got one doubt you could write whatever you put your mind to. You've always been a force to be reckoned with. But, like you've said before, getting recognized for good writing takes time."

"And opportunity. The *Carroll Journal* and *Mt. Airy Gazette* won't take me seriously, because I'm a nineteen-year-old *woman* instead of a thirty-five-year-old *man*. Seems all I'm fit for is sentences and paragraphs about spools and thread and lace."

"Keep tryin', Ava. You have it in you." He quoted his own words back to himself. Keep trying. Continue being her friend. And maybe, when he had himself established like a proper independent man, she'd see the good of the match too. "Maybe you just need to find somethin' new to write about. Somethin' that makes folks smile like your ribbons do."

Well, that sounded about as dumb as dumb could get.

Silence sprang the tension back to life. Of course, he wasn't sure what else to recommend for her creativity. She knew a lot about trails in the mountains from trapping with her daddy for so many years, and she could debate better than anybody. He stifled a groan. Yep, she had no problem with debating.

"Are you going to the shuckin'?"

Her question drew his attention back to her face and resurrected the lump in his throat. "I was plannin' to. The Edwards invited me."

She nodded and turned back toward the dark silhouette of the mountains on the horizon.

He worried the reins again. "Would you need a ride? I can pick you up at the Temples', if you want."

"I'm goin' early to fix the Combs girls' hair before the party or else I'd appreciate the company."

He nearly bent from the strange combination of relief and disappointment hitting his stomach. Maybe *he* was the crazy one.

"How 'bout I save you a dance or two?" She touched his arm, his attention settling on her smile for much longer than normal. With the golden glow from the lantern on her face and those loose curls swirling

21

around her cheeks, he couldn't seem to find his voice to respond. In fact, what crossed his mind had little to do with talking at all.

"You've always been one of the best dancers around. I reckon you'll have a whole slew of girls wantin' to take to the floor with you."

But only one really mattered. "I didn't think you were much of a dancer."

Her smile brightened and she shrugged. "Well, it ain't so bad if I dance with you, especially since you're the one who taught me how and all."

The least he could do in return for all the tutoring she'd given him in school.

A soft glow rose in the distance as they rounded the turn in the road. The only place with acetylene lights anywhere near Fancy Gap, Sid Allen's grand house perched like a mansion on a hill. Its pale exterior radiated ghostly white in the moonlight, and the tower room rose up into the night like one of the castles Jeremiah had once seen in a storybook. He knew almost every piece of that house, after working on it with Mr. Dickens for the past six months. Eight rooms. Oak floors, except in the living room; plaster interior walls; and a slate roof with a porch wrapping all the way around the front. It was like nothing else in the entire county and was paid for by Sid Allen's hard work and luck from his travels to Alaska, if rumors held any truth.

Jeremiah sat a little straighter. He'd used what he'd learned from working on that house to improve his own.

"Can you imagine having lights that glow like that? And running water *inside* the house?" Ava's voice lowered as if in awe. "Mr. Temple said someday all the houses will have it, but I can't even imagine. I got plumb tickled when Daddy piped water from the pump into Granny Burcham's house so she wouldn't have to walk out to the pump all the time, but to have the water come directly into the sink. That's a wonder."

Jeremiah's lips twitched with a waiting smile. His house would have running water, for certain. Acetylene lights? Well, he wasn't too sure about that one yet. He was still figurin' on how he could afford an inside outhouse.

"I reckon the more folks start bringing those types of things into the mountains, the more we'll have access to 'em."

"Would you ever take me inside that house, Jeremiah?" Her shoulder pressed against his, her gaze boring into his profile. "Just for a peek. Mrs. Temple says the walls are covered with flower paper and there are carvings on the mantels."

"There are."

"Did you do some of those carvings?"

His lips quirked. "Some."

She sighed back into the seat as they neared the house's drive. "Wouldn't it be something to write about the house for the paper? Regular folks like me want to know what it looks like. I heard some people say there are secret passages to underground tunnels."

The rumor mill at work. "I ain't seen no secret rooms, and I've worked on every foot of that house."

"Well, I've got to think of something to write about so the newspaper will take me seriously."

Jeremiah raised a finger to his lips to quiet Ava's chatter and leaned over to douse the light of the lantern as they jingled quietly up to the barn. A tension chilled the air and quieted his voice all the more. An unnatural stillness breathed over the night sounds. "The Allen women are likely asleep, so I'm gonna unhitch the wagon here in the shed so the timber will be protected, and then you can ride with me down to the Temples' on horseback."

"I can walk by my—"

Thankfully, she must have recognized his glare, even in the faint evening light, because she clipped her lips closed and glared right back. Without another word, he helped her down from the seat. The slight whiff of lemongrass and lavender, evidence of her granny's homemade soaps, wound its way from Ava's hair to his nose, tempting him to hold her a little longer before allowing her feet to touch the ground.

He cast an inward prayer for strength heavenward and then turned to unhitch the horses, keeping his motions as quiet as possible. The hair on the back of his neck raised, and Jeremiah glanced around the barn, peering into the shadows for the origin of the sensation. Was someone watching them? He kept his ears perked for any unusual noises as he took care of the horses. Sally, his mare, nuzzled up against him in gratitude for releasing her from the heavy load, as Ava carefully finished the same job with Clyde, one of Mr. Allen's excellent stallions.

"What do we have here? A couple of thieves?"

The unmistakable sound of a revolver's hammer clicking into place along with the deep male voice chilled Jeremiah to a halt. He shifted his body in Ava's direction. What had he gotten them into?

Ava made out the sturdy silhouette of a man in the doorway of the barn, the shiny end of his revolver poised with purpose and glimmering in the moonlight. She looked over at Jeremiah, who turned so his body shielded hers, his expression unreadable. In the shadows of the barn, she couldn't make out the man's face. A thief who'd noticed their load and followed them?

"I advise you to lift your hands in the air so I can see 'em and take your time turning all the way around."

The tone in his voice, the timbre, carried a familiar quality. Ava followed Jeremiah's lead in raising her hands, and with a careful turn, they came face-to-face with the man.

"Now, let's see who we've got here." A flicker of light bloomed from a match at the man's fingertips as he lit a lantern near the doorway. Sid Allen.

Ava nearly collapsed with relief.

"Mr. Allen, I'm sorry I came in late." Jeremiah turned toward the owner of the massive house. "The road was slow up from—"

"Boy!" The word burst from the man's lips like a curse, and he lowered the revolver. "What on earth are you doin' comin' in without alertin' the house? I told you to *always* let someone know if you come in after dark." He made a cutting gesture with his hand. "It's a good thing I don't shoot first and ask questions later."

"It bein' so late and all I—"

"When I say somethin', I mean it. You know the way in these parts. And there's been riders out of late." The man's face lit with the glow of the lantern, his pale eyes, the trademark Allen blue, aflame. "You hear?"

Jeremiah pushed a palm through his dark hair and lowered his head. "Yes, sir."

Mr. Allen took the lantern in hand and shifted its beam toward Ava. She squinted against the light. He narrowed his eyes. "Ava Burcham? What on earth are you doing out this time of night?" He moved his gaze to Jeremiah. "It's too late for decent courtin', and I always took you two for the decent sort."

"Oh no, sir." Ava nearly jolted forward. "We ain't a-courtin'."

A snapping sound followed her declaration, and she met Jeremiah's gaze. He jerked at Sally's saddle strap, his expression none too welcoming. Likely, he was still nursin' his irritation about Ava getting shot at.

"Pulled a little too hard, that's all."

She tilted her head and examined him a second before continuing her defense. "I was in town. . .near the library, and lost track of time." She hoped her smile looked more believable than it felt. "Jeremiah offered to give me a ride home and—"

"The library doesn't stay open this late."

Jeremiah's raised eyebrow heckled without words, and Ava's entire body bristled in response. The last thing she wanted to do was confess her attempt to catch moonshiners to any Allen in the county. If rumors proved true, most of them had been in the business of blockade liquor for decades, even if some didn't practice anymore.

"I. . .well. . ."

"Never mind." Mr. Allen cast a look over his shoulder, his brows furrowing into deep grooves. "The two of you need to get out of here and back to your homes where you belong. Now."

The edge in his voice spurred Jeremiah into action and he finished with the horses. Ava nearly ran toward the barn door. She'd barely made it to the threshold when Mr. Allen caught her arm. "Where do you think you're going, Miss Burcham?"

Her feet froze to the spot and she looked up at the tall man. "The Temples'. It ain't a mile to walk if I cut across—"

"Not tonight, girl." Mr. Allen's expression tightened as he nudged her toward Jeremiah. He sent another look out the barn. "Get on the road directly, and have Ava hold the lantern as you ride, so. . ." He released a stream of air through his nose and growled. "So folks'll be able to notice who you are long before they come upon you."

Some unspoken message passed between Mr. Allen and Jeremiah that Ava didn't fully comprehend, but she figured out enough of it to know that danger waited in the dark tonight. Danger Mr. Allen knew something about but didn't want to disclose.

If Ava had been up for a fight, she might have questioned Mr. Allen further, but her track record for the evening didn't bode in her favor. Jeremiah already waited for her, his fingers braided together to give her a boost onto the horse. Without a word but with a rather audible sigh, she followed his cue, with Jeremiah mounting behind her a second later.

"I don't want to see this happen again, you hear?" Sid Allen raised the lantern so Ava could reach it. "Courtin' or not, the darker the days, the less likely folks are to keep sober, and that means likely trouble of a night."

He didn't say more, but the warning hit too close to home. Liquor soothed a lot of restless Appalachian men in winter. Some bore it better than others.

Some loved their drink so much, they killed for it.

The thought awakened the familiar ache in Ava's chest that never disappeared for too long. Twelve years old, and all she'd seen of her daddy's assailant had been a special flourish of his wrist as he pulled his Colt and stole her daddy's things off his lifeless body.

A shudder trembled through Ava at the memory as she and Jeremiah left the barn, and, almost immediately, Jeremiah's faithful blanket appeared. He wrapped it around her shoulders, as far as the lantern would allow, and moved in closer behind her.

Something about his nearness—his presence—eased her posture back against his chest. He'd been her friend for years, one of the few people who knew the truth about her family's terrible tragedy. The one who'd found her lying in a pool of blood beside her dying brother and who fought the boys that taunted her about her mother.

"I know you won't listen to me, but could you try to get home before nightfall in the future?"

His voice brewed low near her ear, and the strangest quake of warmth trembled through her chest, stealing the chill in the air. She closed her eyes, embracing the unexpected feeling with the slightest hitch in her breath. Was this what safety felt like? Belonging? It'd been so long since she'd felt it, she couldn't remember.

"Ava?"

She didn't answer immediately, holding on to the idea for a second longer before she switched the lantern to her other hand. "I want to help."

"Ava."

"And no one believes me."

"That's not true."

"Of course it's true." She stiffened away from him. "They all think I'm like my mama."

"Sheriff Webb believes you. He was one of your daddy's friends." Jeremiah's voice remained calm, smooth, pouring over her agitation like warm honey on a biscuit.

"He's a friend to everyone," she whispered, her body suddenly tired. She relaxed back against the sturdiness of his chest again, the same sweet, belonging sensation slowing her erratic pulse.

The sound of the horse's movements and Jeremiah's breaths filled the silence for a few seconds. A leather scent mingled with the smell of fresh-cut pine, which always accompanied Jeremiah, enveloped her as much as the blanket. She must be extra tired tonight, because she wished to linger just a mite bit longer than the ride allowed.

She sighed. The lantern's glow swayed against the darkness around them. Jeremiah didn't believe the lies. Never had.

"I'm sorry." She cleared her throat, the stinging in her eyes a sudden nuisance.

A soft brush, like a breath, moved over her shoulder. Had he touched her hair? The idea pearled into a fleeting thought. Could Jeremiah. . .care about her?

"It's okay if you just live your life, Ava. You don't have to keep trying to fight for them."

She blinked against the moisture gathering in her vision. "If there wasn't any blockade liquor, my daddy wouldn't be dead."

"Messin' with the moonshiners is a dangerous business. Let the law do their job." He brought the horse around to the side of the Temples' store, the whitewashed building part residence, part shop.

Her throat closed around a sob, refusing it access. She'd not cry in front of Jeremiah Sutphin. Or anybody.

"Thank you for bringing me home, Jeremiah." Without another word, she pushed the lantern into Jeremiah's free hand and slid from the horse before he could respond.

"Ava!"

She darted toward the Temples' back door, tears warming her cheeks. How could he understand, really? Even if he tried. Once inside, she slid to the window and peered out. Jeremiah sat on his mare, staring at the house, the lantern lowered to his side and casting a glow against his stoic expression. He pushed a hand through his hair, upsetting his disheveled appearance even more, then turned and, with another glance her way, rode into the night.

"God, keep him safe," she whispered against the pane.

What had he said to her? *"It's okay if you just live your life."*

She wiped at the tears slipping down her face. Live? How did she do that? She'd been surrounded by ghosts for so long.

She waited by the window until Jeremiah's lantern light disappeared in the distance and even the moonlight faded behind the clouds. *God, help me!*

Chapter Three

Sometimes, girl, you gotta live life like a squirrel. Jump,
even if the limb looks too far, 'cause the one you're
standin' on is bound to break, if you don't.
Granny Burcham

The mantel clock in the workroom of Temples' Alteration shop kept time with Ava's pulse. She refused to look at it again. The last time she'd snuck a glance, the hand had only moved three minutes. At this pace, she'd die from going plumb stir-crazy if she didn't keep busy, but she'd waited all week for this day. Longer, truth be told.

Her smile spread wide as she double-knotted the last two cloth buttons on the back of Elsie Combs's dress and stretched to a stand, refusing another look toward the mantel. With a careful fluff of burgundy and lace, she held the frock at arm's length. Elsie had offered to pay seven whole dollars if Ava could manage to make puffed sleeves. She'd already paid four as down payment.

Ava carefully pulled the dress over the nearby wire form, her smile spreading so wide it pinched into her cheeks. Flounced ruffles, like a cascade of clouds, poured down each sleeve. A blouson front so frothy it almost inspired Ava's laughter, and a beautiful spill of lace and cloth almost touched the dusty wooden floor. She'd never made anything so delicate and expensive before, nor got paid half as fine.

Ice frosted the single window in Ava's workspace, despite the fragile warmth of the midmorning sun. Thankfully, the little potbelly stove kept the small back room warm enough for Ava's fingers to remain nimble for her task. Perhaps once other girls saw Elsie's dress, Ava would have more orders, especially from the girls in town. She only needed to work some extra jobs or write a few more articles to purchase the secondhand typewriter in Sid Allen's mercantile. *Then* she could pursue more than sewing articles. Something more important.

Jeremiah had suggested she find something new to write about and, sure enough, she had. Maybe it wasn't exactly what he had in mind, and perhaps she added a few innuendos to give the story a bit more flair than was necessary, but for good or ill, the *Carroll Journal* took the piece.

A chime bled into Ava's thoughts. *The* chime! Her gaze shot to the mantel. Ten o'clock. She slipped to the doorway that separated her workroom from the front space of Drury Temple's alteration shop. *Oh, please don't let the first frost slow down the newspaper boy!*

She shook her head at the thought. Pete had made it through worse in these mountains. Lots worse.

With a quiet step, she peered around the doorframe and glanced past the bolts of cloth and a few shelves of lace and ribbons until her attention landed on the front counter. Mrs. Susie Temple stood with her gray-and-brown head bent over pages of sales figures. Not a paper in sight.

The clock chimed again. A chair scraped at her right, and Mr. Temple stood from his spot in a rocking chair and tapped his pipe against his knee. Time for his morning walk down to Top Side for a cup of coffee with some of his fellow businessmen, which would free Ava to confiscate the paper before Mr. Temple took it away. The two had given her a place to live when she was orphaned, closer to school than her granny's mountain cabin afforded, and they'd taught her a viable trade, but it had never felt like home. Not like Granny's cabin. "Susie, I'll be back directly." Mr. Temple took his well-worn fedora from a hook by the door and gestured toward his wife. "Gonna meet the boys."

The door slammed closed behind him, leaving the room in a dust of silence. Ava waited a half second and then approached the counter where Mrs. Temple continued her work, the scraping of pencil on paper the only sound in the room.

Ava pinched her fists at her sides and teased a step closer. The editor had told her. . .well, he'd told Mrs. Temple in her place that he'd publish the article in today's paper, so it should be in there.

Mrs. Temple didn't look up, but the slightest lift to the corner of her lips gave off the hint she knew exactly why Ava had emerged from the sewing room. *Someone* had to know her secret in order to deliver the article without suspicion of it being written by a female, and Mrs. Temple had proven a willing accomplice.

As Ava reached the counter, the front door burst open, bringing in a swirl of December cold and the fresh scent of winter wind. Ava nearly jumped forward, expecting the fiery-headed paperboy, but instead, Cleaves Murphy ambled inside with his two daughters. The Murphys and Temples had been friends for time out of mind, even though the Temples had moved up the social ladder in Fancy Gap and the Murphys still barely made it from one season to the next. The two girls wore dresses a size too small and threadbare at the bottoms. Each carried a delicate basket, likely handmade by their mama. The youngest girl, Alice, was wearing a coat that had so many patches and reworked stitching it couldn't have blocked much of the cold.

"Well, what a nice surprise." Mrs. Temple's smile bloomed with welcome and she rounded the counter to greet them with a handshake. "What brings you all down from the mountain?"

"We come for a bolt of cloth for the misses. Simple. Cotton."

"Of course, of course." Mrs. Temple leaned near to Ava as she passed. "What did you do with that coat I gave you last week? The one you repaired?"

Ava blinked, following Mrs. Temple's gaze to the young girl. "Oh!" Ava grinned. "Why, it's in the back."

"Would you run fetch it?"

Mrs. Temple's expression spoke volumes. She planned on getting that coat into the hands of that young girl some way or other. "Yes, ma'am."

The coat hung in a closet in the back room with some other finished clothes. Mrs. Temple had gotten it from Amethyst Carter, a well-to-do young woman from town. Amethyst had heard of Mrs. Temple's excellent embroidery skills and had hired her services on a new coat she'd purchased. When Amethyst came to collect her newly embroidered coat, she cast the old one she was wearing to the floor without a second thought. It had a few worn spots around the cuffs and required a little doctoring up on the buttons and seams, but as a whole the black wool looked excellent.

Ava snatched the coat from its place and started for the door, when her attention fell on her workstation. A pair of woolen gloves, made by Granny Burcham in mingled purples, sat on the edge. With a quick sweep of her hand, she grabbed the gloves and shoved one in each pocket of the coat before returning to the little group in the storefront.

"Ah, here we go." Mrs. Temple took the coat from Ava and handed the cloth and the coat to Mr. Murphy.

His bushy brows took an uptilt. "We can't take this, Mrs. Temple. We just come for the cloth."

"Your daughter can't go traipsin' around in winter weather without proper coverin' either."

Mr. Murphy's frown deepened. "We ain't gonna take no charity." He nodded toward the youngest, whose lips were as pale as her face. "She'll be all right once we get back in the wagon and can huddle up. Right, girl?"

Alice looked from her father to the coat and then back to Mrs. Temple with a slow nod. "Yes, sir."

Ava's gaze fell to the baskets.

Mrs. Temple bounded a step forward. "Cleaves Murphy, if that ain't one of the most half-crazy, muleheaded—"

"Of course we don't plan on any charity, Mr. Murphy." Ava looked at Mrs. Temple, the woman's mouth stopped mid-insult. "We were hoping to trade the coat for one of those handmade baskets your girls are always carryin'."

Mr. Murphy looked from the baskets to the coat, his dark brows raising up his tall forehead.

"Why, my Granny Burcham would go plumb wild over one of those Murphy baskets," Ava continued, hoping her smile gave the appropriate incentive. "Baskets are excellent for decorating as well as being practical. Ain't that right, Mrs. Temple?"

The woman snapped her lips closed and did little to hide her grin. "Exactly right."

Mr. Murphy's lips firmed into a line as he examined the coat then the baskets. "Well, that won't do at all. That coat's worth at least two baskets." He nodded toward his girls. "Give 'em up to Ava there, girls. We'll make a fair trade."

Alice's face fairly glowed. "Yes, sir."

Ava leaned over to her. "Check the pockets for something to give to your sister as a peace offering, since you're the one getting the fancy coat."

"And we'll trade the old coat too, won't we, Ava?" Mrs. Temple added. "You might as well leave it here for Ava to fix up so we can make another good trade in the future."

Alice giggled as she removed her tattered coat and handed it to Ava. Her big sister made a courageous attempt to cover her wistful stare as the younger pulled the coat over her worn, calico dress.

"I ain't never felt anything so fancy in all my days." She breathed out the words.

"Well, you'll take a turn lettin' your sister wear that coat every once in a while, won't you?" Mrs. Temple's gentle encouragement brought a light to the elder daughter's gray eyes. "Till we can make us another trade?"

Alice shot Ava a knowing grin and nodded. "Yes, ma'am."

As soon as they left the store, Mrs. Temple patted Ava on the shoulder and returned to her place at the counter. "You got a right fine head on your shoulders, you know that?"

Ava's grin bloomed with some added warmth to her cheeks.

"Now if we can just get you to do some work."

The smile dimmed, but only slightly, since the corner of Mrs. Temple's mouth tipped to hint at her teasing.

The woman raised her gaze to Ava, pointing with her pencil toward the baskets in Ava's hands. "Whatever are you going to do with them two baskets?"

Ava examined each one, both simple but lovely in their own right. One large, the other a more medium size. "I'm going to decorate them with some lace and dried flowers and sell them in your store."

Mrs. Temple's eyes widened with her grin. "Are you now?"

"If we can mend and resell dresses so people can buy something nicer than what they have, why not baskets too?" Ava stood a little straighter and tipped her chin at Mrs. Temple, causing the woman's smile to burgeon into a chuckle.

"Girl, you're somethin' else. You know that?"

Before Ava could answer, the door burst open again, almost

sending one of the baskets to flight. In with a rush of scattered flurries walked Peter Pickett, complete with a satchel full of papers. Red curls peeking out from beneath his cap almost matched the color of his nose, but even the cold air failed to dampen his smile.

"Good morning, Ava." He nodded his greeting. "Wind's comin' up from the south."

"There'll be snow in its mouth." Mrs. Temple finished the old saying, drawing Peter and his bagful in her direction.

Ava followed behind as if hanging on the scent of fresh-cooked biscuits.

"Just hopin' the new snow waits till after the shuckin'," Peter said, placing his bag on the counter. "I've got some ladies to spark and a hankerin' for a good dance or two."

"You and your sparkin'." Mrs. Temple waved her hand at him. "You change your spark 'bout as often as a squirrel stays in one place."

He offered a helpless shrug as he pulled a coveted paper from his bag and placed it on the counter. "What's a man to do when there're so many pretty girls in Carroll County?" He shot a wink toward Ava.

She rolled her eyes but laughed. "You'd know, since you're all over the county with those papers. You probably know everybody and everything that's goin' on."

The gleam in the young man's eyes dimmed with his expression. "I reckon I do know more than I want to some days."

Mrs. Temple glanced at Ava and lowered her pencil. "What is it, Peter?"

"You ain't heard, then." He shifted his feet and looked behind him, as if someone might be listening from behind the door. "And I ain't too sure it's fittin' for ladies' ears."

A chill descended over Ava's body that had nothing to do with the wintry weather.

"You better go on and get it off your chest now, boy." Mrs. Temple rounded the counter, her expression brooking no refusal. "We're bound to find out anyhow."

Peter took in a deep breath and set his bag on the floor, aging ten years as he did. "Solomon Dunn was found dead in a ditch by the road four nights ago."

"Dead?" Mrs. Temple's hand went to her chest. Ava froze in place, a vision of the stocky, white-bearded man flicking to mind.

"Shot in the chest. His money taken. Even his shoes."

Ava weakened from her head to her knees, a memory from eight years ago nearly buckling her to the floor. Mrs. Temple came to her side, subtly supporting her.

"Some say he was part of the Lightnin' Boys, but I can't make no sense of Old Man Dunn throwing himself in with that lot."

Neither could Ava. He certainly didn't seem the blockade liquor sort.

"All I can figure is he got caught in the wrong place at the wrong time, catching a sale between two groups."

Four nights ago? Her breath caught. The night Jeremiah brought her home?

Ava's throat tightened with an unvoiced whimper. It could have been them! Sid must have known about the liquor run or else he wouldn't have warned them. Was he a part of it too? She always hoped he'd stayed above the likes of some of his kin, but he'd known *something* was happening that night.

Peter picked up his bag and gestured with his chin toward the counter. "You can read more about it, if you like. Front page. I reckon it's a good thing Old Man Dunn was on his own after comin' in late from town. Can't imagine what it'd have been like with any of his family along too." With a sad shake of his head and a tap to his cap, Peter left the room a bit colder and a lot quieter.

"Come on, girl. Sit down over by the counter and I'll get you a drink of milk."

Ava allowed Mrs. Temple to guide her to a nearby stool, where she collapsed. Her hands shook as if she still sat hiding in the overturned wagon, watching her daddy bleed to death in front of her.

"Now, now, it ain't the first time something like this has happened, and we both know it won't be the last. It's the darker part of these mountains." Mrs. Temple took Ava's cold hands into her warm ones, holding Ava's attention. "Don't go back to what you can't change, girl. There's no help in it." She rubbed Ava's hands and lowered her chin as if her advice ended any argument, but as Mrs. Temple disappeared to the back, Ava pressed her palm into her stomach. Another family left fatherless because of an all-consuming business some of these mountain folks clung to like breath. A moneymaker. Easy money.

"Here we go." Mrs. Temple rounded the doorway, cup in hand. "This warm milk will chase that cold news away."

Ava's stomach curled against the thought, but she took the cup between her hands, allowing the heat to bring warmth through her palms and up her arms. She barely took a sip.

"Now we can see to that news you've been waitin' for all morning, can't we?"

Ava blinked up at her, comprehension coming like it had molasses clinging to it.

"Your article in the paper?" Mrs. Temple beamed a little too brightly and brought the newspaper from the counter.

Ava pushed the hollowness away, as she'd grown accustomed to doing, embracing the day. The now. And blocking her daddy's lifeless face from her immediate thoughts.

"Right. The article." Ava stood, bracing herself against the counter.

Mrs. Temple strategically flipped the front page out of view and slid the paper in Ava's direction. "Come on, now. What are you waitin' for?" She raised a brow. "Tomorrow?"

Ava cleared her throat and tugged the paper closer. There weren't a whole lot of people who knew this secret. Granny, of course, because, well, Granny had a way of finding out everything. But not even Jeremiah knew. The idea had come to her so fast, she hadn't had a chance to tell him, especially after the way they'd parted four days ago.

And she hadn't seen him since. Which left a knot in her stomach if she thought about it too long. Had he made it home safe and sound? Surely, she'd have heard if anything—

Mrs. Temple released an audible sigh, but a mischievous light shimmered to life in her eyes in contrast to her crumpled frown. "So, what's the latest news?"

Ava forced her expression into a smile and her fingers into motion. She peeled apart the leaves of the paper, breath lodged in a lump in her throat. At the top of the second page, there in black and white, was an article by Cameron Birch entitled FANCY GAP THIEF

FINALLY CAUGHT RED-HANDED.

Ava blinked down at the paper, the long-awaited tinge of excitement dulled beneath Peter's news, but she seized the moment. Held it. Allowed the thrill to replace the numbness of the last few minutes and memories.

"There...there it is," she breathed, going over the words she'd typed out on Mr. Temple's typewriter while he'd been in town. But even as she read it again, the sense of pride she'd anticipated never came. She'd reworked the story, exaggerated the plot, embellished language, and overemphasized nuances. She'd written it from the perspective of the fictional observer, Cameron Birch, who watched the incident from the window of the hotel. But now something felt wrong. Fake.

But how else would she be seen as a serious writer? What more could she do to make a difference in this culture filled with so much hardship and struggle?

She shook the melancholy away. No, she'd finally earned a serious spot in the paper. Something more than ribbons or cotton or fashion and bobbins. Something that could bring attention to a real problem in their community.

"How come you published as this Birch person instead of your given name?"

"They ain't gonna let no woman write *serious* articles for the paper around here. Or leastways, the editor they keep sending me to won't. The first time I asked if I could submit a piece for the paper, one talkin' about the poverty of our times, they offered me a spot writing about 'best recipes of the mountains.'" She groaned. "Nobody wants to eat my cookin', let alone have me write about it."

Ava sighed back down at the paper, her words printed right there in black and white. Even if her name wasn't listed as the author, the sentiment came through. Desperate folks do desperate things. And even if she'd dramatized a few things here or there, she brought awareness to a real problem. Her stomach tensed a little at the thought. Giving a little more excitement in certain places didn't hurt anything, did it?

She doubted Jeremiah would approve.

The front door burst open again, ruffling the pages of the newspaper until it almost blew out of Ava's hands. Land sakes alive! Was everybody in the state going to visit Temples' Alterations today? With a stifled growl, Ava looked up.

As if he'd heard the call of her thoughts, Jeremiah Sutphin stepped through the doorway, a little wild looking with his jacket loose, cap in hands, and his dark hair wind-tossed, and she immediately did two things at the same time. Wondered when he'd started looking so dashing and. . .hid the newspaper behind her back.

Chapter Four

It's the woman that drives you crazy the most, is the one you
can't live without. Or at least, that's what I've figured.
Granddaddy Sutphin

I f he hadn't been sent to gather some special materials from Mt. Airy, Jeremiah would have relieved the ache in his chest from his last conversation with Ava rather than let four days go by, but his tardiness couldn't be helped. Just like the broken wagon wheel, delayed arrival of materials, and the slow travel snow added to everything. . .except sledding. But it was nigh impossible to sled uphill from Mt. Airy with a wagonload of lumber against the wind.

Then as soon as he'd made it to Sid Allen's house with materials, he'd overheard Sid and his brother, Floyd, talking about the incident with Solomon Dunn, and he dropped everything and set off at a dead run toward Temples' Alterations. The situation sounded too similar to Ava's past.

As he burst through the shop's doorway, his gaze immediately met Ava's wide eyes. She froze, except for the drop of her bottom lip, and then, with a wild flourish, she snatched a paper off the counter and pulled it behind her back.

"Jeremiah!"

"I came to see if you were all right." He stepped forward, but the sight of Mrs. Temple kept him from drawing as close as he'd like.

"All right?" Her gaze searched his, and then understanding dawned. "You mean about the news of Mr. Dunn."

Her countenance flickered. The fear he'd grown to recognize shimmied to life in her expression for a split second before setting itself into a firm-lipped grasp which boasted, "I will be fine on my own." He hated when she blocked him out. Hated the hurt that led her to this undying necessity of self-preservation.

"Well, I'm fine, as you see." Her smile shone too brightly. "Was there anything you needed?"

The tiniest bit of hope flickered to life in those eyes. Would he ever get her to see how much he cared? How she didn't have to face life on her own?

Mrs. Temple's hawkeye landed on his profile. He could feel her scrutiny needling into his cheek.

"It's just that. . .well. . .the whole thing with Mr. Dunn might have caused you to—" He tilted his head and lowered his voice. "To remember, and I wanted to make sure you're fine, especially since we didn't part ways well the last time."

Her expression thawed, eyes rounding, and her mouth opened ever so slightly, but no words emerged. He'd breached the wall, if only for a second.

He reckoned he ought to finish up what he'd come to say then. Good or bad. "I know you want to help people, and that's a good thing. It's one of the reasons I. . ." He cleared his throat. "Why you're special."

Mrs. Temple made some sort of sniffly noise and Jeremiah couldn't handle the audience one more second. He took Ava by the hand. "Excuse us, Mrs. Temple. Ava will be right back." He pulled her across the room and out the side door, onto the enclosed porch.

As soon as the door closed behind them, he turned, and Ava ran into his chest, burrowing deep, paper crinkling between them. His breath caught from the impact and the unexpected. The last time she'd lowered her guard like this was when her dog, Red, passed away. Most times, she'd find her way to be near him, talking about everything and nothing, but the times she hurt the most, she *showed* him how much he meant to her, even if her head didn't know it.

Or at least that's what Jeremiah wanted to believe.

He wrapped his arms around her, allowing the silence to settle the distance between them. She smelled of apples and soap, and her vulnerability with him dissolved every frustration from a few nights before.

"I'm sorry." She pushed back, wiping at her face with her free hand while the other clutched what looked like a newspaper. "I. . .I'll be fine."

Her warmth against him dissipated too quickly. "There's nothing wrong with taking the compassion and care of a friend, Ava." The words barely made volume from his throat to the air, scratchy and raw as they were.

She studied him and then shook her head and moved farther away. "It. . .it was just so familiar. So much like. . ."

"I know."

"Do you. . ." She lowered her focus to the paper in her hands, brow creased into wrinkles. "Do you think it could have been the same man?"

He drew in a breath, shaking his arms free from the memory of holding her. "As the one who killed your father? That was eight years ago. It would be impossible to know."

She pinched the paper in her hands to her chest, nodding like the lost little girl she seemed to be sometimes. How could he help her?

"Is there anything you remember about that man?"

Her gaze shot up to his. "I. . .I don't know. Not much."

"What is it? What do you remember?"

She turned and paced the length of the porch. "I didn't think I remembered anything extra." Her gaze came up to him. "I don't know why I'm remembering it just now. Why not back then?"

Jeremiah rubbed at his chin, the prickles against his palm reminders of his long hours on the road. "I've heard tell that sometimes the mind can only bear so much emotion at once. Maybe there's been enough time passed to bring certain pieces to light."

She nodded, her attention focused on the distant scene of crystallized hillsides.

"What did you remember?" He touched her arm and drew her to a hand-hewn bench against the wall. "Your father?"

She lowered to the bench, almost in a trancelike state, and rested her head back against the wall of the shop, eyes closing. "I told you two men on horses started chasin' our wagon when we stumbled on their meeting spot?"

"Yes." He sat down beside her, watching her placid profile, her long braid resting over her shoulder.

"And then. . .and then Daddy took a curve too quick and the wagon tipped, turning over and throwing us from the seat?"

"I remember."

"I should have run for help." She pressed one palm against her forehead. "I knew Daddy was hurt from the crash, but he pushed me back into a dark corner of the flipped wagon and told me not to make a sound, no matter what happened." She looked over at him, eyes glassy. "But I should have. I should have gone for help."

"Ava." Jeremiah placed his hand over the one she had wrapped around the newspaper. "You were only twelve years old. How could you have known what was gonna happen?"

His words didn't seem to dent the frown puckering her lips. "I couldn't see much from where I was. Daddy's boots. But I heard the horses come up, heard loud voices, and then a gunshot." She flinched. "Daddy fell to the ground right outside my hiding place, lookin' at me. I could tell he was still alive, because when I started to move toward him, he shook his head."

Jeremiah knew what would come next. The assailant would reach into her daddy's jacket and her daddy would fight back, resulting in a pistol whip to the head which likely led to his death faster than the stomach wound. And then the men would ride off with his money, horse, and any portable goods he'd had in his wagon, leaving Ava to be found by a passing traveler after hours of hiding.

"You don't have to relive that, Ava. Just try to focus on whatever memory is new." He squeezed her hand and she blinked at him. "The man's voice? A face?"

"I can't remember his voice. Not with any distinction." She shook her head and narrowed her eyes, as if trying to recall something deep in her memory. "His accent was real thick though. Not refined, like Sid Allen's from all his travels."

"Okay, that's something new."

"And. . .and his hands were young hands." She looked down at Jeremiah's hand wrapped over hers, examining it. "I didn't know that as a child, but looking back now, I can see them. Strong, young hands, and he fumbled a lot, like he was nervous. He dropped my daddy's pocket watch about three times before he finally tucked it into his coat."

Could her daddy have been the first man the stranger had ever shot?

Her gaze flashed to his. "And there was a scar on the inside of his. . .his right wrist."

"A scar?"

Her eyes widened, as if seeing some vision beyond his face. "Like a fishin' hook. On the inside of his wrist. I saw it because he had to remove his glove to get my daddy's wallet from his jacket pocket."

"That's something we didn't know before." He gave her hand another squeeze. "But it's been years, Ava. Even if we could find the man, what could we do?"

Her gaze found his, a cold, dark stare. "Bring him to justice. Who knows how many other people he's killed! How many other families he's broken."

"Ava—"

"And we get the news out about awful men like him so it doesn't keep happenin' to more families like mine and the Dunns'." She shook the paper at him. "Someone needs to do something, Jeremiah, and I'm not afraid to try."

He looked from her face to the paper in her fist. "Zat so?"

She sighed and squeezed her eyes closed. "I reckon I ought to be the one to show you, since you'll likely figure it out after a while anyway." She smoothed out the paper and placed it in his lap.

What on earth was she talking about? A headline in bold drew his attention. The thief? The one police had been after for a month or more?

He stared down at the paper and then back to Ava, slowly taking it from her to read over the article. He flinched at a few parts, especially some outright names mentioned. Whoever wrote this article put themselves on the wrong side of some of the biggest names in Carroll County. And the writing? Sure, it oozed with the drama of recent fiction, lathering on exaggeration to create enough sensation to sell a few more papers, but the sentiment was a good one—calling the people of Carroll to see how poverty, power, and desperation could lead folks to step outside the law for help.

He searched for the author. Cameron Birch? Who in the world was—

His gaze zoomed to Ava's, and a replay of Sheriff Webb's words about someone shooting at Ava went through his mind. "*You* wrote this?"

She gave a wary nod. "It's my first serious piece in the paper."

"Serious?" He read back over it with fresh eyes. "You used your middle name as this Cameron Birch to pretend to be some man who witnessed the whole thing from the window of the hotel?"

"They wouldn't have published it from a woman. You know that."

"But why did you write it with such. . .I don't know. . . Drama?"

Her body stiffened and she scooted away from him on the bench. "What do you mean?"

He raised the paper and began reading, " 'A look of pure desperation consumed his features, like a lonely desperado on the western plains trying to etch out his existence. What had this man had to promise to secure his family's safety from some of the most notorious of Carroll County?'" He looked over the paper at her. "That *must* be Cameron Birch 'cause it don't sound nothin' like Ava Burcham."

She jerked the paper from his hand and stood. "I knew you wouldn't understand."

"Wouldn't understand?" He faced her. "Ava, you nearly got yourself shot—"

"Joe didn't mean to fire his gun." She pulled the paper from his hand. "He was scared."

"He didn't mean to fire his gun? Ava, shootin' by accident or on purpose is still shootin'. You could've been killed." He groaned and pushed a palm through his hair. "And these names? Allens, Hawks, Daniels. Did Joe hint about which folks he was beholden to?"

"No, but the whole county knows the names circulating in the moonshinin' industry around here. Someone needed to be brave enough to say them loud enough for the whole world to hear."

"Ava." He shook his head and took hold of her shoulders. "Part of being brave is being smart. It may take awhile for folks to figure out who the author of this article is, but what happens when they do?"

Her face paled. Good. At least, maybe, he'd scare some sense into her.

"And what about Joe? If some of these folks think Joe confessed—"

"He didn't, though." She grabbed his arm, eyes wide. "He didn't tell, but most folks know the clans around here with the power to instill fear. *Someone* is threatening him, or he wouldn't—"

"He's old enough to make his own choices, good or bad. If he needed money, there are folks in town and several of the churches who'd lend a hand."

She backed away from him, the shimmer in her eyes nearly derailing his ire. "Joe'd never take charity. He's not that sort of man, like most people in these mountains."

"He'd steal from unescorted young ladies instead?" He growled out a breath. "What does that tell you about his character, I wonder?"

"I knew you'd react like this. I knew it. You want me to be quiet about these problems like everyone else." She edged a step closer to him, fire lighting her multihued eyes into a smoky gray. "You should be thankful I'm drawing attention to a real problem in our county. Fear." She pushed past him to go back to the store, but he blocked her path.

"I'd never try to stop you from doing the right thing, only the dangerous thing. And you're a better writer than this." He jabbed a finger at the paper she held. "State the facts; those are crazy enough. You don't have to pull speculations into the truth to make it better or more exciting. It tends to cause more trouble than—"

"He's not the only person I've talked to who's under somebody's thumb for funds they can't pay. There's real fear in their faces, Jeremiah. They need help."

"Then they're gonna have to swallow their pride and go to the places who offer to give them help. Maybe your next article could feature a few of them instead of sensationalism."

Look what good coming to talk to her did! None. Maybe he wasn't the right fit for Ava Burcham. She needed someone a lot softer or a lot handier with a pistol than he was.

"I gotta get back to work." He started for the steps and turned around. "But if you don't listen to anything else I've said, hear this."

She turned her back to him, stiff and silent.

"If you want to make a real difference, then find a way. *Make* the difference. Stirrin' up rumors and puttin' yourself in harm's way will only cause more trouble." He rested his hand on the stair railing, breathing out a sigh. "I may not know much about writing, but I know you're smarter, braver, and a much better writer than that."

She spun around, peering at him, eyes narrowing. "No, you don't know about writin', do you? Never have."

Her words jabbed him right in the center of his lifelong struggle. And what's worse, she knew it.

"I'm gonna leave before you say a few more things to regret later." He crammed his hat back on his head and finished his descent down the steps, but her thick head needed another reminder. He pivoted at the bottom to face her.

She pulled the paper into her chest, her frown less stubborn and a little more. . .guilty.

"If you're gonna change the world around you, make sure you're not the one changing to fit. You've always been the sort to make a difference for others. Your kindness. Your encouragement. From school days to now. Your heart is as big as all those ideas in your head. But becoming somebody else?" He pointed to the paper and shook his head. "You're better than that and you know it."

~

"Ava's here." Welcome shouts came from inside the Combs' house Ava had frequented for years. Callie Mae emerged through the narrow doorway of the white clapboard house at a run, her blond curls dancing around her rosy face. Laura Alice lagged behind her big sister, the same sunlit hair bouncing around her smile as she nearly attacked Ava with a hug.

"You brought some ribbons for us, Ava?" The little cherub face looked up with wide blue eyes blinking. "So we'll look purdy for the shuckin'?"

"She always brings 'em." Callie Mae frowned down at her little sister. "She carries 'em with her in that satchel all the time."

Laura Alice's big blue gaze dropped to the bag hanging against Ava's hip.

"You don't need ribbons to look pretty since you're already about as pretty as can be." Ava leaned close and tapped the youngest's nose. "But what do you think, Laura Alice? You think I brought 'em?"

"You brought 'em. You always bring 'em." Laura Alice squeezed Ava's waist to punctuate her excitement. "Will you put 'em in my hair for the corn shuckin' tonight? Will you?"

The bountiful exuberance of the girls' welcome smoothed out the rough edges of the uneasiness Jeremiah's last visit left behind. He didn't understand, of course. He was a man. Things came easier for him. But even as she attempted to justify the way she'd written the article, she couldn't shake a tinge of disappointment hovering on the edges of her victory. . .and at her response to him. She'd been mean. He didn't deserve that.

She ignored the thought as Laura Alice tugged her by the waist toward the front porch. "Can you use four ribbons in my hair? I got enough hair for four, I think."

"Law mercy, let the poor girl get herself up the steps before you go botherin' her about them ribbons." Rosie Combs rested her palm against the doorway, her thin frame wrapped in a blue calico dress and well-worn apron. Her weary expression softened into a smile as her eyes met Ava's. "Well, Miss Ava, if you survive to the kitchen, I'll let you taste some molasses cookies I just fetched from the oven."

Ava's stomach pinched at the sight of Mrs. Combs's kind domesticity and relaxed mothering. She'd never known such a mother. Happy, strong. Sound.

"You don't have to ask me twice." Ava pulled away from the girls and followed the little entourage up the steps into a house at least five times bigger than Granny Burcham's mountain cabin. Of course, the Combses had five times the people to fill their house too.

"Elsie should be down in a minute or two. She wanted to have her dress on for this evenin' so you could match the ribbons in her hair with her frock. What a fine job you did on that dress too, Ava. Mighty fine work." Mrs. Combs disappeared through the narrow hallway toward the kitchen, Ava moving at a slower pace with Callie Mae and Laura Alice trying to peek into her satchel.

"It's easy when Elsie looks lovely in anything I make," Ava called after Mrs. Combs. She sent a glance up the stairs, a little excited to see how the dress fit on her friend.

Not three steps into the house, a tall shadow fell over Ava accompanied by the sickeningly sweet smell of tobacco snuff mixed with liquor. "Mighty fine to see you here, Ava Burcham."

A chill swept over Ava's shoulders as she turned. Why did it have to be Keen Gentry? Somehow, he always showed up at the most unexpected times, his large, boxlike frame towering over almost everyone else. A fact he seemed to take a great deal of pride in.

He stepped from the adjacent parlor room and sauntered toward her, his murky-gray eyes as inviting as his smell.

"Keen." She nodded but kept her smile tight. "What brings you around here?"

"Been helpin' out on the Combs' farm. Good work. Savin' for my own place." He took off his dirty fedora and dusted it against his thigh, his gaze trailing down her without one hint of mannerly subtlety.

Ava pulled her jacket more tightly around herself, if nothing else to block his view. How did he have the power to make her feel he could see through every piece of clothing she was wearing? And her coat was wool, even!

"Well, I'm sure you'll be proud to get your own place." Ava took the girls by the hands and attempted to bypass him, but he stepped in her way.

"What's your hurry?" His grin creased beneath his unruly beard, his words taking a languid turn his gaze didn't emulate. "We ain't visited for a while, have we?"

Ava pushed the girls around Keen's right, so they could slip down the hall away from whatever direction this conversation turned. Knowing Keen, it'd likely be downhill. "I don't reckon we have a lot to talk about."

"Don't ya?" He edged a step closer, the poignant scent of unwashed hardwork mingling with the sweeter odors to turn Ava's stomach.

"I didn't take you for a bobbins and cotton-talkin' sort of man."

Her reference barely paused his approach. "Naw, I ain't a cotton-talkin' sort of man a'tall. In fact, what I had in mind don't require a single word."

"I ain't interested." She cringed and stepped back. "Not even a little."

He moved closer, undeterred. "You won't know unless you give it a chance."

"I don't need no trial to know, without a doubt, you're one of the last men on this earth I'd ever spark, and definitely ever marry." She waved him away. "So get on back to your other gals and leave me alone."

"I didn't say nothin' 'bout matrimony." His finger slid down her arm, his sneer taking an even darker turn. "Ain't no man want to marry a woman with bad blood, which makes you the best kind o' girl. You can give all the fun without the noose."

Bad blood? Ava flinched at the reference to her mama, a chill, but she refused to quell beneath Keen's accusation. "Get your grubby hands off me." She smacked his palm away. "My daddy taught me better than to mess with hardheaded, empty-hearted fools like you."

His jaw tightened, and he leaned so close, his breath nearly brought up her breakfast. "Your daddy?" His lips took a nasty tilt up on one side as his palm fisted around her arm again, drawing her closer. "I reckon someone had to raise you, didn't they? Your mama was no count."

"Stay away from me, Keen Gentry, or I'll introduce you to the back of my hand."

He chuckled. "Your daddy was likely glad to leave this world after living with such a woman. Good thing she done her crazy self in not long after he died for the sake of everybody else—"

Ava stopped Keen's painful words with a fist to his mouth. She attempted to retreat down the hallway, but he grabbed her by the wrist, twisting until she winced. "No woman strikes me without feelin' a sting."

Ava felt a sting, all right. Her knuckles burned from the impact, but the trail of blood coming from the side of his lip made the sting worth every bit of future bruising. And he'd have a swollen lip for the corn shucking. Yes, sirree, totally worth it.

"Keen Gentry, you get your hands off that girl." Rosie rushed forward, skillet in one hand, and the other taking hold of Keen's arm.

Keen didn't so much as budge. His fingers only dug deeper into Ava's skin.

"Keen." Rosie's voice hardened. "If you don't let her go, I'll take my frying pan to that hard head of yours. And once I tell my husband about your antics, he won't hire you another day of your life."

This threat shook loose Keen's grip, and he took a step back.

"Now, git on out of here until you can learn some manners, boy." Rosie waved the skillet at him until he skulked out the door, but not before casting another threatening glance in Ava's direction.

As soon as the door closed behind him, Ava's knees nearly gave way, but thankfully the tears didn't.

"Fool of a boy. He ought not speak ill of the dead." Rosie shook her head at the closed door and then turned to Ava, brown eyes soft. "Come on, girl, let's have a cookie or two and leave the stink." She gestured toward the door with her chin. "Outside."

Ava followed Rosie toward the kitchen, Keen's words ushering up a whole host of unwelcome memories. Fits of rage. Hiding in the cellar. Daddy's soft voice calming the wildness of Mama's screams. Heat rose into Ava's face, blurring her vision. How could the memories impact her from the distance of so many years? She looked down at her hand as it quivered just the slightest, a habit inspired by her mother's unpredictable behavior. Bad blood?

She paused outside the kitchen, the little girls' happy chatter slicing into her shadowy thoughts. Her own family? Her own children? She closed her eyes to the thought, to the sliver of hope in the dream.

She'd heard the whispers her whole life. Kept the doubts at a distance from her future, but she'd never faced the reality of caring about a man enough to contemplate marriage until recently. . . .

Jeremiah didn't see her as bad blood, did he? Had her mama possessed a clear head when she was younger? Did the madness start after she got married? Had children?

Ava's breaths pulsed shallow, eyes burning. Did she have the madness in her?

She squeezed her eyes closed and swallowed through the lump gathering in her throat. She couldn't chance it, could she? Place

Jeremiah, if he even wanted a future with her, in a position where she'd ever hurt him the way she'd seen her mama wound her daddy.

Her nose twinged from the effort to keep her tears in check. No, she'd have to be enough. Make her own way. Rely on herself.

Because who would ever want to marry a woman with bad blood?

Chapter Five

A kiss is a powerful thing. 'Specially if a body means it.
Granddaddy Sutphin

A corn shucking may have brought people together from miles around, but it didn't make those people like each other any more than they had the day before.

Jeremiah cast another glance around Hubbert Easter's barn, taking in the distinctly drawn lines between the group of menfolk gathered to work through a massive pile of corn. Amid their congeniality and jokes, one side kept wary watch on the other, with Jeremiah and a few other men straddling the midline of a silent war.

It'd been this way as long as Jeremiah could remember, and having a lawman for a father, he'd heard more stories than he liked about both sides. Men from different political sides. The haves and have-nots. Above-the-mountain folks. Below-the-mountain folks. Allen. Goad. Hawks. Daniels. Why couldn't lines just make their way across the middle toward each other instead of always causing a divide?

He shook his head and patted the page from the newspaper he'd placed in his pocket, bringing his thoughts to sweeter places. Cameron Birch struck again, except this time, "he" announced that Temples' Alterations was offering to buy gently used clothes for cash money or trade-in for mended clothes. An idea, he felt pretty sure, originated with a certain hardheaded, softhearted friend of his. If he didn't know better, he'd say she was trying to find a way to keep folks from getting as desperate as Joe.

His grin tipped as he looked toward the barn door, the lights of the Easter house propped pleasantly on the hillside nearby. Somewhere up there, Ava helped the other ladies prepare food to bring down to the barn for everyone to enjoy.

He'd much rather keep his thoughts Ava-ward than partake in the underlying tension between the two groups sidling up on either end of the barn. The two sides even started a competition about who could shuck the most corn in half an hour, a feat that proved helpful for those waiting on shucked corn, but only incited a few more glares when the Allens and their party beat the other folks.

No, Jeremiah knew enough to steer clear of sides in this particular place, because all too often right and wrong started taking convoluted shades of revenge, pride, and family ties over truth. His daddy had always said, "Keep your head steady, your eyes open, and your heart true."

"I reckoned you'd be sittin' on *their* side now that you work for the Allens."

Casper Norris flashed a ready smile and took a seat.

Jeremiah stripped another ear and tossed the husk and the ear into their respective piles. "I don't mean to take sides. Seen too much on both ends to commit to one or the other."

Casper laughed, his full head of black hair bouncing in time with his shaking shoulders. "You can say that again. Betwixt your grand-daddy's run-ins with the law and your daddy trying to keep him out of jail for—" He lowered his voice. "Blockade liquor. I 'spect you've seen your due."

The mention of Jeremiah's family history, with a daddy who'd been a deputy and a granddaddy outlaw, shone as out of place as the deputy badge Casper showcased on his jacket lapel. Not quite the best impression to make at an "off duty" social event, but the man likely still puffed with a bit of pride at having been chosen by the sheriff.

Jeremiah picked up another piece of corn, keeping his focus on his work. "What's brought you all the way down here from Hillsville?"

Casper shrugged a shoulder, taking up an ear himself. "Ain't much to do up in Hillsville in the middle of December, so I figured I'd come where the people are."

Jeremiah nodded, his senses piqued with awareness. Years of hav-ing a lawman for a father—hearing stories and seeing things—may have heightened Jeremiah's senses to trouble, or perhaps it was just liv-ing in the mountains, where trouble happened too often when rumors, pride, and a bunch of hotheaded men got together. "Well, I'd say you found 'em." He tossed the husk into the pile. "Looking for anyone in particular?"

Casper's gaze rose to a group of men across the room. A few of the Edwards boys, a couple of Mitchells, and a Combs or two. Casper's grin returned and he nodded toward the open entry of the barn. "I wouldn't mind layin' eyes on Elsie Combs some more."

Jeremiah's shoulders relaxed with his smile. "Well, if that's the reason you showed up, then I think you'll get your wish. The womenfolk should be bringin' the food down in just a bit."

"That's what I'm countin' on." He tagged on a good-natured wink before picking up another ear of corn. "What about you? When do you plan to make things official with Ava? You been sparkin' her as long as I've known ya."

Heat swelled up from Jeremiah's middle into his face, and he tossed the bare ear in his hand to the pile. "I ain't too sure sparkin' is what I'd call it, Casp."

"What else then? Why, I heard one of the teachers recently say the two of you were thick as thieves the last three years of school."

Because Ava tutored him in writing, that's why. Mostly. Then. . . well, then it wasn't about the tutoring as much as the tutor. "We're friends. Good ones."

"And that's all?"

Not if he had a choice. Jeremiah's hesitation called his bluff.

"I knew it." Casper tossed another ear onto the pile. "Surely, she's interested."

How could Jeremiah switch this conversation to less personal ground? "I don't know about that."

"Then she ain't as smart as I thought she was. A solid, hardworking man like you?" Casper waved a husk toward him. "And her friend, besides?"

"I ain't tried to make it plain." Jeremiah rubbed the back of his heated neck. "We've been friends for most our lives and. . . Well, after all that's happened with her family, I don't know—"

"I can't fault you there." Casper's lips took a sour turn. "Takin' on a woman with her family history ain't for the faint of heart, and that's the truth. Can't be too sure the sickness won't reach to the daughter, especially her bein' a girl and all."

"There ain't nothin' wrong with Ava Burcham's mind." The defense shot from Jeremiah before he could stop it. "Nothin' a'tall. She's one of the smartest people I know." He curbed his tone. "I ain't worried 'bout her mind." Her curiosity, maybe. Her zeal? For sure. But not her mind.

"Well, once she sees that house you're workin' on, she'll set that sound mind in the matrimonial direction. You know that's what most women want. Stability." His smile took a syrupy slide as he drew a little closer to Jeremiah. "Speakin' of houses, I ain't never seen the like with Sid Allen's castle on the hill. Lights, even! Some say he's usin' liquor money to pay for it."

All the warmth from their previous camaraderie chilled. So this conversation wasn't just for conversation's sake. "I can't say I know anything about that sort of thing, Casp. The Allens have always been good to me and my people, but I wouldn't know about his personal business." Despite the rumors of the "Allen clan" skimming the edges of justice by getting out of lawsuit after lawsuit by force or manipulation, Jeremiah and his family had always had good dealings with them.

"Come on, now, Jeremiah. I reckon Sid gave you a few side jobs for added incentive." Casper nudged Jeremiah with his shoulder, his grin not matching the darker turn of his expression. "Of the less upright variety? Or, working as close to him as you do, you've overheard a few things here and there?" Casper reached his hand into his pocket, jingling some coins. "I can make it worth your while. Information to uphold the law is worth every cent."

Jeremiah breathed out his frustration through his nose and allowed some silence between them. The reason Casper Norris left one side of the barn to sit with Jeremiah in the middle didn't have anything to do with friendship, but information. Well, Jeremiah wasn't interested in giving him any, especially when he didn't have any to give. "I heard tell you were deputized a few weeks ago. I never figured you for the sort."

Casper's stare sharpened, but he held to his grin. "If you can't beat 'em, join 'em, I say." He took up another ear. "Runnin' liquor ain't got as much security in it as it used to. Not with all the revenue officers everywhere and the Hawkses taking over most of the business below the mountain. Besides, I'm less likely to be shot as a lawman." He gestured toward Jeremiah with his chin. "Your daddy's case was an exception, of course."

Jeremiah refused to respond to the reminder of his father getting caught in the cross fire of a family feud, with nary a person charged in the case due to the fact that no one could be pinpointed as the culprit. But that wasn't new in these parts. People were shot every day. Sometimes the culprits were found and prosecuted. Sometimes, nothing ever happened, but most times law was taken into private hands and folks turned a blind eye to the results.

"Besides, with my colorful background, I know about everybody and place in Carroll County, so Sheriff Blankenship brought me on before he resigned to help keep a lookout for illegal moonshinin' and watch out for. . ." His attention turned back to the boys across the room. "Trouble."

A small group of musicians gathered on the far side of the barn began a lively medley of fiddle, banjo, and guitar. A good sign. Meant the food, and ladies, were coming soon. A welcome distraction from the direction of the current conversation. "So this visit is more for business than pleasure."

"Ain't no reason I can't enjoy a little pleasure along with the business." He raised an ear of corn in salute.

"Speakin' of business." Jeremiah tossed another ear into the growing pile. "How's Joe Creed doing? His mama and sister are beside themselves with worry, last I heard."

Casper shot Jeremiah a look. "You don't know, then?"

Jeremiah's hand paused on the husk between his fingers, heat slowly slipping from his body. "Know what?"

"Joe was found dead in his jail cell yesterday mornin'." Casper raked a palm over his smooth chin and gave his head a slow shake. "By his own hand. Hanged himself."

Processing came slowly. Joe Creed killed himself? "But. . .but he wasn't no more than twenty years old. He had his whole life ahead of him."

"Guilt don't have an age requirement, I reckon." Casper tossed another ear into the pile. "All I can guess is he couldn't bear bringin' such shame on his family with what he'd done."

"But since his daddy ran off, he'd been takin' care of his family. Shame or not, he wouldn't have left his mama and sister on their own."

"Ain't much he could've done to take care of them from behind bars, Jeremiah." Casper shot him a frown. "With attempted murder and thievery on his record—"

"Attempted murder?"

"He fired a shot at Ava Burcham. Surely, you knew that already."

Jeremiah jerked up another ear of corn, squeezing it in his fist. "I heard tell it was an accident."

"Well, we can hear tell a lot of things, but I saw it with my own two eyes."

Joe had been a schoolmate. Good, quiet fellow. Maybe some of Ava's notions bode with a little truth. What sort of desperation took a man and turned him to crime. . .then suicide?

"I know, it's a travesty." Casper placed a hand on Jeremiah's shoulder. "Some just can't come back from the roads they've taken. But that's why the law is here—to help keep people from going too far."

Jeremiah leaned forward, resting his elbows on his knees. The whole idea fit like the wrong piece of wood. Joe Creed? Suicide?

The music bled into his thoughts, the familiar melody of "Come All Ye Fair and Tender Ladies." As if called by the melancholy tune, a procession of womenfolk entered through the open doors of the barn, their hands laden with platters and bowls as varied as the dresses they wore. Near the back of the line, where the younger women followed the elder, Ava walked beside Elsie Combs, her familiar smile wide in a laugh. She'd worn her hair down, in long, brownish-walnut waves, each side tied back in one of her famed ribbons. Red today, likely to match the stripes in her blouse.

His chest squeezed out his breath at the sight. What would she say if she could read his thoughts? If she saw how much he admired her smartness and generosity, her beauty? Would she laugh at him? Run away?

"Jeremiah Sutphin. Seems to be your lucky night." Casper whistled low and gestured toward the half-shucked ear of corn in Jeremiah's hand. "Lookie there."

The marbled red and orange kernels of the corn peeked through the last veil of the husk. Heat slipped from his face to his feet and back again. *Red.* He'd found a red ear of corn. First in his life. He blinked, bringing his attention up to Casper. "It's red."

Casper laughed. "Sure thing, it is." He patted Jeremiah on the shoulder and then turned to the crowd. "Got the first red ear for the night, y'all. Jeremiah Sutphin."

The crowd responded in unified applause, with a few rowdy calls added on by some of the younger men. Jeremiah's head must have been full of cotton, because it took way too long for him to make the connection between the red ear of corn and. . .what happened next.

"Well, Jeremiah." Casper gave the room a long, steady look, encouraging a few more calls and some laughter. "Who's the lucky lady?"

"Pick your gal!" someone yelled from the right.

"Ain't got no time for bein' yella, boy," came another call.

Casper leaned close. "This is the time to put that sparkin' into action, Jeremiah."

Jeremiah's face flamed. No wonder the word was called sparkin'. Somethin' akin to lightning shot through his entire body, shocking him to his feet. Maybe it was partly the goading of the crowd and partly a hankering he'd nursed for years, but the red ear in his hands gave him license to kiss any girl of his choice. His gaze zeroed in on his best friend.

And he knew exactly what to do next.

≷

Ava had just placed a bowl of boiled potatoes on the makeshift table in the barn, when a roar of applause burst from all around. Casper Norris stood up from the crowd, saying something about a red ear. Ava rolled her eyes heavenward. What a strange tradition, but at least it was one that played fair. If a gal got a red ear, she got to choose a fella as well. Who on earth Casper Norris would choose, she didn't care. Ava caught Elsie's brightening expression and sighed. Of course! Half the men in Carroll County were in love with Elsie and her pretty face, and her dark hair particularly fetching in lavender ribbons.

Well, if Ava ever found a red ear of corn, she might just break the thing in half and toss it to the ground. Her stomach pinched. She frowned over at Elsie, whose eyes only grew wider as they locked with Ava's. What was wrong with her?

"Ava?"

Ava turned around. Jeremiah stood in front of her, looking rather dashing in his white button-up and suspenders. He wore the strangest look on his flushed face, like he was nervous or something. "What's wrong?"

His grin slid crooked and he raised his right hand, which held an ear of corn. A *red* ear of corn. She looked from the corn to Jeremiah, trying to sort out the odd situation. What was Jeremiah doing with Casper Norris's red ear? And then reality clicked into place, especially when Jeremiah took a step closer to her. . .and the crowd's fury grew louder.

Ava's bottom lip came unhinged.

Jeremiah Sutphin planned on kissing *her*. Her body stiffened in preparation. She'd seen countless kisses over a red ear. Most times, the men moved in like they were branding a woman for life. She closed her eyes to brace for the onslaught.

The gentlest warmth slid against her cheek, soft, and bringing the scent of sawdust and soap. Her eyes fluttered open. Jeremiah cradled her cheek with one hand, his gaze searching hers, asking for permission, maybe? She wasn't sure, but her breath quivered out of her as he breached the distance. His lips, firm and warm, brushed against hers, inciting a cascade of swelling warmth. Was this sweetness, this tender touch, what a kiss was supposed to be? She'd never experienced anything so intimate and alive in all her life. Every muscle stood on edge... waiting. For what? Her fingers wrapped around his jacket. For a little more.

He tarried, his breath trembling as if his body shook from the contact too. Was he as mesmerized? Could a kiss shake a man like the quake running through her? Surely men took something like this as commonplace.

But when Jeremiah pulled back, his thumb gently caressing her cheek before he released her, the tremulous smile on his face confirmed all her questions. The contact had impacted him with as much unexpected. . .rightness as her. She blinked up at him, her eyes swarming with a fresh sting of tears.

"Tradition?" he whispered, with a half shrug, but his lingering gaze said so much more.

He was so good. Her heart thrummed into a slower beat, a steady ache growing in the center and branching out. Too good for her.

Another burst of shouts rang out, jarring her from her stare. She flinched out of her kiss-dazed stare at Jeremiah, thoughts coming in slow motion. On the far side of the barn, Wesley Edwards, one of the Allen crew, raised a red ear as a trophy to the room.

All eyes moved to Maude Iroler, Wesley's longtime gal, the same jeering as with Jeremiah rising from one side of the barn to the other. Maude's face flushed such a deep hue of crimson, Ava could see it across the barn. But perhaps the fog of Jeremiah's kiss still permeated her thinking, because instead of Wesley taking the few steps toward his regular gal, he marched across the barn toward Ava and Jeremiah. Ava froze. Jeremiah's kiss was one thing, but she had no interest whatsoever in a kiss from Wesley Edwards. But Wesley turned toward the dessert table and, without hesitation, swept Rebekah McCraw into a hearty kiss.

The crowd roared with encouragement. Will Thomas, Rebekah's beau, jumped up from his seat and rushed forward. Sidna Edwards came to his brother's side while a dazed Rebekah McCraw stumbled back against the wall.

Maybe Wesley's mind was more muddled than Ava's, because he'd just kissed the wrong girl.

"Get away from her." Will shoved a grinning Wesley away from Rebekah and gestured across the barn to a rather pale-faced Maude Iroler. "What are you doin' kissin' *my* girl when you already got one of your own?"

"No need to get so riled." Wesley tossed off the comment with a lazy glance back to Rebekah. He waved the red ear. "Ain't nothin' wrong with a little fun for tradition's sake, and who's to say it'd do your girl some good to get a worthwhile kiss for once."

Ava cringed from the toenails upward. Those were fightin' words if ever words were spoken.

Will surged forward, fists at the ready, but Jeremiah jumped in between, bracing his palm against Will's chest. "This ain't the time or place, boys." His gaze narrowed on Wesley. "Joke or not. We'd do wise to treat Mr. Easter's invitation with the respect it deserves."

"Ain't no disrespect at all, Jeremiah." Wesley swept his cap low with a bow. "Some folks just don't have a sense of humor's all."

Will growled but backed away, his hands still balled so tight that the white of his knuckles shone against the lantern light. "You Allens think you can take whatever you want and no one'll stop ya, but times are changing, and that's a fact." A cool sweat broke out on the back of Ava's neck as Will's ruddy face took on a deeper and contorted shade. "Just 'cause your kind prances around these parts high on the hog, don't mean you deserve it. Never have. And some day you'll get your due." His warning ground out like thunder before a storm. "Make no mistake 'bout that."

His words left a tension sizzling in the air, a foreboding. She'd seen the same kind of anger too many times to ignore the possible consequences. Whether from boyhood folly or a less benevolent intention, Wesley Edwards sparked a flame that had been simmering for years. Ava prayed the fire stayed low and died quickly.

But the expression on Will Thomas's face as he glanced back toward Wesley before taking Rebekah out of the barn didn't bode well for dying flames.

Chapter Six

Pride and youth go together like a spark and dynamite.
Just make sure you keep your distance or you're bound to get a sting.
Granddaddy Sutphin

What a horrible way to end a mighty fine kiss.

Jeremiah followed Will Thomas toward the barn door to make sure the boy created some distance between himself and Wesley Edwards, his own irritation pricking an underlying heat in his face. One minute he was staring down into Ava's face, her eyes as warm and welcoming as winter sunrise, her lips just as inviting, and the next, he was keeping Will Thomas from tearing apart boneheaded Wesley Edwards for playing with fire.

Boys will be boys, some said, but once those boys turned fourteen, they started carrying Colts around in their pockets, and childhood humor could take a swift and dark turn. What's more, Wesley had offended Will's honor in front of a large group, and if there was anything that bordered on being as important to the mountain folks as family and faith, it was honor.

"Why did you do it, Jeremiah?"

He turned from his place outside the barn door to find Ava standing beside him, her narrowed eyes searching his face with a look of utter distrust. Her nose crinkled like the little girl he'd once known.

He worked hard to tamp down his grin. "Do what?"

"You know good and well." Her hands landed on her hips, but she lowered her voice. "Why did you kiss me?"

He studied her upturned face in the moonlight. After the kissing, the sight seemed to be a little bit sweeter than before. "Tradition?"

"Which means you could've picked any girl." She waved a hand back toward the barn. "Wesley sure did! Why did you pick *me*?"

He shifted a step closer, his grin slipping free just a little bit. " 'Cause you're the only girl in the whole barn I think is worth kissing. For me, anyhow."

"You shouldn't have kissed me like that."

"Like what?"

Her brow puckered. "Like you. . .well, like you meant it."

A sudden swell of compassion nearly buckled him at the knees, but he hung on to his grin. "I did mean it."

"You shouldn't mean it, Jeremiah." She lowered her head with a slow shake, her hand reaching back to stroke her loose hair. Her nervous habit. " 'Cause I'll only break your heart."

"How do you reckon that?"

She tightened her chin and met his gaze. "I ain't never gonna marry."

He paused his forward motion and searched her face. "You sound pretty sure."

"I *am* pretty sure."

Her confidence doused the sweet warmth resurrecting in his chest from their kiss. He hadn't practiced kissing a whole bunch; in fact, his experience was practically nonexistent unless he counted Prissy Ingle in fourth grade, on a dare. And that was nowhere near as pleasant as kissing Ava. But surely his skills weren't so bad as to put a woman off marriage forever. Truth was, Ava hadn't seemed to mind his kiss one bit. The only other option would be. . . "Because I ain't good enough for you?"

"No, it has nothing to do with you." She rolled her eyes and groaned. "In fact, you're *too* good for me. That's why I'd never tie you to somebody like me. I'd. . .I'd never want to hurt you like that."

"What do you mean?"

She turned to walk away, but he grabbed her by the hand. "Ava, is this about your mama?"

Her lips tightened into a line as she dropped her head. "It may not seem like anything to you, but I seen what it did to my daddy. How he wearied over time from having to take care of a woman like her. The fear and helplessness of a man as good as you."

"Ava, you ain't your mama."

The tear-filled eyes she raised to his tore at his heart. "But what if whatever happened to her is waiting to happen to me?"

He pressed her cold hand, trembling slightly between his palms, and leveled her with a stare. "I don't believe that."

"Not believing don't make it untrue." She jerked her fingers from his hold.

"And believing don't make it *true*." He raked a hand through his hair and breathed out as she folded her arms across her chest and looked away.

He knew the stories about her mama. In fact, he'd been with his daddy when they discovered Ava in a house full of death. He cringed at the memory of the pale, trembling face of a twelve-year-old Ava, sitting motionless in a bloodstained dress, beside him in the wagon. But even with the pain of her childhood, he'd never worried about her soundness of mind. Sure, she'd made some ridiculous choices, like writing up some clan names in the newspaper, but each act could be traced back to a clearheaded and, usually, bighearted intention. "Do you want to be married one day, Ava? Have a family?"

Her refusal to answer only confirmed his suspicions.

"Well, then, there's only one thing to do."

She looked up at him. "And what's that?"

"I reckon you need to do some investigatin', Miz Reporter. Don't you?"

"You ain't makin' no sense."

"The only person who knew much about your mama when she moved here, besides your daddy, is your Granny Burcham, and there ain't no clearer-headed woman alive."

Her brow furrowed with her frown. "What do I ask her, Mr. Know-It-All?"

"Come on now, Ava. You can figure that out, I'm sure."

He stepped close to her, her glossy eyes widening like large gray-green saucers in the moonlight. "I know you care about me. You wouldn't give up a future for me if you didn't." He raised a palm to her cheek, her skin as soft as the satin ribbons she always carried. "And I care a whole lot about you."

"Jeremiah," she whispered, her gaze beckoning him to close the distance. "I *can't* care about you like this. I won't be the woman who breaks your heart."

He ran his hand down to cup her chin and gave it a little squeeze. "That's just because you're afraid and you don't believe in yourself enough yet."

Her frown deepened as a tear slipped down her cheek. "What's that supposed to mean?"

"Someday you'll see who you really are. Not what the fools say about the whole bad-blood nonsense. No. How I see you. How God sees you." He swallowed, pushing the desire to kiss her away. "And you'll be ready to trust me. . .to love me back without being afraid."

Ava's mind raced all night after the corn shucking. She forced her body still as she shared a bed with Elsie in the Combs house. Her thoughts revisited the scenes, over and over again, especially Jeremiah's kiss. . . and his challenge. If she didn't ask her granny, Ava could live in blissful ignorance of any symptoms she may develop over time, but she'd also forgo the opportunity to be a wife to a good man. . .and one day, a mother. Was ignorance worth that loss? Living in the fear of what-if?

Morning came too quickly, and before long, she'd loaded up in the Combs' wagon for the short ride to church, each of the Combs girls displaying new ribbons in their braids, even Mrs. Combs. Laura Alice cozied up to Ava's side, her little, pudgy arm linked through Ava's as the wagon bumped along the dirt road. Her sweet warmth, pressed close, pinched at a soft spot in Ava's grand plans for singleness.

Oh, how she wanted a family—to have the opportunity to cultivate one that didn't involve fear and deep-riveted wounds. But how could she trust her wants when the very real memory of her mother lingered in every corner of her mind?

The white steeple of the church-schoolhouse rose ahead of them, like a beacon into the sunny December morning, turning Ava's thoughts in a more heavenly direction. God had always seemed so far away, so distant, from the shadows waving a sinister hand over the works of the world. She'd asked Him into her heart as a little girl, but with so much brokenness in her past, could she really trust Him with her future?

A few voices from inside already carried the strains of a melody.

What was it? "Leaning on the Everlasting Arms"?

The song sliced through the murky recesses of her history, resurrecting a memory of her daddy singing to her before bed after one of Mama's more difficult nights had led her to violence and too much drink. He'd never had what some would call a good voice, but it was his, and that was what mattered. He'd place his palm on her head and whisper the same words every night when he was home. *"The Lord your God is in your midst, a mighty one who will save; he will rejoice over you with gladness; he will quiet you by his love; he will exult over you with loud singing."*

It had been a long time since she'd heard her daddy singing, but. . .could God be with her in her daddy's place? Could He "quiet" her heart with His love? She'd given up on receiving good from Him when her life fell apart at twelve. He didn't seem to be with her, or rejoice over her, but if He was mighty to save, could He save her now? Especially if it meant saving her from herself?

As Laura Alice chattered on about how much more beautiful her ribbons were than the other girls', Ava's heart tugged with a sliver of hope that just maybe He hadn't given up on her after all. She'd experienced a "quiet heart" before, but never for long. With her daddy. Her brother. Her granny, and. . .yes, with Jeremiah. Had God given her those memories, those people, to reveal His presence in scenes from her childhood? Her adulthood?

Heat invaded her vision. She'd never thought about the people in her life in such a way before.

Ava followed the Combses into the church, the school desks pushed out of the way to make space for simple benches. Because they'd come in later than most other folks, Laura Alice and Ava took seats in the back near the door. Most of the folks from the corn shucking filled the pews, with a few additional parishioners Ava didn't recognize. A potbelly stove stood to the side, making a failed attempt at staving off the December cold. Ava pulled her jacket closer around herself and focused on the song as it continued on for another verse, the words confirming her inward revelations.

I have blessed peace with my Lord so near, leaning on the Everlasting Arms.

Blessed peace? The closest she'd ever known peace was when she was with her brother at the fishing hole, or the times she'd walk through the woods with her daddy on one of his trapping adventures, or sitting by Granny Burcham's fire listening to stories and eating molasses cookies. But those were just memories, barely whispers in a life. This song spoke of God's arms of unfailing strength and constant peace.

Some whispers in life are made of paper, and some are made of steel. She'd always thought her granny's adage referred to bad memories, but what if she'd meant the good ones?

"I just can't see how Wesley Edwards can waltz into his uncle's church this morning."

Ava's ears perked to the harsh whisper ahead of her in the pew from an older lady she'd noticed last night at the shucking. "Like he ain't shamed the Thomas family enough with his kissin' the McGraw girl last night."

"You're makin' a fuss over nothin'." The neighboring woman consoled. "Boys'll do anything to make a scene."

"Especially that one. Once his daddy died and Floyd Allen took over the rearin' of them Edwards boys, there was no hope left for 'em but to come out just as headstrong as their uncle."

Just the mention of the patriarch of the Allen family sobered Ava's thoughts. Although Floyd and all of the Allens had always been kind to her, she'd heard tales of their darker sides. Shoot-outs—even between brothers—and then using their influence with the higher-ups to get out of jail, and some of their tougher ways of obtaining payment for debts accrued.

But she'd also seen Sid Allen's big heart in making sure Jeremiah had quick successions of carpentry jobs when he started out on his own. And, of course, the simple fact that Sid had traveled to so many places beyond Carroll County made him a little more fascinating than most. She sighed. How on earth did one decide what to believe about another person?

She certainly didn't want people assigning her mother's reputation to her, even though, from the conversation with Keen, she knew some folks did.

A movement at the door caught in Ava's periphery. Framed by

the gray morning, Will Thomas stepped over the threshold without removing his cap. He scanned the congregation, his attention finally landing on a fixed point ahead. Ava followed the direction to Wesley Edwards, who'd taken a seat just behind the preacher's stand, likely due to the fact that the preacher was his uncle Garland. . . or the fact Wesley liked being noticed. Sidna, the quieter of the two brothers, sat beside his brother, looking about as comfortable as a cat in a rainstorm. Ava cringed. Sitting facing the congregation wouldn't have suited her either. Wesley's rich voice rose above the others around him, and he seemed completely oblivious to Will's presence. Hopefully, he'd stay that way. Any meeting between Will and Wesley couldn't end well with the events of the previous night still humming among the conversations in the room. But the storm cloud on Will's face came with persistence.

Wesley looked up then and gave a shake of his head, raising his hymnal as if to tell Will he had something better to do. Ava almost gave a sigh of relief, but something else exchanged between the two that she didn't quite catch, because Wesley snapped his hymnbook closed with enough force to garner his brother Sidna's attention, and then he weaved his way out from behind the pulpit and down the aisle.

Will stepped outside, letting the door close before Wesley reached it, and something hitched in Ava's pulse. She looked back at Sidna, who'd stopped singing and was staring at the closed door.

Raised voices were heard from behind the door.

Ava squeezed her braid, attention sliding from Sidna to the door, and then, without making a sound, she moved from the pew and out the door. Laura Alice and a few others followed on her heels, to find Wesley standing in the middle of the churchyard, three men surrounding him and Will Thomas, who was on the ground with a bloody nose. Will Thomas's daddy, one of the three, lunged forward to help Will to his feet while the two other men, one being—Ava paused in her forward movement at the sight—Casper Norris? What was he doing getting involved in a brawl like this?

Wesley had his gun out, but so did one of the other men, as he attempted to pistol-whip Wesley, who dodged the attack with the fluidity of well-honed practice. Casper's fist didn't miss, though, and slammed right into Wesley's unprotected stomach.

Ava took a few steps forward.

Four on one? This wasn't fair a'tall!

Wesley rallied and vaulted into Casper like a man on fire, while Will and his father began an approach to Wesley's unguarded back.

A growl surged from behind Ava just before she felt a force lunge past her. Sidna Edwards lit in on Will and Mr. Thomas with the fury of vengeful kin, taking the elder down with a single punch. A flying rock came from the direction of the Wesley-Casper fight, barely missing Ava's nose, but bouncing off Clementine Thomas's tightly rolled hair. The young woman paused for a second, blinked over at her brother— who'd been downed by another punch from Wesley—and slid into a slump on the grass with a whimper of tears.

A whole host of ladies flocked to her side, but the rock hadn't hit with any force, especially with the amount of hair Clementine boasted. Ava rolled her eyes. You'd think Clementine had been shot in the head.

"Stop this at once," came the rough baritone of Rev. Garland Allen, Bible still in hand, as he emerged from the crowd standing in the doorway of the church. "This ain't the place nor time for such commotion."

Sidna's fist paused before dropping another punch to Bud Easter's pulverized face. Heeding the words—or maybe more so the wrath—of his uncle, he pushed Bud so hard the young man fell to the ground. Wesley stood from his kneeling position beside Mr. Thomas, the point of his blackjack shining from his hand.

"Who started this disruption to our public worship?"

"Will Thomas." Wesley picked his cap up off the ground, returned his knife to his pocket, and faced his uncle. "He called me out of church and set me up for a floggin'."

The preacher's icy blue eyes stilled on Mr. Thomas as Will helped him to a stand. "That so, George?"

"We come to get an apology for your nephew's offensive behavior last night, Garland. We didn't come for no fight."

Four-on-one didn't match that statement.

"They came at me first, Uncle." Wesley stepped closer to Garland. "Ain't gonna let them wallop me without defendin' myself."

"You refused to make amends, boy." Mr. Thomas's finger jabbed the air.

"I didn't do no wrong." Wesley shrugged, his grin taking a rascally turn. "Just havin' a bit of fun."

"George, you got no cause for this." Garland stepped closer to the Thomas patriarch, his voice taking on a gentler appeal. "Wes didn't mean no offense in plucking some fun last night. You know how boys'll be—"

"You Allens think you own this mountain." George Thomas raised his finger to Garland like a weapon, his right eye nearly swelled closed. "You've been offendin' folks for years without consequences, but there's a change in the law round here, and you won't get by with it no more."

A chill shot up Ava's back at the unveiled warning. She scanned the crowd. One man slowly rose from the ground, Will kept his arm around his father as they turned to walk away, and Casper Norris? He was nowhere to be seen.

Wesley turned to the waiting crowd, wiping the back of his hand across his bloody smile as his assailants dissipated. "Well, I hope that's taught 'em who the better man is, at any rate. What'd you say we get back to some singin'?"

A few in the crowd chuckled at Wes's attempt at levity. Sidna dusted off his suit jacket and frowned over at his brother. From the look on his face, Garland shared the same sober sentiment as his elder nephew.

Something sinister permeated the morning air like the thick humidity of a summer afternoon. A terrible foreboding rife with long-held anger and blind rage breathed out from the crowd, with fingers from the past twisting half truths and hard hearts.

How could something as simple as a kiss set ablaze a scene with the scent of murder?

Ava pressed her palm to her chest and squeezed her eyes closed. *Kisses were mighty powerful things.*

Chapter Seven

When you don't know who you are, you spend more time
stumbling in the dark than findin' your feet.
Granny Burcham

Ava had barely spent a moment with Jeremiah since the corn shucking. Not that he'd been far from her thoughts, though. He and his kiss seemed to show up at every unoccupied moment, reminding her and her pulse rate of a question for which she had no answer.

They'd met in Sid Allen's store on Wednesday while she picked up supplies for Granny Burcham, but that was enough time to pass on news neither wished to share. Jeremiah's came with the deepest sting.

Joe Creed was dead. And at his own hand?

It didn't seem possible.

The entire situation with the churchyard brawl appeared minor in comparison to the loss of such a young life. Ava gave a gentle nudge to her mule, urging his pace up the steady incline of the mountainside. Dooley grunted his response but increased his pace...a little. She hated making him work so hard to weather the ridges and valleys to Granny Burcham's, but riding cut her journey in half, and it already took the better part of an afternoon to make it to her granny's secluded cabin.

A new path spread out to her right at the foot of the mountain, resembling the makings of a road. She scanned the forest around her and peered down the trail, trying to make out anything in the distance. She'd visited granny a few weeks before and there'd been nothing to hint at someone moving back here. It proved a good location, though. The river circled in all directions on this mountain, and a person could get to town in only an hour or so by fast horse.

Ava looked up the narrow mountain path toward Granny Burcham's.

She still had a good two-hour ride to make the ridge by nightfall, but every minute was worth it, to know she still had one person left in the world whom she could call family. She grinned at the idea of her weathered and wiry grandmother, cast another look down the new trail, and then began the trek deeper into the woods.

Not long after Ava's family died, she'd tried to convince Granny Burcham to move closer to town so Ava wouldn't have to live with the Temples to attend school, but Granny's house had been in her family for generations. Memories, sweat, wounds, and celebrations etched into the very walls of the tiny cabin, and after just one week in town, Granny had nearly worried herself into a frenzy.

No, Ava knew her granny would die there, and happily so. The place, the generations, permeated through her to the quick, and no other place would be home. It's the way things were in the mountains, how the land clung to a heart, and a heart clung back.

Light barely topped the trees with its molten colors by the time Ava reached the familiar log-hewn cabin. Residual snow glistened like silver among the towering pines, and the thinning winter foliage gave glimpses of cascades of fields down below, trailing all the way to another set of mountains, and then another—some sprinkled with the fairy white of snowfall and others ablaze with the fiery light of sunset. The trees ached and squeaked in the breeze, welcoming the evening with their broken moans, and the world suddenly felt larger and broader and more beautiful than it had before. Was this God's view? Did the world seem so small to Him?

Daddy had lived as a man who'd felt seen and heard by God. How could Ava find such an understanding when she'd felt nothing but insignificant to His plans for so long? She grasped for the tiny hint of peace she'd recognized earlier. *The Lord God is in your midst. A mighty one to save. He will quiet you with His love.*

"I thought I heard you creepin' up the trail." Granny Burcham emerged from the dusk-covered front porch, her wiry salt-and-pepper hair spun back in its usual tight bun. "Get on in here afore the chill sets in."

Ava smiled, dismounted, and took her bags from the mule, leaving Dooley to find his way around the house to his usual place in the makeshift lean-to. The warmth in Granny's voice gave no room for chills or shadowy thoughts, and Ava breathed in the belonging like a hungry child who'd found bread. Family. Home.

"I can smell the fried apple pies from here."

A familiar chuckle guided Ava up the steps and into ready arms. Granny Burcham stood a foot shorter than Ava and often joked that she'd started shrinking when she turned sixty and had been losing an inch every year since.

"You don't reckon I'd leave you without your fried pies now, girl?" Granny patted Ava's back and led the way into the small cabin. A large bed stood to the far corner, covered with one of granny's quilts passed down from her mama. Ava could practically feel the straw-tick mattress scratching up against her skin. She'd share the bed with Granny until she returned to the Temples.

Two ladder-back chairs sat pulled near the fire with a small table between, and from the attached kitchen on the back side of the house came a more potent whiff of apples and cinnamon and...?

"Did you make some peach ones too?"

Granny Burcham chuckled, took the bags from Ava, and scurried off to the kitchen like a peddler ready to show his best wares. Her simple calico dress hung to the dusty brown boots Ava had purchased for her from Sid Allen's store two winters ago. The product of one of her first hefty paychecks from Temples'. "I found a can of 'em in the cellar yesterday and got to studyin' on how to use 'em." She shot a wink over her shoulder. "And you're the best excuse I got, girl."

Ava's smile brimmed as she lowered her hood and shimmied out of her coat, welcoming the light and warmth of the fire in more ways than one. Within minutes, Granny had Ava sitting by the fire, tea in one hand and fried pie in the other, quilts covering their legs.

Ava raised the tea to her lips but barely got in a swallow.

"Now, what's the latest goin's on?"

Ava sighed back into the chair, mulling over her response. Maybe she should ease into the news about Joe. "There was a churchyard scuffle on Sunday at Garland Allen's church."

Granny crinkled her leathery face in a frown and waved the news away. "That ain't no news a'tall. Folks is always a-fightin' round these parts."

"Maybe it'd make a difference if I told you it was between the

Allens and the Thomases over a shuckin' kiss."

"Woowee, now you've caught me and right good too." Her pale eyes glittered, with a little extra help from the firelight. "Kisses are powerful things, 'specially if a body means 'em."

Heat climbed up Ava's neck, scorching her throat, and she shoved a piece of the apple fritter into her mouth.

"So, who done the kissin' and who done the fightin'?" She chuckled. "Ain't too surprised when they come together."

Ava took her time chewing the cinnamon-apple goodness and hoped the shadows in the room covered the pink in her cheeks from the mere mention of kissing. In fact, she could even feel it all over again, if she closed her eyes. *Have mercy!*

"That must be a mighty fine apple fritter from the way you're moonin' over it."

Ava's eyes flew wide and she pushed through a swallow before offering a grin. "You know how much I love your fritters."

"Hmm." Granny cradled the teacup between her wrinkled hands. Her gaze, clear enough to draw the secrets out of anybody, let Ava off the hook by returning to the fire. "Keep on tellin' the story. It ain't fittin' to leave a granny in suspense over a kiss."

Ava lowered her chin to hide her growing smile. Her granny's curiosity bordered on insatiable, and no wonder, since she spent all of her time tucked away in this isolated cabin. Without further ado, Ava divulged the entire tale, from Saturday night into Sunday morning, with Granny asking clarifying questions here and there.

With a few tsks, Granny leaned back in her chair and shook her head. "There's been trouble brewin' 'tween the Allens and the Courthouse Clan for years, Ava, and there's naught to be done about it as far as I can tell. 'Ceptin' prayer and a good dose of humility on all sides."

"Do you think this could lead to more trouble?"

Granny lowered her cup to the little table and guided a weathered finger across her lips, focus trained on the firelight. "There's folks that have a way of makin' trouble and those who end up steppin' right in the thick of it. I'm afeared we got two sides of troublemakers in this fight." Her gaze drew distant, her profile almost a statue. "Bitterness is a wicked poison. Fogs up the head and sickens the heart till folks call wrong right and right wrong."

"Granny?"

She blinked and turned back to Ava, taking up her cup with a renewed smile. "I've gone on and darkened the mood of this mighty fine evenin'. What else can you tell me about news?"

"Nothing that will brighten the mood, I'm afraid." Ava drew in a deep breath and took a long sip of her tea, now tepid. Talking about death never came easy. "Joe Creed died in jail last Friday night."

"What?" Granny sat up straight, her chair giving a squeak in protest. "How?"

The words faltered on Ava's tongue. She took another sip before continuing. "Hanged himself, from what I heard."

"Have mercy." Granny's palm went to her chest and she quickly set her cup back on the table. "What in the world?"

"I know. It's so sad. So unexpected."

"Sure is, and downright wrong." Granny stood, her hand still pressed to her chest, and began pacing back and forth in front of the fireplace. Her little black-and-gray bun, so tightly wound at the back of her head, gave the slightest bob in response to her shaking head. "Joe wouldn't do a thing like that, surely."

"Well, Jeremiah got the news straight from Deputy Norris."

"But that boy was the only breadwinner for his mama and little sister. I can't think of any desperation or shame big enough that he'd put himself above them." She paused, giving her head a firmer shake. "No, sirree. Somethin' ain't right."

Ava lowered her own cup, the fire's heat suddenly losing its potency. "What are you sayin', Granny?"

"Just studyin' on it, I reckon." Her words came slow, soft, as if she spoke more to herself than Ava. She picked up a poker at the side of the rock fireplace and gave the logs a little nudge. "Deputy Norris told Jeremiah, you say?"

Ava folded her hands together, to attempt to warm them from a sudden chill. "That's right. Casper Norris."

Granny tilted her head closer but didn't turn to look at Ava. "Enoch Norris's boy?"

Ava raked through her memory for an answer. She didn't know

Casper very well. He was older than her and had lived most his life below the mountain. "I think so. Why?"

Granny sighed and placed the poker down before returning to her seat, her body bent more than before. "Nothin', likely. He's from a rough lot, but if Lew Webb saw fit to keep him as a deputy, then maybe he broke out of the Norris mold."

Ava stared into the flickering flames, Granny's words rekindling her internal argument from the past few days. Was it possible to break from the mold? To separate from the horrors of the past?

"Now look, I've cast gloom on you, and I'm sorry for that." Granny covered Ava's hand with her own. "My heart just aches for Joe's mama and sister, is all. Tragedies like this don't make sense to the human mind."

Ava battled voicing the questions she'd been contemplating since her talk with Jeremiah. Did she want the answers? Granny would tell her the truth, dark and all. Was Ava's future stained with her mama's brokenness?

"Granny, do you believe in the notion of bad blood? That we can't escape the sicknesses of our people?"

Granny's brows furrowed beneath her crinkled forehead, and she took her teacup back in hand. "You know Jeremiah's granddaddy was one of the biggest moonshiners in the county, don't you?"

Why was Granny asking about Jeremiah's granddaddy? "Yes, ma'am."

"And, far as anyone can tell, he's got blood on his hands from his dark deeds, just like many of the folks who fall in love with money shine-makin' brings. In fact, there's some folks that say the rascal had his second wife killed just because she didn't cut his hair the way he liked it."

"Granny!" Ava sat up straight. "Those are just rumors." Ava's hands pinched more tightly together. "Ain't they?"

"Larson Sutphin was a mean man in his younger days, Ava. There's no tellin' what sorts of awful truths the shadows would show, if they could." Granny shook her head. "But would you ever be afraid that Jeremiah carried the same meanness as his granddaddy?"

"Of course not."

Granny's thin lips crooked ever so slightly and she gave Ava's hand a squeeze. "You can't keep livin' in fear of her. She only has the hold you give her."

"Her blood flows in me. I know what it was like to watch her rail and scream and act like some kind of wild animal." Ava's voice scraped over her throat, harsh, breathy. "I'd never want to hurt the people I love the way she did, Granny."

Granny tilted her head and examined Ava. "You forget you got Burcham blood in you too, and we're a sturdy, solid-minded sort."

"Granny." Ava sniffled and pulled her hand away to wipe at the moisture on her face.

"I see. Someone's called you out on it again, ain't they?" She stood and walked to the kitchen, only to come back and refill the teacups, the sweet scent of mint rising in the air.

Ava lowered her gaze. "Something like that."

"Hmm. . ." Granny took her seat again and pressed back in the chair until it gave another creaking noise. "Your mama was never a strong-willed woman. Even when she first came to live in the mountains, she'd stay in such a state of fright 'bout everything, your daddy wouldn't leave her alone, so he'd bring her here when he'd have to go trappin'." Granny's smile gentled. "And your mama hated bein' back here in the hills. So your daddy started findin' jobs to do closer to home, but that still didn't seem to suit her. She took to drinkin' right after your brother was born, but even before then, Ava, she lived in fear all the time. That kind of fear leads to a nervous and unsteady mind."

"And then. . .when Tucker was born?" Ava had heard the story.

Granny studied Ava's face before her gaze turned back to the fire. "She got worse. She never physically hurt nobody, but she just wouldn't take care of the baby. Tucker and you ended up staying with me more than you ever did your mama when you was wee babes."

"And she got even worse after I was born." The statement didn't require an answer. Ava knew. Something about Ava being a girl triggered her mama's anger more than it had with her brother, and from the time Ava could remember, her daddy never left Ava alone with her mama. Rarely left Tucker alone with her, but as he got older, he developed the same kind of soothing voice as Daddy used to calm her.

"She was broken long before you were born."

"But me bein' born seemed to make whatever was wrong with her mind worse." What if that was the trigger for Ava too? What if she felt fine and lived life fine until she had her first baby and then. . .

"Fear don't speak truth, never has. You'd be wise to not heed it." Granny tapped Ava's knee. "Your mama came to these mountains as a broken woman from a broken family. Years after your daddy married her, he learned the shameful things that went on inside her house growin' up and why she'd been so keen to marry him quick as a whip, just to get out of there."

"I—I don't want to hurt the ones I love like she did, Granny." Ava pinched her eyes closed and tucked her wobbling chin down. "I'd rather die alone than bring that type of pain to somebody else."

Granny's eyes shimmered with uncustomary tears, and she reached her weathered palm to cup Ava's cheek. "I reckon we all got bad blood, if you think about it, girl. But. . ." She raised her long narrow index finger along with her brow. "We got something else that's a marvel."

"What's that?"

"Do you believe what the Good Book says about Jesus covering you with His blood, Ava?"

She'd heard it her whole life, felt the truth of it deep in her soul even when the circumstances screamed that she was too broken and too alone to feel His love. Her daddy and granny had shown her what grace looked like, and Ava had embraced it so freely years ago, in the quiet of a nightly prayer with her daddy. "I hope so."

"Oh girl, you don't have to hope. The Bible says it's for certain, no matter how much bad blood we got in our past."

Ava pinched her trembling lips closed as Granny continued.

"And if I figure it proper, the blood of Jesus is only *good* blood. The best there is. And He washes the bad blood away forever."

"From my mama's influence too?"

Granny's smile crinkled at the corners of her eyes. "If He took on death, hell, and the grave, girl, don't you think He's strong enough for all those worries spinnin' in your head?"

Ava wiped at her eyes again. "If the Good Book says all this, why don't more people believe it?"

"That's a great question, for sure, and I can only say that most folks believe exactly what they want to believe, whether it's true or not. Makes it easier on fragile sensibilities and bigheaded pride." She winked. "Which means you got the choice too, don't you? Hold on to truth or ride the wind of fear?"

Ava sighed back in the chair and closed her tired eyes, trying to hold to the peace Granny's words offered. A sudden weight hit her knees and she looked down to find a worn Bible sitting on her lap. She looked over at Granny, who only tapped the book. "Truth douses fear, Ava. Truth and perfect love. The only way to keep your heart and head"—Granny touched Ava's forehead—"in the proper place, is to know both."

Chapter Eight

*I've outrun a lot of things in my time, but I've never been able to
outrun a guilty conscience, an achin' heart, or the judgment of God.*
Granddaddy Sutphin

We're wanted men, Uncle Sid. They got three warrants on me.
Three."

The back door of Sid Allen's dry goods store slammed closed,
bringing Jeremiah's head up from his place unpacking Sid's wagon to
clear it for lumber use.

"And brother Sidna's got two, and he barely did anything in that
fight."

Sid Allen marched toward the supplies with his nephews on his
heels, the older man's clean-shaven chin stretched taut with his frown.
"You've told your uncle Floyd about this."

"He's the one who told us to get over the state line in a hurry."
Wesley, the shorter and younger of the two brothers, pushed forward
to his uncle's side. "Sent us here for supplies."

"Uncle Floyd's down with pneumonia or he'd go make things right
on his own, but there's no time," Sidna added, his hat in his hand,
looking more like a child than a man. "He said all we can do is get over
the line and wait until he gets things sorted."

Sid ran a hand over his face and shot Jeremiah a glare. "This is
what happens when folks like your daddy ain't a part of law in town
anymore. Lies."

Jeremiah had seen Sid Allen's temper flare a few times, particularly
with folks trying to get out of the debts they owed him, but the heat
behind those steely blue eyes matched the rumors a little too well for
Jeremiah's peace of mind.

As if he'd voiced the question, Sid stepped closer. "You tell me if
this is fair or not, Jeremiah. These boys have been charged with assault,
attempted murder, and disturbin' public worship, but what did the other

boys get?" Sid leered, holding Jeremiah's attention and the silence for a few seconds. "Nothin'. Not one charge placed against the boys who picked the fight. Not one." He growled, his fists tightening at his sides, and for the first time since knowing the man, Jeremiah braced himself. "You tell me what that says about those in charge in town."

With a heavy sigh, Sid pressed his palm against his forehead and turned back toward his nephews, his stance relaxing a little. "I hate them boys turned a little fun into somethin' like this." He steadied a steely look of ice blue on Wes, an expression Jeremiah remembered all too well from his own father. "Did you pull your jackknife *and* Colt, like the warrant said, Wesley?"

"Yeah, but I didn't use 'em." He waved a hand back behind him as if gesturing toward the incident. "Every man there was carryin', so I wanted to show 'em I wasn't scared, and I had no intention of bein' so."

"Come on, now, Uncle Sid." Sidna stepped closer, searching his uncle's face. "We ain't never had no trouble with the law. Not one bit. And this here? Our first time over Wes kissin' the wrong girl? That just ain't right. Besides, Will Thomas showed off his Colt just as much as Wes did, and none of us put out a warrant for his arrest."

"That's because we didn't think the Thomases would cause such a ruckus over a kiss." Sid's arm sliced the air before landing back on his hip. "What person puts out a warrant for an arrest over a kiss and a schoolyard fight? Nobody."

"Except folks with a plan against us from the start." Wes's lips tightened into a deep grimace that aged the twenty-year-old. "Uncle Floyd said we ain't gonna get no fair treatment from the lawmen." Wes looked over at his brother. "So we gotta get out of here until he can talk to them. Let things cool down."

"That's the truth. There's nothing to do about it until Floyd can talk to folks for some help. He's an appointed lawman for these parts anyhow and he knows what to do." Sid shook his head and waved toward the store. "Go get what you need to take with you. I reckon it'll only take a week or so for Floyd to work it out and y'all will be back home. It'll likely take longer for the courts to work up an extradition order to cross state lines for you, so don't be idle. Get you a job right away until Floyd calls for you."

The boys started toward the store.

"Wesley." The younger of the two boys turned back in response to his uncle's call. "You ought not have pulled your Colt first, boy. That don't look good on no man when no one else has pulled theirs. You hear?"

"Yes, sir."

The two younger men disappeared into the back of the store, while Sid turned to help Jeremiah finish unloading the stock, his brow a series of deep ridges to match his frown. They worked in silence for a few minutes, and Jeremiah's thoughts skimmed through things he'd heard for years from both sides. The Allens and the "Courthouse Clan," as some called them, and two folks in particular caused the biggest rivalry, if he remembered correctly. William Foster and Dexter Goad. Some history over politics, pride, competition, and whatever else created a rift that had just grown deeper as years and offenses piled up.

Jeremiah released a long sigh. No wonder the refrain of forgiveness played such a massive theme throughout scripture. The repercussions of its absence rocked nations and severed relationships like few other things.

"They've been tryin' to pick a fight for years."

Jeremiah's attention met Sid's, acknowledging his statement.

Sid patted the side of the wagon with an agitated huff. "We ain't got cause with most of them, but some will stop at nothin' to ruin us."

"Times are changin', Sid," Jeremiah offered. "Even when my daddy was a deputy, folks were looking more to lawmen to take over keeping the peace in Carroll County rather than men having to be laws of their own." A truth Jeremiah had hoped would have taken place before his daddy had gotten caught in a backwoods rivalry, but as far as he could see it, real change to the mountains was still years off. "Maybe it would help keep more folks alive like Joe Creed. . .and my pa."

"I ain't got no trouble with lawmen doing their jobs. Never have. I have three brothers who've done their part as lawmen of this county. But I don't like folks messin' in business that ain't theirs." Sid tucked the final box up under his arm. "But I can tell you one thing. Just like those boys back there." His pale blue gaze settled on Jeremiah as he thumbed over his shoulder toward the direction Wesley and Sidna had disappeared.

"If the Courthouse Clan starts somethin' against us, you can be sure, the Allens are gonna finish it."

The simple, white clapboard house at the end of the road held a time-less charm, likely due to Jeremiah's tender care of the place that held so much of his history. By no means large, the three-room house still carried an air of simple class passed down from its caretakers, Amos and Gloria Sutphin, to their son. A small covered front porch lined the front of the house, painted in white to match the rest of the exterior. Truth be told, Ava had always loved Jeremiah's house because it looked exactly as a home should, especially the porch, and in the days when Gloria Sutphin lived, it had given Ava a comforting glimpse into a world where mothers loved their children well.

Of course, it wasn't really Jeremiah's. His parents had rented it from Jeremiah's uncle, and within the next few months, Jeremiah's cousin, Ellis, would take the house as his own. But where would Jeremiah move? Surely he wouldn't stay with the newlyweds?

Would he move all the way to Hillsville? Her lips pinched into a frown. Town meant more distance between them, and despite the awkwardness a kiss and confession brought to their friendship, the last thing Ava wanted was distance from another person she cared about.

She clutched the warm dish close to her stomach as she neared the house, when the sudden sound of hammering pulled her attention across the way to the barn. The steady rhythm carried across the open field. She cast a look toward the path through the trees that led deeper into the mountains and then turned her feet toward the barn.

A gentle lowing softened the intermission between the hammer's work, and as Ava peeked her head around the doorway of the barn, she caught sight of Jeremiah's lone cow, Lulu. Jeremiah stood in the middle of the barn, carefully attaching spindles to the back of a chair, his hair a disarray of curls and his focus on his task. She'd never thought of him as husband material. In fact, she'd never contemplated a future with anyone, but after that unexpected kiss at the shucking, her school friend had suddenly become something. . .more.

His body turned away from the door, lithe frame and sturdy

shoulders bent over his work, his strong fingers fitted a last spindle into place. He took such care, such focus. She'd been the recipient of his steady attention and gentle care before, but what would he be like as something even sweeter? She leaned her head against the doorframe, releasing the fear long enough to allow a little bit of that hope her granny talked about to make its way into her daydreams.

Loving him would come so easy.

Wolf must have caught her scent, because his gray ears perked and he turned his head to settle his pale blue eyes on her. With a little yelp, he bounded from his place across the barn and nearly knocked Ava over with a welcome. She clung to the dish with one hand and gave the dog a welcoming scrub with the other. "Good to see you too, boy."

"Well, well, this is a surprise." Jeremiah untied his apron and placed it on the worktable nearby. "What are you doin' out this way?"

Ava pulled her attention away from his open-collared shirt, the late December day taking on a summer swelter. As if she hadn't seen him wear an open-collared shirt before. Heaven sakes! What was wrong with her?

She stepped around Wolf and gestured with her chin toward the pot in her hand. "I'm takin' a meal to Joe's mama and sister, and you just happen to be on the way."

"That's mighty kind of you." He pushed a hand through his hair, leaving it even more tousled and then placed his newly finished chair on the barn floor. "I went out and checked on them yesterday, but they weren't up for visitors."

"Well, I wasn't plannin' on stayin', just wanted to show some kindness." She shifted closer and studied his handiwork. "This is beautiful, Jeremiah. Your skill just keeps getting better and better."

He was trying not to smile. He pressed his lips tight, rubbing a palm against the back of his neck before waving toward the chair. "I've gotten a few orders for some, but this set's made special for me."

"For you?" Her palm made an absent skim across the smooth maple of the chair's back, a delicate design curving the rim.

"Ellis has asked me to leave as much of the furniture with the house as I can, so I'm trying to get some of my own pieces made." He gestured for her to follow. "I just finished this rockin' chair. Wanna see?"

His boyish excitement pulled her forward to the other side of the barn, where a beautiful, high-backed rocking chair sat. Intricate carvings of leaves and berries weaved over the oak wooden back, and the chair shone with a fresh coat of stain. Her fingers reached to follow the smooth wood grain of the oak armrests and trail over the delicate designs. "I ain't never seen any rocking chair as pretty as this." She looked up. "I knew you could create pretty things, but this. . .is beautiful."

"And that back piece came from one of the knottiest pieces of oak I've ever seen. Didn't reckon it would make much of anything, but once I started sanding back some of the rough spots, it showed its character." He slid a hand over the back of the chair. "Just needed a little time and care, I reckon."

Her gaze locked with his. Was he still talking about the chair? She stumbled through a distraction. "And what about all of your parents' things?"

"I've packed up the most precious things and stored them in the cellar until I get my own place."

"And your mama's lace curtains?" The question slipped out unbidden.

His grin quirked up on one side, studying her so thoroughly her cheeks heated. "You've always liked those curtains."

"She made them with her own hands! Irish lace." Ava sighed, stepping around the rocking chair so it provided a little buffer between her and her friend. The softening toward him kept tempting her into kissing thoughts, and she wasn't going to make a fool of herself and flat out ask for another try. "Do you realize how hard it is to find someone who knows how to make Irish lace? And she loved doing it so much." Ava's fingers glided over the dips and edges of the carvings. "I wish she'd lived long enough to teach me what her Irish granny taught her. I could have learnt."

"I wish she'd been able to stay longer too."

His gentle response quelled the fire in her cheeks and she scanned the barn, allowing the quiet to press between them. Three identical chairs stood near a small, square table with carved legs. A bedstead leaned against another wall, with simple adornments of flowers across the top. Jeremiah's house would end up looking every bit the place his mother would have loved. She always made each room like something from a storefront window—all family-heirloom lace, Old World china, and carefully crafted furniture. Jeremiah was a loving combination of his daddy's gentleness and his mama's creativity. Her throat tightened. He was such a good man.

"So, have you decided on where you're going to move?" She shrugged a shoulder and watched him from her periphery. "Town?"

"You think I ought to move to town?"

"No." She answered quickly and then cleared her throat with a smile. "I mean, town is pretty far away from here."

He raised a brow, the sparkle in his eyes somehow reigniting the heat in her face. "And you don't want me to be far away?"

"You're my friend. I'd. . .I'd never want you to be far away."

He slipped a step closer, his hand coming to rest beside hers on the back of the rocking chair, their fingers almost touching. "You know I want to be even more than friends, Ava. Don't you?"

She stared down at their hands, her breath pulsing into a higher pace, before she met his gaze. "I know."

He nodded and allowed the silence to thicken the space between them.

"I. . .I just can't right now."

"All right, then." He shifted closer, his fingers grazing hers, and his lips crooked into a smile. "I don't mind waiting for later."

Half of her wanted to stand still and see if he'd breach the distance and kiss her again. The other half was terrified he'd do just that. . .and she'd take to kissin' like a squirrel to tree hoppin'.

She wasn't sure her heart could handle too much of kissing Jeremiah just yet, especially with both of them alone at his place. Didn't bode well for what folks might think. Not to mention the fact that she hadn't even sorted out if she was a good fit for such a kind man.

She squeezed the pot more tightly against herself and stepped back, breaking the pull his closeness had on her reason.

"I better head on to the Creeds before it gets too late." She took a few more steps back toward the barn door. "But before I go, I was wondering if you'd like to come to Granny's for Christmas dinner."

Instead of answering, he reached for his jacket folded over a nearby stall and slid it on.

"She's makin' her famous cherry cobbler."

"Tell your granny I'd be much obliged." He crossed the barn toward her. "And I think I'll walk with you to the Creeds, if you don't mind. I'd like to see if they need firewood. I got plenty I can provide."

She paused in her turn out the barn door. She'd always welcomed Jeremiah's companionship, but this new "understanding" between them left a strange but pleasant fluttering in her stomach. It would be a simple step into sparkin' him for real. He made it so easy. A long-time friendship probably helped, but the what-ifs kept her wary of embracing the sweetness. She'd seen too many nightmares in daylight. Lived the horrors of a broken mind and ravaged family. What Jeremiah offered felt too perfect to believe. After all of the tragedy, could God truly offer her a quiet life with this gentle friend?

"Stay here, boy." He ushered Wolf back into the barn and turned to Ava. "Mrs. Creed ain't fond of dogs."

Ain't fond of dogs? What sort of person didn't like dogs? Well, her mama didn't, but most folks kept them as guards, if nothing else.

Jeremiah fell in step beside her as they started down the path past his house and through the forest. Winter birdsong brightened the gray day with its piccolo notes, and the brisk December air cooled Ava's heated face into clearheadedness again.

"I reckon I ought to tell you something before you find out about it by other means." Ava kept her face forward to make her confession, dodging a fallen log along the trail.

"Well, that's always a promising start to a conversation with you."

She shot him a mock glare, but it bounced off his ready grin, and the flutters in her chest shot into horse-race speeds. "You keep stickin' around, so I reckon you don't mind so much."

He shrugged, his hands pushed into his pockets. "Nope. I don't mind at all."

Her gaze locked with his for a second longer, his tender look nearly unraveling her into teary eyes. Loving him seemed *too* easy. Why couldn't she just let go?

"The newspaper took another one of my articles."

He nodded, keeping his attention focused on the trail ahead.

"Nobody had given an account of the corn shuckin' or the church-yard brawl yet, so I—or rather Cameron Birch—gave them a short piece about it."

"A shuckin' and churchyard brawl made the news?" Jeremiah's humored voice rang out through the tall pines. "They must not have a whole lot to print nowadays."

"Hush." She jabbed an elbow into his arm. "I just know how to write it so it's interestin'."

He leveled her with a raised brow of doubt. "No exaggerations or conjectures this time around?"

"Nope." She raised her chin and turned away from him. "Just some excellently placed wording to increase suspense."

"Maybe you should write a novel instead of the news." He chuck-led and raised a palm in front of him like a headline display. "The Untold Stories of Mountain Mayhem and Mischief."

"Ain't you the funniest thing since a lopsided turtle." She rolled her eyes heavenward, but his continued chuckle peeked at her grin.

"That's why you like me so much."

"Since you seem to stick around, I figure I'd better get used to you."

"Sounds mighty fine to me."

She pinched back her smile as the tiny Creed cabin came into view. Jacob Creed had run off a few years earlier, leaving his wife and two children to fend for themselves in these backwoods. Never an easy task, but folks had come around to help, and Joe had picked up his daddy's mantle with a soberness few boys of his age possessed.

The reality of his death, the pain it must've caused his mother, pierced through Ava afresh. Granny Burcham once said that when you've felt the sting of deep loss, it creates a deeper understanding and compassion. She looked over at Jeremiah. He felt it too. He understood.

Their footfalls clipped up the two steps onto the porch, and Ava reached the front door first. No response came from her first knock.

"Mrs. Creed!" Ava knocked again, and the door creaked to a slow open.

Ava looked over at Jeremiah, a sudden iciness creeping over her skin. He placed an arm in front of her and stepped through the door into the dimly lit room only to run headlong into the steel end of a double-barreled shotgun.

Chapter Nine

Shadows don't fall without reason.
Granddaddy Sutphin

Jeremiah's body and breath froze for a split second as the gun leveled directly at his face. He stiffened, waiting for the impact of a shot. As his vision adjusted to the gray room, he changed his focus from the barrel of the gun to the bearer of the gun, and his heart thrummed back into a rhythm, though an uneven one. Sadie Creed, Joe's little sister, peered with large brown eyes over the top of the weapon, her face ghost-pale in the shadows.

"Sadie?" Ava whispered at his side. "Sadie, it's me, Ava Burcham, and here's your neighbor, Jeremiah." Ava's words soared into his hearing, more confident than anything he could work up at the moment.

"I know who y'all are." Her small voice quivered. "What do you want?"

A hardened edge clung to the twelve-year-old's question, and Jeremiah felt the strange and sudden urge to weep. Long ago, he'd found another little girl dealing with tragedy, and the long shadows of her past still carved scars into her present.

"We brought some food," came Ava's answer from Jeremiah's right. "In honor of your brother."

The simple phrase hit some unseen mark in the little girl. With a sudden weakening of her bottom lip, the gun began to shake. Just before she collapsed, Jeremiah grabbed the shotgun while Ava ran to Sadie's side. The girl quivered into Ava's arms, whimpering like a frightened puppy.

Jeremiah searched through the front room of the house, keeping the gun at his side. The strong scent of human waste rose from the back, so he braced himself, with a hand to his nose, and stepped over the threshold. Mrs. Elmira Creed, or what he thought was her, lay among the quilts on a rickety, iron bed.

"Mrs. Creed?"

Jeremiah didn't reckon his quiet voice would call the woman to the present, but her eyes fluttered open, pale blue with dark shadows beneath. Her skin shone, slick with sweat.

"Ava Burcham and me have come to help you and Sadie."

"You can't," she whispered, her voice hoarse, broken. "Nobody can. They're gonna come get the money. We're done for."

Jeremiah crept closer. "Who's comin'?"

She slowly turned her head toward him, her lips so pale they appeared almost white. "They came for Joe. They'll come for the money next."

Her eyes closed, and Jeremiah turned to exit the room only to find Ava standing in the doorway, arms crossed and gaze fixed on him. "Sadie says her mama's sick with grief. Been abed for five days and hardly eatin'."

"Something feels wrong here, besides the obvious."

Ava nodded and stepped closer to Mrs. Creed. "Sadie mentioned some money Joe had been saving to pay for his family to move away from here." She glanced over at the sleeping woman and hushed her voice to a whisper. "Mrs. Creed has some folks in Kentucky, and Joe was plannin' to take them there."

"To escape?"

Ava's locked stare confirmed his words. "Whoever was holdin' somethin' over Joe's head has struck fear in the whole family—enough to have them ready to leave the state."

Like the Edwards boys? The thought niggled a silent pain in Jeremiah's head. "And fire upon the first people to walk through the door."

Ava's frown deepened. "Sadie said something about the men comin' for the money soon and she and her mama was going to try to leave, but her mama got struck with heart sickness." Ava rubbed her arms as if cold. "I think we need to help them get out of here before somethin' worse happens."

Jeremiah nodded, his mind racing through possibilities. Mrs. Creed didn't look fit to be moved. And it wasn't proper for him to stay there overnight. He raised his gaze to Ava. "Where's the money?"

"Sadie knows where it is." Ava ran a palm down her braid and glanced back toward the woman on the bed. "Almost forty dollars, she said."

"Forty dollars!" He quickly lowered his voice. "How on earth did Joe get forty dollars?"

"Not by legal means, if you ask me." Ava sighed and hugged herself again.

Quiet filtered into the dark room. Did he alert the police? The Allens?

"I got an idea." Ava whispered into the silence. "But I don't like it."

Good night, if she didn't like it, there was no way he'd like it. He squeezed his eyes closed and waited for the revelation.

"Someone needs to stay here and get Mrs. Creed back on her feet. Clean things. Cook healin' foods. Make sure Sadie has somebody to help her."

His gaze locked with hers. "But if that money stays here too, it will put you all in danger."

"Exactly." Ava didn't move her attention from his, as if trying to prepare him for the next words. "That's why *you* should take it to keep it safe and I stay here to help the Creed women."

"What?"

She stepped closer to him, mere inches away. "You know as well as I do that Mrs. Creed ain't goin' nowhere but heaven unless she gets some help. I can stay here and try to nurse her so she can be fit for travel, and if you take the money, we can honestly say it ain't here if someone comes callin'."

"Ava—"

"Hear me out, Jeremiah." She took his arm, searching his face. "You and me both know the dangers of bein' on the wrong side of folks in these parts. From what Sadie's said, Joe was part of a liquor run gone bad and lost a good deal of money for his boss. That's why he was so desperate to steal from women. Whoever he worked for was fixin' to take out his frustration on Sadie or Mrs. Creed to squeeze out whatever he wanted from Joe."

"Blackmail?" Jeremiah spat out the word. "Did Sadie say who it was?"

Ava shook her head, her gaze lowering to Mrs. Creed again. "But if they think there's money here, they'll come back for it. Especially if they couldn't get Joe to talk."

The implication shone a fresh light on Joe's death. Murder settled more securely within Jeremiah's conscience than suicide, which was a sobering thought all on its own. "I can't leave you here, Ava."

"And you can't stay neither. We have to get that money away from here, and someone else needs to know about what happened besides the folks inside these walls." She waved toward the bed. "Mrs. Creed won't be fit to travel for a while."

"But it ain't safe here."

"Where in this world *is* safe, Jeremiah?" The question shook, as if pulled from her soul. "Besides, like I said, if the money's not here and someone comes for it, we can rightly say we don't know where it is. I'll just say I came to tend the bereaved, which won't seem out of place at all, and it *will* be what I'm doin'. I don't have to lie."

"Ava—"

"And then we can meet in. . ." She studied Mrs. Creed for a few seconds. "Three days, at noon. I got a whole arsenal of concoctions from Granny to get Mrs. Creed on her feet in a hurry."

Jeremiah cringed at the idea of half the "creations" he'd heard Granny Burcham describe for one ailment or another, and he suddenly felt a lot sorrier for Mrs. Creed than he had a moment before, and that was saying something. "What if these moonshiners *do* show up and they're not the kind who are respectful of ladies? I know my granddaddy was one of the biggest runners in the mountain, but he'd never hurt a woman. Not all of them were like him."

She raised a brow. "Do you have a better idea?"

His shoulders slumped with resignation. "If we could move her to. . .to. . ."

"Exactly. The closest place is your house, and I'm not even sure we could make it there, even if folks wouldn't give a big holler about a single man having a widow woman stay in his house."

His gaze locked with hers. "Three days. That's it. And if you can get her to leave sooner, you send Sadie down the path to my house as quick as lightnin'."

She nodded and turned to walk with him back to the front room, where Sadie sat stoking the fire and watching a steaming pot.

"Sadie, Jeremiah said he'd take the money and keep it safe so no one will find it here. Will you trust him with it?"

The young girl looked from Ava to Jeremiah, nodded, and then disappeared into the back room.

"I have her boiling water so we can start cleaning up her mama and this house." Ava leaned closer to him, lowering her voice. "No reason for keeping a house in this state when you don't have to. My granny would be livid as a jealous rooster over the likes of this place."

Sadie returned with a small white jar and, after a moment's hesitation, gave it to Jeremiah.

"That's real good." Ava patted her back. "Once your mama's on her feet, we'll get the two of y'all on your way to a safer place." Ava gestured back toward the pot. "Would you see if you can drum up some lye soap for us, Sadie? I'm gonna walk Jeremiah out."

Ava followed him onto the porch. He breathed in the crisp, fresh air, welcoming the pine scent over the stifling stench of the Creed cabin.

"Jeremiah, is there anyone you can trust to tell about the money?" She stepped closer to him. "And the doubts on Joe's death too?"

Yes, she was thinking along the same lines as he'd been.

"Not the Allens. I don't think they'd hurt the Creeds, but I'm not sure who they'd tell or what they'd do about it."

"No, the only person I would consider is. . ." He paused to run a palm down his face, his eyes burning from the struggle against this complete sense of helplessness. "Maybe Lew Webb."

"Sheriff Webb?"

"My father always trusted him. They were good friends for years."

She looked off in the distance, her mind whirling so hard he could almost hear it. "Then I think you ought to get his opinion. We need more than just us knowin' about this." Her attention shot to his face. "Oh, and we'll miss Christmas dinner with Granny. Can you get word to her?"

"I'll ride out that way at first light."

He started for the steps, but she grabbed his arm. "No, talk to Webb first. We need someone on our side who understands the law."

"All right, but maybe I can get both done tomorrow. I don't want your granny worryin'."

"Tell her we can make it up next week." She waved a hand toward the front door. "After all this is sorted out."

The evening breeze blew with a deeper chill, and Ava wrapped her arms more tightly around herself.

He nudged her in the arm. "Get on back inside."

She nodded, almost absently, and took a step back from him, her profile pensive. . .lost.

"And I'll come day after next to bring firewood." *And check on everyone.*

"All right. And maybe some milk from Lulu?" Her large eyes rounded, beckoning him to stay. But she knew he couldn't, not if they were going to keep the money—and by extension, Mrs. Creed and Sadie—safe.

His heart twisted as tight as a fishing knot.

"You'll be all right, Ava." He placed his palm against her shoulder, stopping her turn. "I know you will. You're one of the bravest people I know."

A tender look moved across her features and settled in her eyes. She almost smiled. "You think I'm brave?"

"You've always been brave, even if you didn't believe it." He tugged at her braid before moving toward the porch steps, casting another glance at the house. "I just don't like leavin' you here with some unknown and angry men likely to come at any moment."

"Would it help if they was *known* and angry men?"

He growled and shook his head. "I've a mind to send Wolf down here to keep watch." He straightened. "In fact, that's exactly what I plan to do. You know if I tell him to find you, he'll sniff you out."

Best tracking dog Jeremiah had ever seen.

Without warning, Ava rocked up on tiptoe and planted a kiss on his cheek. He shocked still and raised his palm to cover the cheek she'd kissed. "What was that for?"

She unleashed her smile, his favorite feature on her face, though she had plenty of lovely features, for sure. " 'Cause I'm just grateful to know you, Jeremiah Sutphin." Those glowing eyes of hers glistened with an added sheen. "Your mama and daddy would be so proud of you."

He couldn't do much more but stare at her upturned face, which was no hardship at all, because he'd never seen her look prettier than when she was lookin' at him with such admiration. In fact, he felt ready to take on a whole gang of known or unknown angry men.

"Get on, now." She cleared her throat and waved toward the forest. "It'll be dark soon, and you need to get that jar to a secret place."

He slipped a step back, reluctant to leave. "Make sure the guns are handy."

"I will."

"And look for Wolf. I'll send him as soon as I get back home."

She held to the porch railing, keeping her gaze on him as he backed away. "I'll save him the ham bone."

Jeremiah tried to smile. Danger lurked in the mountains every day of the year, but between the Allens' situation and the new information they'd learned about Joe, a deeper, more sinister shadow fell over the workings of the Blue Ridge, and Jeremiah had to leave the girl he loved to unforeseen trouble. . .and a hidden enemy.

~

Just pulling Mrs. Creed out of her filthy bedclothes and giving her a good dose of willow bark and calomel tea brought the woman to a sitting position in no time. She still didn't talk a great deal. Of course, Ava never knew her as the talkative sort, but her dark eyes held a brightness they hadn't possessed a few hours before.

Sadie quietly ran errands and religiously applied camphor salve to Mrs. Creed's temples at intervals Ava designated, but the young girl spoke about as readily as her mama. The night grew long and starless, and Ava drew all the curtains to keep the blackness from inspiring unneeded fears. There were plenty of legitimate ones as it was.

Not long past nine, a sound of footfall on the porch shook Ava from her musing stare into the fire. The sound came so softly, she would have missed it, had she not been sitting in the rocking chair by the front window. Sadie slept curled in a small bed in the corner of the room, bone weary from the events of the past few days, no doubt, but Ava's mind had kept a steady alert. Waiting. For what, she still didn't know, but the footfalls came again, nearer to the window.

Ava gave a noiseless push up from the chair and pressed her body against the solid log wall between the window and the front door as a shuffling sound gave the door a little shake. A cold wave started at Ava's forehead and cascaded all the way to her ankles, her breath lurching to shallow.

Someone was at the door.

She slid a step closer. *The Lord is in your midst. He is mighty to save.* The verse filled her mind, half prayer, half mantra.

The door shook again, and Ava heard a faint scratch of wood on wood. She set her focus on the shotgun leaning against the wall on the other side of the door, and then she heard another noise. A whimpering against the door, followed by another scratch.

An animal?

She released her clenched air as a little nip sounded from the other side. A dog. Her body slacked against the wall. Wolf.

Praise the Lord.

With as quiet a hand as she could, she removed the board securing the doorway and opened just far enough to allow him to slip inside. He rubbed his nose against her leg, his whimper increasing until she patted his head. "You found me, boy." Her voice scraped over her tightening throat. "I saved a ham bone for you."

As she ran a hand down his gray fur, she noticed a white cloth tied around his neck like a handkerchief. A piece of paper had been knotted within the folds. She glanced out the door into the darkness, as if she could see the two or three miles through the trees to Jeremiah's house, but something caught her eye. A glimmer of light through the trees. A lantern?

She blinked and then the light vanished. Had she imagined it? If it had been Jeremiah, he would have accompanied Wolf to the door. If it was anyone at all.

With quick movements, she secured the door back in place and turned to Wolf, who sat by her side as if waiting for the promised reward. His presence curbed a bit of the edge off the dark unknown outside the windows, and the fact Jeremiah sent him made the whole scenario even sweeter. Maybe this was another example of God using people—her gaze dropped to Wolf's furry head—and animals to show His presence in her life. They became His hands and feet. His care.

She reached for the knotted paper and walked to the table to retrieve the ham bone she'd saved for Wolf. He took it with a gentle tug from her hand and found a warm spot by the fire in which to enjoy the spoils of his travels as Ava stepped close to the fire's light to open the paper.

Jeremiah's familiar, unsteady hand greeted her.

I took the rode to town tonite so I cud meet with Lew furst thing in the mournin. Staying at the hoetel if yu need me. I will chek on granny and Lord willin be back to see yu by tomarra nite. Be safe, Jeremiah.

The paper blurred. Ava swiped a hand over her eyes. She knew the time and frustration it took for him to pen those words. The humility of knowing she'd have to sort through his spelling. She sniffled and looked up from the page, only to see Wolf staring at her, bone between his paws.

"I know."

The dog's ears perked and he raised his nose, as if he doubted her.

"I'm serious. I do know. That's why I have to be sure, because he's so. . .so. . ."

She sighed. *Gentle. Kind. Honest. Comforting. Tenderhearted.* How could she even think of bringing more hardship into his life than what he'd already lived through? She grabbed a blanket from the end of Sadie's bed and placed it on the floor in front of the fire. Wolf repositioned himself against her legs and continued to gnaw on his bone as Ava drifted off to sleep.

Ava sent Sadie to gather eggs at first light while she added most of the soiled cloths to a giant pot boiling out in the backyard between the house and the tiny corncrib tucked at the edge of the forest. With a long stick, she stirred the cloths, dispersing the acrid scent of lye into the foggy morning chill. Well, at least the soap's pungent odor proved better than the weathered quilts and towels she'd pulled from the house. Half of them really weren't fit for saving.

After midday, when her shoulders were weary from the constant tasks, Wolf caught her attention. He'd been chasing after the smoke swirls from the fire and suddenly froze, his pointy ears raised to alert. Ava paused in her stirring, the hairs on the back of her neck rising in response. Someone was watching her.

As if he'd read her mind, Wolf released a low growl and moved to her side. And that someone wasn't Jeremiah.

She pinched the stick between her hands and turned in the direction of Wolf's attention. A figure walked forward from the wooded path. Tall and lean, a man emerged at a slow pace, his long coat flapping behind him as he walked, his derby pulled too low for Ava to make out his face.

Wolf shifted at her side.

"It's all right, boy," she whispered. "He don't look like he's come to hurt us." Or at least Ava hoped. Him coming on his own seemed promising.

"Good morning," she called first, to give Sadie a little warning from her place at the back of the house. "Can I help you?"

The man took a few more steps forward without a word and then pushed back the tip of his hat. "Good mornin', Ava."

Ava released her tense air into a stream at the welcome smile of Deputy Casper Norris. Could Sheriff Webb have sent someone already? That seemed nigh impossible. She steadied her expression. It *was* impossible.

"I didn't expect to see you out this way, Deputy. Don't you got more pressin' matters than traversin' the hills?"

His smile spread at her words. "Keepin' folks safe is a pressin' matter, as always, Miss Ava." He dipped his head in deference and stared down at Wolf, whose fur bristled, body still tense. "But I see you got some help to keep you safe."

Ava lowered a palm onto Wolf's head and one of his ears twitched, but he didn't move his attention from Casper. She hadn't expected the lovable pup to transform into a guard dog right before her eyes. Of course, she'd never seen him meet someone new before either.

"What do you mean, keepin' folks safe? Were you expecting trouble?"

He looked away to study the house. "I'd heard tell that Joe had built up some enemies. I tried to get him to give me names, but he wouldn't. Faithful to a fault, I suppose."

"Or terrified," Ava offered, studying his profile. "The right kind of threat in these parts can prove as certain as a death sentence."

He turned his attention back to her, his smile wavering a little. "True. That's why I'd feel better if I could talk to Mrs. Creed to see if she could shed any light on the situation."

Mrs. Creed had barely spoken a few sentences when Ava had checked in on her before coming outside, and the idea of Casper upsetting her even more than she already was seemed more hurt than help. "She ain't up for talkin' just yet." Ava gestured toward the soiled cloths in a pile by the pot, the stench still strong enough to make an impression. "I've barely been able to get her to eat somethin', let alone talk. She's been abed for days without. . .without taking care of herself. I came by to bring her a meal in her bereavement and found her in such a state as this."

Casper grimaced and took a step away from the pile. "When do you think she'll be up for a visit?"

Something didn't feel right. Like Casper wanted to say more, but didn't or maybe. . .wouldn't.

"I think what she needs is to get out of this mountain. She's had so much loss, between her two babies, her husband, and now Joe? It would do her heart good to be near her people."

He slowly nodded, surveyed the house again, and then turned those dark eyes back on Ava. "I'm sure that would be good for her, but it ain't cheap to make a trip like that and start over. It's gonna take some time." His smile returned. "What if I come back in two or three days to see how everyone is doing? Will that suit?"

Ava looked to the house. A slight movement of pale blue at the back corner gave away Sadie's hiding spot. She quickly moved her attention back to Casper. "We can only hope."

He studied her a moment longer and then tapped the bill of his cap. "Well, then, I'll see you in a few days."

Ava smiled with a tip of her head. "By the way, Casper, I know stealin' got Joe into a heap of trouble, but somethin' else must've pushed him to take his own life. Did he say anything else?"

"Not everybody's as they seem, Ava, and Joe's secrets finally caught up with him. Best stick to tendin' the sick instead of spendin' too much time musin' over a lost boy." He raised a brow and doffed his cap again. "Good day."

Chapter Ten

Some whispers in life are made of paper and some are made of steel.
Learning which to listen to makes a heap o' difference.
Granddaddy Sutphin

I don't know that I have any information to help you, Jeremiah." Deputy Lew Webb tapped his wooden desk in the front room of the two-story jailhouse and leaned back in his chair. "Joe was unconscious when I checked in on him before leaving for the night, and then he was dead by morning."

"You mean you didn't get a chance to talk to him at all?" Jeremiah slid down into the seat across from the older gentleman. "Who talked to him?"

"Well, I know Casper had to knock the boy out to get him to the jail. He fought him the whole way." Deputy Webb shook his head. "And by the time morning came, well, it was too late for answers."

"Surely, he wasn't here alone though?" Jeremiah leaned forward, fingers braided in front of him. "Somebody was keeping watch over the jail, weren't they?"

"Pink Samuels was on watch, but said the boy was sleepin' when he checked in on him at midnight and then, well, by morning. . ."

Jeremiah stared over the older man, trying to make sense of the situation. Had Deputy Samuels missed something? "And Pink didn't hear anything? See anything odd?"

Webb looked up. "What are you implyin', boy? You think somethin' is wrongful just because of the way his mama and sister was actin'?"

"You said yourself you were surprised that Joe would take his own life when he was responsible for them. It just raises questions about—"

"Desperate folks ain't the clearest-headed sort, Jeremiah." The deputy's stare bore into Jeremiah's. "Some things may be best left alone."

A warning? Out of concern, or defensiveness? Surely, more concern. Sheriff-elect Webb and Jeremiah's father had been on good terms.

Friends, even. "My granddaddy used to say if you leave somethin' alone too long, it might boil over."

Webb grunted. "I don't know that your granddaddy is the one you ought to be listenin' to."

"Was Pink the one who discovered Joe in the morning?"

"That's right, but don't expect to get much out of Pink. The sight tore him up somethin' awful." The older man winced. "It sure ain't somethin' easy to come upon, especially when Joe had been hangin' for hours."

For hours? And no one heard anything? Or checked on the prisoner?

A loud slam from the door of the jail's entrance nearly brought Jeremiah to his feet. In walked Sheriff Joe Blankenship, his brown fedora tilted back on his head to show off his graying hairline.

He grazed Jeremiah with a glance and then focused his attention on Deputy Webb, bringing his full presence between Jeremiah and Webb as if Jeremiah wasn't even in the room. "I sent a telegram to Sheriff Haynes in Mt. Airy last week, and he's located both boys just over the state line."

"Mt. Airy? Well, that makes sense they'd stay close." Webb leaned forward, folding his hands in front of him on the desk. "Maybe hopin' it all would blow over."

Jeremiah had the gnawing feeling he ought to slip from the room, but with Sheriff Blankenship blocking his path, he didn't see a way to avoid the conversation. Not that either one of them minded Jeremiah's presence. He'd sat in this room with his dad for dozens of "law talk" moments, but the older he grew, the more uncomfortable the situation became.

"It ain't gonna blow over, and that's a fact. We got to teach the next generation of Allens they don't run the county." The sheriff sliced the air with his palm, his voice rising to the conviction of a preacher. "I plan to wire Sheriff Haynes in the morning to bring those boys to the line Friday, once all the Christmas festivities are over."

"You want me to go collect 'em?"

"No, you have plenty to do getting ready to be sworn in as sheriff next week." Blankenship shook his head at Webb and took a few steps back toward the door. "No, send Pink. He lives near the line anyhow and can leave from his house early to get the boys up the mountain to town before dark."

"Will do." Webb gave a nod and sent an apologetic look in Jeremiah's direction.

The sheriff reached the door and turned to point at Webb. "And tell Pink to keep his wits about him."

"You expect trouble? Those boys don't have one stain on their records."

"They're Allens." Sheriff Blankenship sniffed. "I always expect trouble."

The sheriff doffed his fedora at Webb, gave a nod to Jeremiah, and left the building. Jeremiah took the hushed transition for his cue to depart. After all, he still had to make it to Granny Burcham's, drop some crates of his parents' things at his new place on the way, stop by Temples' to let them know Ava would return in a few days, and then make it back to the Creeds' house in time to check on Ava and the Creeds before too late. One glance out the window at the sun's placement in the sky warned him he'd be cutting his plans mighty close.

"I appreciate your time, Mr. Webb." Jeremiah offered his hand and the deputy stood to accept.

"You're always welcome here, Jeremiah. Always have been, as long as it's on this side of the bars." Webb chuckled at his own joke, inspiring Jeremiah's smile, but the man refused to release Jeremiah's hand.

"Be careful, boy."

Deputy Webb's gaze locked with Jeremiah's, his voice firm, his eyes pleading. "There are certain times when it's all right to ask questions, and other times. . ." He released a sigh. "Other times it ain't. You're your daddy's boy. That's a good thing, but, well, don't end up like him in the end."

Caught between two feuding stills. Clans. That's what the sheriff-elect meant.

Why did searching for the truth often end up as a trade-off for your life?

Jeremiah nodded and stepped back. No, he'd be careful, but if innocent people were in danger and he could help but did nothing?

Well, what sort of life was that anyway?

≈

"Your mama ate more eggs this morning than most menfolk I know." Ava scrubbed at the iron skillet in the washbasin, careful to keep the water from splashing all over the floor.

Sadie Creed's giggle warmed the room along with the morning light through the windows. A sound not heard very often, Ava guessed. The young girl's smile had made its appearance more frequently over the last few hours. She'd even let Ava fix her hair with lavender ribbons to match her careworn dress, but this was the first laugh Ava had heard.

"I ain't never seen her eat so good."

"Well, a woman goes without eatin' for a few days and her stomach decides to make up for lost time." Ava's wink incited another laugh as Sadie took the freshly washed skillet from Ava and began drying it with a threadbare towel.

Ava studied the petite girl with her beautiful dark hair and matching eyes. That yellow frock Ava had been working on back at Temples' would suit Sadie just fine. Maybe Ava could send it with her when they made it back to Fancy Gap before heading out to the depot.

The two of them had spent the previous day cleaning up the house some more and packing a few things for the journey, only the most precious. A few china cups passed down from a grandmother from the Old Country. A shawl, handmade by Mrs. Creed's mother. A quilt from Sadie's daddy's side of the family along with Joe's favorite derby. Their meager collection of clothes with a coat each for the winter chill. No, there wasn't much to leave behind that couldn't be found in Kentucky, and hopefully Mrs. Creed and Sadie would discover happiness again too. Safety. Freedom from a few years' grief.

"She sure does look healthier this mornin'." The girl glanced over her shoulder toward the room where her mother rested. "You really think we'll be able to get her to the sitting room for lunch?"

"We had her sitting up for three hours yesterday, didn't we?" Ava handed her a plate she'd just washed. "I reckon with the eggs she's eaten, she'll have enough strength to walk a few steps."

105

"I hope so." Sadie's expression sobered, her dark eyes rounding with a misty sheen. "If she...if something happened to her too—"

"Now, we ain't gonna turn our thoughts in that direction, Sadie. Not when we got sunshine and hope on our side, right? Ain't no good settin' your mind on the what-ifs when you have the most likelys happenin' right in front of you." Ava paused and replayed her sentence—words parroted from her father. Was it really that easy? Just turn her own thoughts in a new direction? Embrace the hope in her granny's words and faith? Trust not just the most likely, but the definite truth of God's hold on her life?

He will quiet you with His love.

Ava tiptoed out onto the emotional hope-ledge and handed Sadie another plate. "I know it's hard to see God's work in the middle of the dark." *The Lord is in your midst.* "But He's still working. The dark is as bright as day to Him, so He knows what to do next."

Sadie didn't look up from her task but quietly dried the next few dishes without comment. The ticking from a small, family heirloom clock whispered a rhythm into the silence. Wolf yawned from his place by the back door across the room.

"You think. . ." Sadie's voice came small, hesitant. "Do you think God was with Joe...at the last?"

A flash of memory crossed Ava's vision. Waking to her brother's body pressed against her, his gaze watching her, his face pale. What had he whispered? *"You're safe, Ava Marie. I'm...I'm so glad."* She'd whispered his name, begged him to stay, but he'd only smiled, a look of beautiful peace crossing his young face. *"God will guide you back to me and Papa in His time. You won't be alone."* Those had been his last words before the door to their cabin came open and in walked Jeremiah and his father. God hadn't left her alone. In fact, when she really thought about it, He'd never left her alone. Not through the years of loss or loneliness. Not through the tears in the dark or the fears inside her own head. He'd sent the Temples, Jeremiah and his parents, Granny Burcham.

She swallowed through the tears gathering in her throat and rested a palm against Sadie's shoulder.

"God never leaves His children alone, Sadie. No matter where they are, or what they've done. If they belong to Him, there's nothin' that can snatch them from His hands, ever."

Tears welled in Sadie's large brown eyes and she turned away, sniffling as she put another plate in the cupboard. Ava had needed to speak that truth as much as Sadie had needed to hear it. Maybe even more so.

She cleared her throat and took inventory of the room. If she figured right, they had enough rations set aside for two more meals, and then she'd gather a few things for them from Sid Allen's store on the way out to the depot. She could fetch the yellow dress along the way too.

"Sadie, I know you didn't want to talk much about Joe yesterday, but Jeremiah and me want to try to protect you and your mama." Ava kept her head down, scrubbing an iron saucepan. "Make sure y'all get away without any trouble on your heels."

The young girl paused in her movements to put another plate away but didn't turn.

"Do you know anything about what trouble Joe had gotten into? With who? A name or two?"

Sadie turned, her fingers fidgeting in front of her as she glanced toward her mama's room.

"I don't mind askin' your mama once she's had a few more good hours."

"No." Sadie's response came quick, her eyes wide. "No, I don't want mama talkin' about none of it anytime soon. I can't see her going back into the bed from grief, at the mention of Joe's wrongdoings."

"All right, then." Ava sighed and turned back to her work. Some things could be coaxed out of mountain women, but once they set their mind to something, well, it was like trying to break a stone with a feather.

Sadie moved back to her side at the washbasin. Wolf interrupted the sounds of sloshing water and clinking dishes with a sneeze.

"It was some crowd below the mountain."

Ava turned to Sadie. What had she whispered so quietly? Below the mountain? That could be a whole host of possibilities.

"I don't know no names, 'cept for Daniels. And Joe spoke of a few connections in Hillsville who kept things workin' from the inside, that nobody would suspect."

Ava kept her breathing steady, even though her pulse hammered in her ears. "And it was just blockade liquor runnin'?"

Sadie swallowed as she fisted the towel in her hand and glanced back over her shoulder. "Joe, well, he'd gotten mixed up in some real bad stuff too. He watched some boys beat a man to death 'cause he wouldn't pay for the liquor. And. . .and he'd. . ."

"Go ahead. It's all right."

Her bottom lip wobbled. "I think he beat up a few folks too. 'Cause, he had to show he was all in, so they'd keep givin' him work." Her gaze shot back to Ava. "But that's when he wanted out. When he saw all the folks bein' hurt or dyin'. And then one of the runs went bad and Joe was blamed for it."

"And was told to pay back the losses or else?"

Sadie nodded. "Mama had told him to talk to Deputy Webb about the whole thing, since she knew him a sight better than some others of the law, but Joe just kept sayin' we couldn't trust nobody. Not even the law."

So he made plans to escape it all, with his family.

"I know folks can be corrupt no matter what side of the law they're on, but some still have the right heart about things." Ava cooed the words, hoping to instill a little faith back in the girl's wounded heart. "Jeremiah's daddy was one of them."

"But he ain't around no more, is he?"

Ava cringed at the edge in Sadie's voice but didn't back down. "No, but there are still others as good as him. Your mama's instincts on Sheriff Webb is right, I'd say. He's one I know better than most, so I would vouch for him, even if I get on his nerves more than not."

Sadie's frown loosened at the needed levity in the conversation. "You're a troublemaker?"

"Sometimes." Ava shrugged and raised the washbasin into her arms. "But for all the right reasons, of course."

Just as she started for the back door to empty the water into Mrs. Creed's winter garden, Wolf popped to his feet, ears pointed like sharp peaks. He paused to sniff the air, and then, after only a slight hesitation, he ran toward the front of the house.

Ava met Sadie's eyes. "I'll see to it." She pushed the pan into Sadie's arms. "Stay here, and if you hear something wrong, run into your mama's room and lock the door."

Sadie's face grew several shades paler, but she nodded, squeezing the washbasin close.

With calculated steps, Ava walked toward the front door. Wolf pawed at the bottom, scratching in an attempt to open the barricaded entry.

"Ava?" A familiar voice called from the other side of the door. "It's Jeremiah."

Ava nearly sobbed. She rushed to lift the latch, Wolf whimpering at her side.

Jeremiah stood, uncertain smile in place, a jar of milk in one hand and the other rubbing Wolf, who'd jumped up to his chest. "I brought milk."

Ava rushed forward and wrapped her arms around his neck, burying her face in his shoulder. "I'm so glad you're here."

After a half second, his free arm slid around her waist and his mouth moved near her ear. "I sure could get used to a greeting like that every day."

The warmth of his breath against her ear shocked his words into comprehension. Heat shot from her quivering stomach up into her face, and she stepped away and pushed back some loose hair from her cheek, stifling a ridiculous chuckle. She'd practically knocked him over, landing on him like hard rain on a roof. What on earth was she thinking? But when she snuck a peek at his face, he didn't seem any worse for wear. In fact, his smile nearly had her jumping right at him again. Lord, help her. Surely, she couldn't feel so much, so deeply for him, with only one kiss between them.

Who was she joshing? They had a lifetime of moments between them. The kiss just started a very new and different conversation.

"It's real good to see a friendly face." She offered an extra-bright smile as she snatched the milk from his hand. "And I'm very happy to see the milk."

"Of course you are." He chuckled and followed her through

the door, leaning close to her. "And it's always a pleasure to see *your* friendly face."

She kept her attention forward as she walked into the kitchen, but her grin spread wide enough to pinch into her cheeks. After a night of uncertain sounds outside, and some strange behavior from Wolf as he moved restlessly by the back door, Jeremiah's presence brought a sense of safety, like a comforting blanket over her shoulders.

Sadie peered around the doorframe, offering a shy smile of relief of her own.

"I hope everything has gone well?" Jeremiah searched Ava's face as she placed the small jug of milk onto the wooden table.

"Mrs. Creed is improving every hour, ain't she, Sadie?"

Sadie's grin brimmed. "Eggs are miracle workers."

"Eggs?" Jeremiah glanced between the two of them.

"Just the happy progress that comes along with good food and excellent company, right, Sadie?" Ava nudged the girl with her shoulder and Sadie ducked her head with another shy smile.

"You sure have helped the conversation round here, Miss Ava."

"Of that, I have no doubt." Jeremiah released a low whistle. "Miss Ava could talk the ears off a corn stalk without catching breath and then argue—"

"I think that's enough flattery for one mornin', Mr. Sutphin." Ava picked up a small metal bucket from the sink and handed it to Sadie. "Would you run to the spring and bring some cold water so we can keep the milk cool? Ice, if you can find it."

Sadie took the bucket with a nod and slipped toward the door.

"Wolf." The dog perked an ear in Jeremiah's direction. "Go on with her."

At Jeremiah's gesture, Wolf tipped his head to Jeremiah then darted after Sadie, her step a little lighter at his camaraderie.

"He's a good dog." Ava walked to the cabinet and removed a few of the dainty doilies Sadie had mentioned her mother would wish to pack. "And he's got a good owner."

"Sweet words? You *must* be glad to see me."

She glanced at him from her periphery, and her lips burgeoned with another grin. "I am glad to see you."

He shifted a step closer, his gaze searching hers. "So, no visitors? No trouble?"

"No trouble." She breathed out a sigh as she folded the doilies into a small stack. "We did have one visitor. Casper Norris."

"Casper? He came all the way here from Hillsville? That's half a day's ride."

She leaned back against the counter and folded her arms across her chest, glancing out the back window to see Sadie slowly making her way back to the house with Wolf at her side. "He said he came to check on the Creeds. He'd heard there might be trouble after what happened to Joe, so he wanted to talk to Mrs. Creed about. . .well, I reckon it was about how she was doin'."

Jeremiah stepped closer and touched Ava's arm, bringing her attention back to his face. "I think the sooner we can get them out of here the better. Do you think Mrs. Creed could make the wagon ride tomorrow?"

Ava looked to the closed door and back to Sadie's approaching form before turning back to Jeremiah. "I'll do everything in my power to have her ready."

Chapter Eleven

You like stories, don'tcha? Then, remember, there's always
two sides. A wise person tries to read 'em both.
Granny Burcham

We need to make this stop a quick one, Ava." Jeremiah whispered from beside her on the wagon seat, his hands guiding the reins as the horses slowed their steady pace toward Sid Allen's store. "Mrs. Creed's already witherin', and I still have two hours yet to go before we reach the depot."

Ava looked back over her shoulder into the bed of the wagon where Sadie sat among some quilts, holding her mama as the pale woman rested her head on her daughter's shoulder. Maybe Ava should have encouraged Jeremiah to wait another day or two, but something in his discussion with Sheriff Webb, the subtle warning, spurred both of them into action.

"I'll just pick up a few provisions, then you can leave me here and be on your way." Ava sighed. "I wish I could ride with you all the way to the depot, but while you're on the road, I can get a telegram to Mrs. Creed's family in Kentucky so they'll be expectin' the newcomers."

His grin crooked a little. "It's good teamwork."

Her heart fluttered in response, half from admiration and a little from the disquiet still pushing at the edges of her full acceptance of a possible future with him. "You have the harder road, I'm afraid. Two hours there and back?"

"Well, it might be a little shorter on the way back since I don't have to drive so slow." He gestured with his chin toward their passengers. "Mr. Allen's just received a new shipment of some special trim work he wants put up in a few of the bedrooms, so I can get to work on that this afternoon."

"And then we have our late Christmas dinner with Granny on Sunday."

His eyes lit with an unexpressed smile. "We do, indeed. Nothin' like startin' off the new year with a Christmas dinner."

Ava offered him a begrudging smile just as the wagon came to a stop in front of the store.

"I'll water the horses while you're inside." He jumped down, and before she could climb to the ground, he'd rounded the side of the wagon. Without hesitation, he slipped his palms around her waist and helped her down, keeping her close for a second longer than necessary. The sweet scent of leather and soap breezed over her as it had when she'd hugged him back at the Creeds. The ache, the longing to belong with Jeremiah Sutphin nearly overwhelmed her. . .and terrified her all at the same time.

She pushed back from his hold and looked over at a few folks standing on the store's porch. "If you keep doin' things like that, the whole town will think we're courtin'."

"I don't see a problem." He winked, and she fought against her smile, instead narrowing her eyes up at him.

"One kiss and you're all sure-fired and sparkin'?"

He leaned in close, his voice swooping low. "The kiss just made plain what I've known for a long time, Ava Burcham."

Her breath caught, his face now temptingly close, as if he just might kiss her again. She worked her words through a dry throat. "And what is that?"

"I've been sparkin' you most of my life, so you might as well get used to the idea of courtin' me."

His closeness, his certainty and words, certainly sparked all right, directly into Ava's pulse. Great day in the mornin'! Kissin' someone you cared about changed everything. Well, she could at least pretend to have some sense. Especially with half a dozen folks eyeballing them from the storefront.

"I'm gonna let you focus all that excellent momentum on watering those horses before your long ride to the depot." She patted his arm and took a few steps back toward the store's steps. "How about that?"

His grin grew large, waiting for one more nudge into a laugh. "My excellent momentum?"

"That's right." She took a few more steps away from him.

"Are those writing vocabulary words?"

She shrugged a shoulder and turned, nearly colliding with Old Man Turner at the bottom of the steps.

"So sorry, Mr. Turner."

"Stop your moonin' over that boy and get your face in the right direction, girl." His eyes twinkled despite the bite in his gruff voice.

"I was not moonin' over that—"

Someone cleared his throat behind her, and she looked back to find Jeremiah staring at her with raised brow. "Mr. Turner, I'd say she was more. . ." He looked heavenward as if searching for a word, and Ava braced herself. " 'Mesmerized'? How about 'enraptured'?"

The temperature in Ava's face soared to new heights.

"Mesmer. . .what?" Mr. Turner shook his head and moved past them. "You book-learned young'uns and your highfalutin words. Just call it sparkin' and be done with it."

Ava released a halfhearted groan and stomped up the steps with Jeremiah's laugh teasing her all the way into the store. The usual murmur of voices greeted her along with the scent of pipe tobacco, cured meats, and licorice. A few rows of shelves stood in the center of the shop, each laden with various items from dried goods to special items, and a side portion of the store held a gathering of secondhand clothes, a new and welcome offering over the last month. Perhaps an inadvertent instigator to Ava's repurposing of clothing too, now that she thought about it.

With a quick check to her cash on hand, she gathered a few pairs of socks, a pair of wool gloves for each Creed and matching hat, a few packs of nuts and crackers, along with some jerky, to help curb hunger during the trip, a small pack of lemon drops, and—she grinned—two sticks of licorice. If she added correctly, her dollars plus what Jeremiah had given her should cover everything without any trouble.

"Are you packing for a trip, Miss Burcham?" Sid greeted her with a smile from behind the counter, his thick hair smoothed back in the latest style, which brought out the signature blue of the Allen clan's eyes. "Or a winter storm?"

Ava chuckled and placed her cash on the counter. "Just helpin' out some friends, is all."

He studied her and cast a look out the window toward Jeremiah's wagon before taking only half of the dollars she'd placed on the counter.

"But, Mr. Al—"

"No fuss, Ava." He placed the items in a bag and pushed it toward her across the counter. "Today there's a discount for goodwill." He leaned forward, his voice dropping. "Get on now. They've got quite a ride ahead of them yet."

Ava pulled the bag to her chest, nearly fit to cry right then and there. "Thank you, Mr. Allen. My friends will be grateful for your kindness."

She turned toward the door just as Peter Pickett burst through, his mailbag swinging so wide at his side, a few letters shuffled precariously to the edge of their container.

"They're. . .they're comin' up the road right now." He pointed behind him toward the open door. "And Pink's got 'em all tied up."

"What are you talkin' 'bout, boy?" a man called out.

"Who's tied up?" called another.

But Sid seemed to understand, because he rounded the counter at double speed and rushed out the door, the rest of the folks on his heels. Ava pushed through the group to make it to the edge of the porch. Jeremiah's wagon still stood where she'd left it, but Jeremiah had moved to the back of the wagon, his body placed almost as a shield between the crowds and the Creeds.

"There! There they come just like I said." Peter's voice rose above the murmurs, and Ava followed the direction of his pointing finger.

In the distance, a wagon trotted forward at a steady pace, not too fast nor slow. Ava squinted against the afternoon sunlight and made out four silhouettes in a horse-drawn buggy. Two men in the front seats and two in the back. As it neared, Ava made out the driver as Deputy Pink Samuels with Sidna Edwards beside him and with Wesley Edwards and. . . Who was in the back? Some man by the name of Easter, maybe? She'd seen him at Temples' once or twice with his wife.

"They got the boys trussed up like hogs," one man called.

"Why would they tie 'em up so?" A woman's voice rose above the grumbles. "They ain't done nothin' worth that, have they?"

A movement out of the corner of Ava's eye drew her attention farther down the road where a lone horseman approached. The stature and gait of the rider labeled him as Floyd Allen long before his white hair and matching moustache became clear. Sid Allen marched down the steps toward the approaching wagon, his face hardened with disapproval.

Ava met Jeremiah's gaze, slowly pushing her way through the crowd to make it nearer to him, which also brought her nearer to the road, just as the wagon passed. Floyd increased his pace, bringing his black stallion alongside the wagon, and in response, Pink Samuels drew his gun, training it on Floyd.

A woman gasped behind Ava, but Floyd didn't so much as flinch. "I already told you up the road, Pink. Put the gun away unless you plan to use it."

"Let us through, Floyd. We're on law business, and you got no right to stall us." Pink's high-pitched voice shook along with the weapon in his hand.

"You got no business tyin''em up in such humiliation as that."

"They tried to escape twice," Easter called from behind. "We had to do somethin' to keep 'em in the wagon."

"I just came from town speakin' with the Commonwealth attorney and told him I'd turn the boys in on Monday." Floyd rode closer to Pink, who kept his pistol high. "Since you already got 'em." His gaze shifted from one of his nephews to the other. "Then they'll follow through with the law, even though they weren't the only boys involved in the churchyard ruckus."

"Then move outta my way."

"I told you we shouldn't come this road, Pink." Easter's harsh whisper grew loud enough for Ava to hear from her place by the road. "We should've taken Ward's Gap, and we wouldn't've had this trouble."

"Hush, Easter. An officer of the law should be able to go anywhere he pleases," Pink shot back, his attention never leaving Floyd. "Get out of the way and let us by, Floyd."

Floyd slid from his horse with ease and sauntered a few steps toward the wagon, not one thread of worry on his brow. "Have you got a requisition for those boys to legally take them 'cross the state line?

'Cause if you don't, I reckon you're not in keeping with the law."

"We. . .we. . .don't need one." Pink's voice quivered. "We got an order from Blankenship."

"Blankenship ain't above the law." Floyd laughed and proceeded a few steps closer to Pink and his gun. "Besides, as far as I can tell, since it's January 1st, Blankenship ain't even sheriff anymore."

Ava squeezed in close to Jeremiah, wrapping her hands around his arm in anticipation for Pink to shake hard enough to fire that gun, and then what? Would Floyd's brother, Sid, pull his own weapon and start a gunfight in the middle of Fancy Gap Road?

"Let the boys loose," Floyd demanded, and as quick as lightning, his hand came up and snatched the gun from Pink.

Easter reached for his sidearm. Wesley, wrists manacled with handcuffs, acted quickly by raising his arms and bringing them down around Easter to keep him from firing the weapon.

Jeremiah ducked beneath the wagon, bringing Ava with him, as a lady screamed from the store porch before running back inside the shop.

A shot fired. Someone swore. From beneath Jeremiah's wagon, Ava watched as three pairs of feet landed on the ground with a few stumbles. She and Jeremiah rose far enough to see Easter running off down the road, Wesley and Sidna Edwards standing by the roadside, and Pink riding off in the wagon, hand pressed to the left side of his face and a blaze of dust following his retreat toward Hillsville.

Floyd marched across the road, his hand pressed against his chest as a red stain grew on his vest.

"You've been shot." Sid ran forward.

"Only in the finger," Floyd growled. "Good thing Easter's a better farmer than he is a shot." Floyd raised his attention toward the small crowd standing nearby and his smile widened beneath his well-manicured moustache. "We're all done here, y'all. Seems it's left to me to get my nephews up to town on Monday after all."

The small group responded with a few murmurs and chuckles as they dispersed, but Floyd and Sid remained close to where Jeremiah and Ava stood by their wagon.

"You shouldn't have hit Pink, Floyd." Sid voiced the concerns filtering through Ava's head. "Even if all it did was give him a shiner, you know he'll go straight to Hillsville with the news."

Floyd rubbed a thumb and forefinger over his moustache. "I wouldn't have hit him if he hadn't shamed the boys by tyin''em up and then took to pointin' his gun at me. Ain't no cause for that. I've worked in the law for years and can count on one hand the times I've had to tie up my prisoners, and that's a fact."

The men moved past, Wesley and Sidna keeping their heads down as they followed their uncles into the store. Ava's shoulders relaxed, and she realized that she'd pressed so close to Jeremiah, her arm linked around his like. . .well, like she belonged that close. With a quick breath, she stepped back and released her hold, but not before he sent her a rather rascally grin. Have mercy! She needed to make sure her sanity ran from the Burcham side of the family before she flung head and heart directly in Jeremiah's future, but the way he looked at her, all tender-like and caring, she almost tossed every bit of caution to the cold January wind.

But rash thoughts led to half-built houses, and if she planned to spend the rest of her life with Jeremiah, she wanted to make sure he got the best end of the deal as possible.

Mrs. Creed's weak voice came from the back of the wagon. "Are we headin' to the depot yet, Ava?"

Ava offered Mrs. Creed a smile and walked around to the back of the wagon. "You sure are." Ava raised her bag. "I've got some things to help you on your trip, and Jeremiah's gonna make sure you make it all the way to the depot without one more stop, if he can help it."

Mrs. Creed nodded and rested her head back against Sadie's shoulder, her gaze locking with Ava's. "The sooner, the better. I won't feel safe for me or my girl till I'm out of this state."

Ava pulled a few things from the bag and then handed it to Sadie. "Don't wait too long before you see what's in the bag." Ava gave Sadie's braid an affectionate tug. "Some of the items might come in handy on this cold day."

"Thank you, Ava." The girl's eyes grew glossy and her words hushed to a whisper. "I won't forget what you done for us."

Ava waved to her and met Jeremiah on the other side of the wagon.

"Be careful."

"You too." He held her gaze, hesitating before placing a hand on the buggy seat. "Promise me you'll steer clear of the Allens for now, just until things are settled with the Edwards boys."

"I promise."

"And don't go near my house or the Creeds' alone."

"Jeremiah." She folded her arms across her chest. "Do I look like a bloomin' fool to you?"

"No, but you're about as prone to trouble as a body can be." His hand slid to hers for a quick grasp before stepping back to the wagon. "And we both know how dangerous things can be without even lookin' for it."

She searched his face, reading their shared history, their losses to the mountains. She offered a halfhearted shrug in an attempt to draw the conversation to a little lighter ground. "I think you should steer clear of the Creeds' too, since I'm not the only one prone to trouble."

A flicker of a grin touched his lips. "Usually only when I'm trying to keep you out of it."

"Jeremiah." She etched a plea into his name.

"I'll meet you for dinner at Granny Burcham's in three days' time." His expression gentled and he held her gaze. "And if I don't get caught up in too much work at Sid Allen's, I may stop in at Temples' to—" He raised his eyes heavenward. "Purchase me some bobbins or some such."

Her laugh broke free. "Do you even know what bobbins are?"

"I reckon I can figure it out."

"Be careful." She touched his arm before he mounted the wagon. "Promise me."

His gaze searched hers again. "I promise."

With that, he took to his wagon seat and headed up the road, Sadie waving her good-byes from the back. Ava sighed as the wagon disappeared from view, and she whispered a prayer for safety. Only three days and she'd see him safely at her Granny's, maybe sooner if he stopped by Temples'.

But they both had lots of work to catch up on from spending those days tending to the Creeds. At least she'd keep busy and. . . She looked back up at the store. Maybe she even had another story to offer the paper. Surely the return of the Edwards boys, and in such exciting form, would prove interesting enough for the paper to find Cameron Birch useful again?

"It's awful nice for Jeremiah to take such care of the Creeds after all they've been through, ain't it?"

Ava turned to find Keen standing much too close for comfort. She shifted away from him, gauging the distance between herself and the shop door. "They could do with some care after all they've been through lately."

His attention never left her face as he raised a dark brow. "All the way to the depot, was it?"

Had he overheard their conversation? Her face chilled. How much had he overheard? "Did you have some charity you wanted to share with the Creeds, Mr. Gentry?" She opened her palm to him, waiting. "I'd be happy to ensure it gets to them."

His smile took a sinister turn, but Ava refused to recoil. "Seems like a sudden trip for them."

"Did you have anything important you wanted to ask, Keen? Because I have a lot of work to do today, and I'm sure my knowledge about the Creeds ain't got nothin' to do with your business."

He leaned close, the scent of liquor, tobacco, and unclean man nearly backing her up a step or two. "If you ain't noticed, Ava Burcham, folks who spend too much time in your company end up dead, so maybe your Mr. Sutphin"—he gestured with his chin toward the way the wagon had disappeared—"should be careful your bad blood doesn't curse him with the same fate."

Chapter Twelve

You ain't responsible for other folks' stupidity, even if you have to
manage the consequences. Your job is to be stupid as little as possible so
you can deal with the ones who don't know how to be anything else.
Granddaddy Sutphin

Jeremiah's mind hadn't been easy since he'd watched Mrs. Creed and Sadie's train disappear down the tracks toward Kentucky. The hairs on the back of his neck stood on edge, as if someone kept a watch on him. Wolf acted restless too. Prowling the inside of the house, like some nervous cat.

Even when he noticed a few of his tools out of place in the barn, and a missing jacket, he dismissed the tension as simple paranoia after all he and Ava had been through over the past few days. Surely no one would worry with them over helping the Creeds now, would they?

He didn't see Ava at church on Sunday morning, which meant she likely rode up to her granny's the night before to help prepare for their special dinner, so keeping on his Sunday best, he loaded up his wagon with another assortment of keepsakes and newly made furniture, as well as a special gift or two, and traveled the two hours to Granny Burcham's, with a quick stop at his new homestead to drop off his items.

It was the largest house he'd ever built, let alone designed. Brick. Two stories, with a porch on both sides, or at least, that was the plan once he had time to build the porch on the back and finish all the inside work. At least, when he moved in two weeks, he'd have working fireplaces and, if he found the time to install it, a cookstove, but if not, he could work on those details in the evenings from his own home.

He grinned up at the building, cradled by two oaks at either side and the back side open to a view of the distant mountains. He'd dreamed of his own place for years, and here he stood. All he needed was a barn, a back porch, and Ava.

With a lighter step, he unloaded the furniture and crates into the house, unhitched the wagon, and saddled Sally for the journey up the mountain to Granny Burcham's. The late afternoon sunlight bathed the small cabin, barely knocking the chill off the early January breeze, but the wintry wind failed to dampen Jeremiah's grin as he unloaded a crate full of Christmas surprises.

Before he could even reach the front door, it swung wide to reveal his favorite face in the world. Ava had her hair down, and it spilled smooth and brown over her shoulders. The sides she'd twisted into braids interwoven with red ribbons. Likely to match her dress. "You're here!"

"I am." Savory and sweet scents wafted toward him. "And it smells awful good in there."

"Granny roasted ham." Ava leaned close, her marble-like gaze alight with welcome. She took his hand to pull him over the threshold. "We're in for some good eats tonight, Mr. Sutphin." She gave his fingers a squeeze. "I'm real glad you're here."

He wasn't quite sure what took hold of him, but with her smile so close to his it just seemed they needed to meet. He dipped his head for a quick touch that ended up lingering a little longer than he'd planned. . .mostly because she didn't move away like he'd thought she might. No complaints from him. Her lips took his with as much softness as they had at the shucking. She even seemed to encourage him to stay.

He pulled back first, and she blinked up at him, clearly a little surprised. But, from the pink shine of her cheeks and the slightest tip of her smile, maybe she hadn't minded so much. Kissing her came as natural as breathing. Maybe as necessary too, if his speedy pulse gave any clue.

"So, where do the presents go?"

She drew in a deep breath, as if his question shook her awake. "Presents? Right." She peered into the box, but he shifted it away from her.

"If I recall correctly, food first. Presents after?"

She rolled her gaze heavenward, but her smile spread. "I reckon you're right." With a wave for him to follow, she led him across the room to a small tree in the corner, decorated with strings of popcorn, some holly, and a few of Granny Burcham's homemade crocheted snowflakes. "You know you didn't have to bring nothin', Jeremiah."

He shrugged and looked down at her, tempted to take another taste of that smile. "I know, but I liked choosin''em."

"Me too." She grinned and looked away, gesturing toward the tree. "You can set those presents right here, by this little tree I cut down yesterday."

"You cut down the tree?"

"That's right, Mr. Sutphin." She raised her chin with her grin. "It may be a little thing, but we womenfolk handled it just as fine as frog hair. Didn't we, Granny?"

Granny Burcham made her way into the room. She boasted her own set of ribbons in her salt-and-pepper hair, likely from Ava's hand-iwork. She wore a mixture of sky-blue and white ribbons twisted around the knotted bun on the back of her head, with extra streams falling down from her bun.

"My, my, Granny Burcham, don't you look as pretty as can be?" Jeremiah set his crate by the tree and gave the woman a kiss on the cheek.

"Oh, you dear boy." She patted his cheek. "Flattery will get you everywhere and then some. And, yes, I saved cherries just to make you some cherry cobbler for Christmas."

Warmth spilled all the way through him. She'd made his mama's favorite dessert. Just like she'd done each year since his mama's death. For him. "You know the way to my heart, Granny."

Her gaze flipped to Ava and back, brow raised. "I reckon I do, but cherries make for a nice extra."

His grin split wide at her clear innuendo. "Doubly nice."

Her eyes twinkled alive. "Wounded hearts beat a more cautious rhythm, but she'll come around, boy."

Ava's response to his kiss certainly added some encouragement. "Thanks, Granny."

"Now, let's get to that ham while it's hot and greasy." She brought her wrinkled hands together and led the way into the tiny lean-to kitchen in the back room, where she'd set three chairs and a table, complete with tablecloth and her own heirloom china.

The fanciest day of the year.

After all the heartache of the past few days, he glanced around the room and embraced his little makeshift family. . .or the family he hoped to officially make his own.

Ava's lips still buzzed with gratitude from Jeremiah's kiss. And here, she'd thought nothing could impress her quite as much as the shucking kiss, but the way his lips lingered over hers, almost like a sweet appreciation for the moment. . . Well, a surge of something like a swoosh of wind on fire waved from her stomach upward and set up residence.

She studied him as the meal commenced. In his white button-up and suit jacket, hair slicked back to bring out his eyes, she couldn't think of a finer man in the whole world. A quiver of doubt slid a chill into the warmth his presence brought. She wanted a future with him, but not at the cost of *his* future. *Oh Lord, help me trust You to make this right. To calm my fears. To keep my mind sound. You are with me.*

"It was awful good of you to get the Creeds to the station, Jeremiah." Granny slid her knife over the ham, her attention keen on his face. "Ava's been tellin' me about all the goings-on down yonder. The pair of you have had a time."

"I hope the trouble with the Creeds is finished for now." Jeremiah took a drink of the coffee Ava had served him with his meal. "But I got a feeling there's something still not right. I just can't shake it."

Granny nodded and placed her silver down by her plate. "You might be onto somethin', for truth. I can't reconcile myself to Joe takin' his own life. Not Joe."

"I still can't understand why the law's caused such a fuss about the Edwards boys." Ava placed her chin on the heel of her hand, brow creased, looking the very image of her nine-year-old self. "Boys have gotten into a heap o' worse trouble, with guns actually bein' fired, but from what the papers say, the Edwards boys have nearly a dozen charges betwixt them with nary a charge for any of the other boys."

"Maybe the judge'll throw it out of court," Jeremiah offered, smothering his biscuit with some of Ava's homemade apple butter.

"I don't know 'bout that, boy." Granny tapped her chin, her gaze growing distant. "If Dexter Goad or William Foster from the Courthouse Clan have anything to do with the charges agin' them boys, I have an inklin' somebody's tryin' to make a point."

"You mean, Goad and Foster want to show the Allens who's in charge?" Ava sat back in her chair and looked over at Jeremiah. "Why on earth would they want to pick a fight with two boys, though, when their trouble's with the generation before?"

"And maybe even the one before that," Jeremiah added.

" 'Cause tryin' to have the Allen menfolk pay for their crimes ain't come too easy, I reckon. But that's partial hearsay and partial not." Granny shook her head, returning to her mashed potatoes. "And some of them courthouse boys have had their sights set on the Allens for years without gettin' their fists satisfied, so maybe this is their way."

"Do they have reason to believe the Allens got out of servin' their time?"

Granny chuckled at Ava's question, an answer even Jeremiah knew from interacting with his father and other lawmen. "Well, sure they have. So has Foster and Goad, as far as what I've heard tell. Ain't none of them blameless. Shucks, Goad's been dealin' in blockade liquor for years."

"I have to take up for the Allens, Granny. Both Floyd and Sid registered their stills with the law, so they can't be called blockaders." Jeremiah took another bite of his biscuit.

Granny raised a brow, which hinted that she didn't quite agree with Jeremiah's assessment but wasn't keen to set him right. "Both sets got power in these parts, and power tends to stand folks a little taller than they really are, so no wonder they're fightin' over who's the tallest. Rough thing about it all is the good and the bad get so mixed together you can't tell them from a peeled turnip in a peeled potato pile."

Granny took another bite of her potatoes, but Ava had lost her appetite. In her short life, she'd never had trouble with either side, but somebody had trouble with the Creeds. Trouble enough to have Sadie Creed pulling a shotgun on friends.

What third party in this messy conflict would want to hurt a young man in his prime or his family? That didn't seem anywhere close to something the Allens would do, from what she knew of them. And the courthouse boys had even sent Casper Norris down to see to the Creeds, so it wasn't likely they had darker dealings with Joe, was it?

Could there be a smaller player in the game of mountain moonshine? Or the gambling rings?

The memory of Keen Gentry at the Allens' store crept over Ava's skin with a residual chill. Who were Keen's people? He'd come from North Carolina, some said, escaping from the law himself. She'd heard plenty of rumors about him running blockade liquor and worse, but which clan did he work for? Himself? Didn't seem likely.

"Don't go looking so sour, girl." Granny's voice pulled Ava from her thoughts. "God ain't took His hands off none of His young'uns, through the good"—she set her full attention on Ava—"or the bad. He's workin', moldin', bendin' us so we'll have our hearts less fit for this ol' world and more fit for the next." She tagged on a wink. "But, since we're in this one, He gave us a heap o' things to enjoy." Her gaze swung to Jeremiah. "Like cherry cobbler and Christmas presents."

The conversation turned in the same direction as the food— sweeter—and soon ended with them sitting by the crackling fire, Granny in her rocking chair and Jeremiah and Ava in their respective ladder-backs.

"Before presents, I brought a special Christmas treat." Jeremiah walked to the crate and, after sifting through the box, drew out a few small containers that looked vaguely familiar.

Ava popped up from her chair. "You brought Dr Peppers?"

His grin crooked and he dangled a box in front of her. "And Cracker Jacks."

"Oh my goodness!" Ava snatched the box and handed it to Granny. "Oh Granny, do you remember when Jeremiah brought these last year at Christmas?"

"Sure do." She shook the box at them. "Eatin' these was worth every ache in my teeth afterwards."

"Oh, I have something that won't hurt your teeth at all, Granny Burcham." Jeremiah pulled out a large item wrapped in brown paper, a simple black piece of yarn tied around it. "This is for you."

As soon as Ava caught sight of the gift's shape in the lantern light, her grin broadened into a laugh. The black handle sticking out of one end helped give it away too.

"You didn't, boy." He placed the package in Granny's arms, and she looked up, eyes wide. "You didn't."

"I heard your old one was causin' more trouble than help."

Granny's fingers slipped through the brown paper to reveal a brand-new cast-iron skillet with a beautiful lace doily folded in the center. Ava looked from the lace to Jeremiah, the implication nearly bringing her to tears.

He offered a one-shouldered shrug. "I figured you could pretty up your kitchen a little with one of Mama's special treats." His expression gentled. "She'd have wanted you to have one, and I should have given it a long time ago."

Granny raised the dainty lace in her fingers and, with the gentlest of movements, pressed the lace against her cheek for a second before lowering it to the pan again. It was one of the most tender responses Ava had ever seen. "I thank ye, Jeremiah." She nodded, clearing her throat. " 'Tis nice to hold somethin' created by a friend's hand, especially when you ain't seen 'em for a long while."

Ava slid into her chair and placed her hand on her Granny's knee, a swift sheen glimmering to life in Granny's eyes before it disappeared. The toughness forged within her Granny from a mountain life often hid the glimpses of grief she bore for the many people she'd lost in her life, but the sight reminded Ava of how much her granny truly understood. How deeply she felt the losses, even if she rarely showed it.

"I'm glad you have it, Granny," Jeremiah whispered, then stood taller, his smile returning as his attention fastened on Ava. "And now, Miss Burcham, I have something for you."

Ava stood with a little squeal, her hands clenched in front of her like a prayer. Jeremiah knew how to give gifts. Last year, he'd bought her the nicest boots she'd ever seen, and as fancy as anything the rich Carters of Hillsville would wear. She'd practically worn them every day since he'd given them to her.

His boyish grin split wide, his gaze focused on her as he reached into the crate and drew out a large, box-shaped item covered in brown paper tied with a red strip of yarn. She looked over at him and back to the gift, attempting to decipher what it could be. From the way he carried it, gentle-like with a tension in his arms, it appeared to be heavier and more fragile than a pair of boots.

"If you sit down, I'll put it in your lap so you can open it." He nudged her with the box back toward her chair. "Besides, I can watch you better from the light of the fire."

Her gaze flipped to his. "Watch me better?"

"I. . .well, I love to see your face when you're excited. Actually, I just like your face in general." He winced and then gave a helpless shrug. "Would you sit down so I can give you this present?"

Why did he have to be so good? If he was just a little bad, the thought of messing up their future together might not hurt so much, but he oozed a gentleness, an affection so authentic and kind, the very thought of wounding him wilted her at the knees.

She lowered herself onto the chair. The box weighed more than she thought it would, and as her hands smoothed over the paper, her fingers helped her guess at the contents.

"Jeremiah." She barely eked his name out on a breath, locking eyes with him. "This. . .you can't. . ."

"Open it." He tugged on the string until it loosened.

Her fingers shook as she slid them between the creases of the paper, popping the string apart. Her gaze found his again, even before the paper fully fell away.

"Have mercy! What is that thing?" Granny exclaimed with a chuckle. "Is it what you showed me from the magazine a few months back?"

Ava's attention never strayed from Jeremiah's, her voice unresponsive.

"I know it's secondhand, but Mr. Allen assured me it's in workin' order."

He blurred in her vision, so she looked down at the black Underwood, front-strike typewriter. Almost as if she might break the metal thing, she slid her fingertips over the keys, marveling that this little dream was hers. It had to have cost him at least forty dollars, and that was only if Mr. Allen gave him a discounted price. Forty dollars!

"There's some paper in the crate for it too. And some kind of smudge marker Mr. Allen included, but I ain't sure what it's for."

Jeremiah's voice filtered into her thoughts and she looked up at him then, a tear slipping over the edge of her lashes. "I. . .I thought you weren't too keen on my writing."

His expression softened and he knelt before her, the firelight making a halo around his silhouette. "You're a great writer. I just want you to be a safe one." He placed his hand over hers against the machine. "And if it's something you love, I'm gonna love it too."

She lowered her head, trying to keep every emotion in her chest from bursting out in an unsightly torrent of sobs. "It's. . .it's wonderful."

"Land sakes alive!" Granny popped some Cracker Jacks in her mouth and grinned. "A fancy thingamajig and a handsome man besides. Ava Burcham, I think you got the best Christmas present this side of the mountain range."

"Maybe even the whole world, I reckon." She wiped at her cheeks and raised her bleary eyes to Jeremiah's face. "Thank you. I know how much this cost you."

"You're a great writer, Ava. Just maybe you'll write some of them Granny stories now and add all your interesting words to make it into a novel, like those you get from the library every week." He'd changed the subject, lightened the moment.

"Now that's somethin' to do, for sure." Granny patted Ava's knee and laughed. "Mountain novels. Just imagine what the world outside of Fancy Gap could learn from the wild stories back here. They won't believe a word of it."

Ava smoothed her fingers over the keys again. Would the whole world want to read those types of stories? Could she even write one? She'd been so stuck on setting the world right through newswriting, she'd never considered that fiction could matter just as much.

Swiping her hand over her eyes, she gently placed the typewriter on the floor and stood, Jeremiah coming to a stand with her. In one sweeping movement, she wrapped her arms around his neck and buried her head in his shoulder. "You shouldn't have, Jeremiah."

"It was worth every penny," he whispered into her hair. She nearly sobbed like a baby directly into his church-wearing shirt.

"Now, we got one more gift to show, don't we, Ava?"

Granny's reminder brought Ava away from the warmth of Jeremiah's arms, a place she was beginning to like more and more with each passing day. "That's right." She sniffled and smiled up at him. "One more."

She almost ran to the cedar chest at the end of her granny's bed, ready to offer more than just a thank-you to Jeremiah, even though her and Granny's gift could in no way compare to an Underwood typewriter. With careful hands, she lifted a quilt from the chest and walked toward him.

"Sit down for your present too." She narrowed her eyes at him as she approached. "So *I* can watch *you*."

"Yes, ma'am." He dipped his head and slid down into the chair she'd just vacated.

"Granny and I knew you were gettin' your own place soon, so we wanted to make you somethin' you could take with you. Somethin' special."

"To pretty up a bachelor's place," Granny added with a crooked grin.

"So. . ." Ava placed the quilt on his lap. "I designed the squares, and Granny quilted 'em all together." Ava smoothed her palm against the cloth. "Some squares are just plain colors, but others, like this one. . ." She pointed to a square she'd designed with a myriad variety of blues. "This one's the mountains, because you've always said if you could have a house, you'd want to see the mountains from it." She moved her hand over to another square with a white background covered in beautiful pink rosettes. "And this one matches a pattern on one of—"

"Mama's favorite dresses," he whispered, moving his fingers beside hers to touch the square.

"That's right." Ava pointed to another. "And that's supposed to be Wolf, but I couldn't get his nose to look just right. And there's the fishing hole you and your daddy used to go to by the big oak, and—"

He grabbed her fingers, squeezing them, and when she looked down into his face, his eyes shone glossy, firelight swirling in a sea of golden brown. "Thank you." He turned to Granny. "Thank you both." His gaze found Ava's again. "It's about as fine as anything I've ever owned."

"It's a way to keep those memories, those folks close, ain't it, Jeremiah?" Granny rocked back in her chair and raised her bottle of Dr Pepper in his direction in salute.

"All wrapped up in their shades of love like a quilt," Ava added, and the words pricked at her imagination, bringing to life one of Granny's stories from long ago about the friendship between Granny's mama and a slave girl. A lifelong friendship and a story to show how people can come together through kindness rather than tear each other apart through hate.

"I think this has been the best late Christmas I've ever had." Jeremiah gave Ava's hand another squeeze, holding her gaze with a look of such tenderness, her fears paled against the love he offered. The hope.

Oh God, help me be brave enough to start a future with Jeremiah Sutphin. Quiet my anxious heart with Your love.

⌇

Jeremiah stayed the night at his new house so as not to make the long trek all the way back to the old place, and though he'd only lit the fire in one room, his new quilt and the memories of dinner with Granny Burcham and Ava had kept his slumber warm and content the whole night through. Maybe it was time to make the full move over to his new place a week before he'd planned. That'd give him more time to finish building the barn too.

Her response to him the previous night gave him all sorts of hope that their future together might start sooner than later, and if everything worked out the way he'd planned, the house should be ready for a bride by early spring.

He topped the hill on the road toward his old house, a spot which afforded a mile's view of the surrounding countryside, and his stomach seized. Billowing above the tree line of the forest against the dusky hues of morning swelled a dark cloud of smoke. . .directly at the spot of his old homeplace. A snap of the reins sent Sally into a gallop over the uneven trail as faint glints of dawn streaked gold through the forest's waning darkness. He didn't have to see the house to know what had happened. Didn't have to watch the charred wood crisp beneath the flames to recognize someone had sent him a clear warning. He'd lived in these mountains long enough to know the cost of stepping over the line of others' perceived just deserts, but he'd never been the recipient of it.

Until now.

As the forest faded away to reveal the clearing of his uncle's homestead, fading flames licked the last remains of the cabin, leaving nothing but a charred chimney rising into a pillar of gray smoke. The house he'd known his whole life. The place he'd been raised. The walls of thousands of memories. The place his cousin was due to bring his new bride in only a few weeks.

Destroyed.

A whimper sliced through the crackle of the dying fire and Jeremiah's pulse careened into a sprint. In the distance, between the burning house and the small, intact barn, lay a bundle of gray fur, motionless.

Wolf.

Jeremiah leaped from the wagon and dashed toward the dog. Wolf attempted to raise his head at Jeremiah's approach but only managed another whimper, his fur stained with blood from his midsection to his back. One leg turned in a crooked direction, clearly broken.

"Hey, boy," Jeremiah soothed, kneeling down by his companion of five years.

With careful hands, Jeremiah smoothed back the fur, examining the stained area. Near the hip joint, Jeremiah found the hole left behind from a bullet. Pistol. At least it hadn't been a shotgun, or there'd likely have been nothing left to do with Wolf but bury him.

Wolf whimpered again. Jeremiah fisted his hands and glanced around the remains. He should have taken Wolf with him to Granny Burcham's. He should have moved everything a week sooner. He should have—

But there was no planning for hate like this. No way to predict the endemic vengeance some folks tended like a garden. Whatever had happened with Joe Creed came with a much more dangerous story than he or Ava had anticipated.

He scooped Wolf up into his arms and marched toward the barn. Likely Lulu had been stolen and most of his tools, but he still had cloth, straw for bedding, and a springhouse with fresh water. He couldn't save the cabin or the things he still held dear from inside, but, while Wolf still breathed, he could try to save his dog.

Chapter Thirteen

You're missin' sunshine? Well, it's always close by.
Never more than a smile and a hope away.
Granny Burcham

I told you I'd get the sewin' done while I was up at Granny's." Ava deposited five items onto the counter in front of Mrs. Temple: two brand-new frocks and three mended items from their used-clothes purchases.

Ava didn't mention the freshly typed article held safely in her satchel, ready for delivery to the newspaper *or* the first chapter of a fiction attempt she'd read to Granny over breakfast. No, this time she'd deliver the article herself and see what the *Carroll Journal* did with it.

"Well, now. I see you've been hard at work while you've been enjoying your festivities." Mrs. Temple raised one of the frocks up to examine it, a periwinkle-blue confection with puffed sleeves and lace trim. "Oh Ava, I'm placing this one in the shop window. Seein' it before you left for your granny's, I had no idea it'd turn into something so fancy. As good as anything from town or otherwise."

Why Mrs. Temple continued to be surprised by Ava's skills failed to make sense to Ava, but whether it was from forgetfulness, distraction, or an easy-to-please temperament, Ava didn't pay no mind. Mrs. Temple's praise was always welcome, and the money, even more so. Though, she hadn't figured out what she was going to use her savings for yet, now that Jeremiah had gone and bought her that typewriter she'd been saving for.

"You just wait till the Greer girls ride by with their daddy." Ava winked and tapped the other frock, a green one of the same design as the blue. "What d'ya bet you'll have 'em sold by week's end?"

Mrs. Temple chuckled and smoothed her fingers over the lace trim of the dress in her hand. "You got a gift for this and that's a fact. It's a shame you've been up in the mountains for nigh four days and missed

134

all the news down here, though."

Ava took up the men's slacks she'd mended and placed them on a hanger. "Mr. Beamer's new puppies? Pete told me about them on my way into the shop this mornin'."

"The puppies is the least of the news." Mrs. Temple shook her head as she slid the blue dress onto a hanger and walked toward the large front window. "The Creeds have moved on after all the trouble they've seen, but I reckon you already know 'bout that. Kentucky, even."

Ava hung the slacks on the rack with some of the other mended secondhand clothes, careful to keep her expression controlled. "Well, that makes good sense, don't it? After all those two have lost, to move up near family."

"I reckon so." Mrs. Temple nodded, positioning the dress so that the skirt flared in a fetching way for passersby to appreciate. "Though it's all a sudden." She sighed and stepped back to look at her work with a smile. "I wouldn't be surprised if those dresses weren't sold by midweek, Ava. I think you ought to make a few more for the window, and that's a fact."

"Is that the only news worth tellin'?" Ava returned to the counter and took a mended sweater in hand. Dark green. A fine color for Jeremiah.

"Well, Floyd took his nephews up to town and turned them into the law yesterday, just as he said he'd do." Mrs. Temple returned to the counter and smoothed out the wrinkles from the dress shirt Ava had mended by shortening the frayed long sleeves. "I sure hope that ends all the fuss betwixt the law and them Allens."

Ava sighed as she folded the sweater and placed it on a shelf with a few other sweaters on display for sale. From the conversation with Granny, it sounded like it'd take a lot more than some trumped-up charges on Allen boys to quell the discontent between the Allens and the courthouse boys.

"By the by, I got a crate full of supplies for you to take out to Jeremiah's when you visit today. I'm sure he'll appreciate 'em. A coffeepot, plate, some sugar, and a blanket." She pulled the crate from behind the counter and placed it up for Ava to reach. "Not much, but something for the poor boy."

Ava looked to the crate and back to Mrs. Temple's face. A coffee-pot? Sugar? "What sort of supplies does Jeremiah need?"

"I reckon about everything he can get." Mrs. Temple picked up a yellow dress from the stack of newly arrived secondhand items and began slipping it onto a hanger. "Mr. Temple said the house burned to the foundation, so there wasn't nothin' left at all."

Ava froze as she replayed Mrs. Temple's last sentence. House burned to the ground? She rushed to the counter, slamming both palms against the wood. "What are you talkin' about? Whose house?"

"Oh honey, I thought you'd have knowed." Mrs. Temple placed a palm to her mouth and gave a slow, consolatory shake of her head. "Two nights back, Jeremiah's house caught afire. Thank the good Lord, he wasn't there, 'cause I fear what might've happened to him if he'd been home. Whoever burned the house shot his dog too."

Air left Ava's body in one whoosh. Wolf? She stumbled back, her mind whirling through comprehension and planning. "Shot the dog?"

"We just heard about it yesterday, but I reckon, you bein' up at your granny's, you didn't learn of it."

Ava forced air into her lungs and her feet into motion. "He'll. . . he'll need clothes too." She stumbled toward the secondhand section, scanning through all the items she'd placed there over the last week. Some brown slacks. They'd be a little long, but she could hem them for him. The green sweater she'd just placed on the shelf. An undershirt. A pair of boots that looked to be his size. Two collared, plaid work shirts. A couple of pairs of wool socks.

"Charge me whatever you need to, Mrs. Temple. I'll pay it. Or dock my pay. Whatever you need to do." Ava marched back to the counter and placed the items in the crate. "I have some of my honey-garlic salve in the back room. I'll take it too. And some extra cloths, for bandages, if you got any."

"Those are good notions for sure."

Ava ran to the back and returned with her cream. "And do you got any tea tree oil? Or calendula? I can make a salve with it, if you have some dried."

"No, neither one." She frowned, scanning the counter behind her.

"Cinnamon? Neem?"

"I got neem leaves. Dried." Mrs. Temple rushed to the counter and drew out an envelope with the word *Neem* written across the front. "Never used 'em, but I have 'em."

"They'll have to do without calendula. They fight infection and help with healin', from what Granny says." Ava placed the envelope in the crate and slipped the coat she'd just discarded back on her shoulders. "I have to go see him."

"Course you do." Mrs. Temple's gaze softened and then she seemed to rally. "Take the buggy. It's hitched to the side." She gestured toward the door. "It'll get you there faster than your mule."

The trip from Temples' to Jeremiah's took over an hour by foot, but Ava pushed the horse over the rugged terrain, halving the time. What had happened? A misplaced lantern? A loose spark from the fire? Why hadn't she known sooner? Had he been alone for the past two days?

And then Mrs. Temple's words came back. Wolf was shot. Which meant, this was no accident.

She pushed the horse a little harder, her pulse moving at the same pace as his hooves.

The smell of smoke hit her as a warning before she reached the forest clearing, but it failed to prepare her for the view. A gasp shocked from her as the trees opened up to reveal charred ruins where a tidy little cabin used to stand, faint smoke still rising from the scorched carnage. A single rock fireplace towered, blackened and isolated above the mangled debris, ashen slashes marking their attempt to take the stone down as thoroughly as the log structure. In contrast to the blackened remains of the cabin, the small barn rose to her right, untouched against the edge of the forest, as pristine as it had been when she saw it last week.

Why would the arsonists burn down the house and leave the barn?

Ava brought the buggy to a stop in front of the barn and listened for any sign of Jeremiah as she retrieved the crate from the back. An eerie quiet settled over the vacant spaces around her, the familiar forest suddenly taking on an unsettling silence. Had they come back to finish off Jeremiah? A whisper of wind chilled her cool face and brought with it the sound of crinkling leaves nearby. She turned, peering into the forest for the origin of the noise. Had it been a footstep? The breeze hushed like a whisper.

Or was it a real whisper?

Fingertips of dread crawled up through her middle and branched over her shoulders. She squeezed her eyes closed. *God, help me. I'm not hearing things. Help me keep my head.*

When she opened her eyes, the rustling in the woods came from a few errant leaves still clinging to the last bits of their tree from the autumn. She pulled the crate into her stomach and walked to the barn door, carefully pushing it open with her hip.

"Jeremiah?"

Silence.

"Jeremiah," she repeated, leaning into the barn.

A tremulous whimper came from a stall at her right. *Wolf!* She caught her breath and rushed forward. The stall, once used for a second horse Jeremiah's daddy owned, had been turned into a storage area for some of Jeremiah's tools, complete with a worktable, but now it served as a bed for Wolf. And, from the blanket and flattened hay beside the dog, a bed for Jeremiah too.

Wolf made another high-pitched whine that pulled Ava closer. "Looks like somebody's taking care of you, boy." One bandage covered Wolf's hindquarters, another wrapped around a splint on one of his bad legs, and a third covered his neck, all stained with old blood.

Ava placed a palm to his head, looking down into those pale eyes. "I'm going to try and help you, Wolf." He closed his eyes as she cooed to him, gently rubbing his forehead. "You're such a good dog. I need you to be strong now, all right?"

She carefully removed each wrapping, tending to the neck wound, some sort of cut, first, replacing the old cloth with fresh. Jeremiah must have shaved some of the fur away from the gunshot wound, which meant he may have been able to remove any bullet already. She hoped. Infection was less likely to set in and the wound would heal much faster.

She applied some of the salve, a combination of herbs to fight infection and encourage healing, and then wrapped his hindquarters with fresh bandages. A careful examination of the broken leg proved that Jeremiah had already set the bone, so she left his work alone.

Carefully, she brought a ladle of water up to Wolf's mouth, and he weakly lapped it up. Then she took a small mixture of ground meat, rosemary, and cloves and offered him a taste.

At first lick, he closed his mouth.

"Come on, Wolf. Granny Burcham says cloves and rosemary will help with the pain." She nudged the bite back toward him. "And we always do what Granny Burcham says."

As if English was his second language, he took a bite of the offered meat. Just one bite. But that was enough. She offered him another drink and he closed his eyes, likely worn out from her work with him.

Ava stepped from the stall and caught sight of Lulu in her usual spot near the back of the barn, no more worse for wear by all the tragedy of the past few days. Well, at least Jeremiah would have milk.

Then she heard it. The rhythmic clap of an ax against wood. Ava poured some water into a tin, took a biscuit from the crate of supplies Mrs. Temple had collected, and stepped out the back of the barn, pausing to locate the direction of the sound.

With quick steps, she marched down the forest trail toward the noise, the tall pines enveloping her on all sides. As she came to a small clearing, she saw him. The white Sunday shirt he'd worn for Christmas now hung damp and dirty over his frame, collar open. His dark hair curled at the ends from perspiration and a few days' growth shadowed his chin. There was a ferocity about his movements, a sober determination in his focus. So much so, he didn't hear her approach, didn't even notice her in his periphery.

Her breath squeezed to the painful point.

He'd felled an enormous pine and already loaded some of the logs from it into his wagon. What number tree was this? Oh, she knew what he was doing. The house belonged to his cousin and it had been destroyed, and now, Jeremiah was determined to replace the loss.

Tears warmed her eyes as she drew closer to him. Two days. Had he been alone with Wolf for two days and no one to comfort him? To help him? To share his grief? She increased her pace, wiping at her eyes.

Well, there was someone here now.

He caught sight of her as he raised his ax to take another swing into the trunk. His body froze and his eyes locked with hers. With a sigh, he lowered the ax, the pain in his expression squeezing out her air on a strained groan.

"I didn't know," she whispered, holding out the tin of water like a peace offering.

He took the tin, his gaze lingering in hers for a second before he took a drink.

"Are you hurt?"

He downed the rest of the water. "No. Only Wolf."

"But. . .but they could have killed you." Just stating the words brought a fresh wave of warmth to her eyes.

"This was a warning." He shook his head and used the tin to gesture toward the path. "They didn't want to kill me."

"How can you know that?"

He took his time answering, wiping the back of his hand over his mouth and handing her the empty tin. "They left Lulu."

The cow? What on earth did she have to do with him surviving? She offered him the biscuit. "They left Lulu?"

His expression softened ever so slightly as he tugged the food from her hand. "Thank you, Ava."

"I didn't want you to be alone." Was that her voice? Weakened and raw? She swallowed to clear away the emotion, but it remained.

His gaze roamed her face and then he looked away, brow wrinkling into a dozen crinkles. "I think you need to stay clear for a while."

The warmth of his closeness dissipated. "What? Why would you say that?"

He closed his eyes and released a sigh before meeting her gaze again. "They won't give another warning, Ava. Next time, it'll likely be to kill. The more we're together, the more they're gonna associate you with me, and. . . Well, to be honest, I can't bear the thought of them hurting you."

"They're going to place us together anyway, Jeremiah Sutphin." She waved a hand back toward the trail as if the whole town stood in that direction. "They practically think we're married as it is."

"Ava, I've already lost all the people in the world I've loved." He frowned and leaned close, taking her by the arm. "I *need* you to be safe."

Her eyes stung, but she wouldn't look away as she covered his hand on her arm. "Then let's do that together."

"Not this time. Not until we figure out who did this and why." He ran a hand through his hair and groaned. "They left Lulu alive and the barn intact because they wanted to warn me to stay out of their business, not kill me." He gestured toward the wood at his feet. "And by burnin' down the house, they knew they'd keep me too busy building a new house for my cousin to get involved in any more of their trouble. They targeted *me*. Only me. For now, I want you to stay near the Temples' or your granny's. Until it's safer."

"Don't you think I want you to be safe too?" He pulled away, but she closed in. "Do you really think they'd try something else? Something more?"

"I don't know, but until I do, I need you to steer clear and be alert."

"Who's to say I won't rescue you when the time comes?" She narrowed her eyes at him and crossed her arms over her chest. "I know about healing plants, I'm a fairly good shot, and I—"

"Ava. . ." The plea in his words, in his eyes, dissolved her arguments like rainwater on a hot day.

She saw it then, clearly. The vulnerability. The stacked-up grief between the loss of his parents, the house, and Wolf's wounds. And the very idea of losing her took this strong, wonderful man and crippled his heart. She knew he loved her. Had known it for a month, if not a lifetime, but the appeal in that one word. . .her name. . .pierced through her arguments.

She lowered her gaze to the ground, new tears gathering where the old had dried. "I left a crate of things next to Wolf. There's some salve for his wounds and new cloths for his bandages too."

"Thank you kindly."

His soft response drew her attention back to his face. She stifled the urge to run directly into his arms but decided on a more memorable departure. "But as soon as this house is done, and when enough time's passed to where concern is gone, I plan to take you up on your offer."

He kept his head down, examining the tree for his next strike. "My. . .my offer?"

"The offer of marriage." She raised her chin, her gaze locked on his profile to catch every tiny reaction. "If you're still keen, that is?"

His head whipped up, brows rising ever so slowly, and his bottom lip slacked till he looked like a fish. Well, at least she could offer a little positive distraction in the middle of all the horrible.

Her grin tempted to spread. "I reckon all this life and death crazy has spurred me in the direction of not wasting any precious time with the ones I—" Her gaze faltered for a half second, almost afraid to speak the word aloud. She'd lost most of the ones she'd loved too. "The ones I love."

He still stood there like a scarecrow, and her brave declaration began to sound a little too brazen.

"And somebody needs to help you take care of Wolf and teach you how to—"

She wasn't quite sure how he'd moved so fast, but right in the middle of her sentence, he'd grabbed her around the waist and pulled her into a kiss to eclipse the previous two. Careful, thorough, and leaving her more than a little breathless and a tad bit light-headed. Have mercy! Kissing sure was a *fine* pastime.

He drew back and stared down at her, a brow raised in playful suspicion. "You're not just sayin' that to make me feel better, are you?"

She cupped his cheek, rubbing her thumb against the rough ridges of his jawline and marveling a little at the freedom to do so. "Well, do you?"

He snuck another kiss, his grin spreading to his eyes. "Heaps."

"Then I reckon that's just icing on the cake, then, ain't it?"

"And you're not just agreein' to marry me so I'll hanker after seein' you when I've clearly told you to stay away?"

She bit down on her bottom lip to catch her smile. "You mean you wouldn't hanker after seein' me anyhow?"

"I have a hankerin' to see you every day of my life, Ava Burcham." He kissed her again, and she laughed against his smile.

Something her daddy had told her a long time ago filtered through her thoughts as Jeremiah made sure she'd have plenty of memories of kissing him while they were apart. *This ol' world is full of dark and light. Dull and bright. Good and bad. God shines in bright colors. So bring as many of those into life's shadows to help you make it through, and His light will change the view in the darkness."*

She clung to Jeremiah as they stood in the forest. . .and embraced the brightness, the hope, for as long as she could.

⤳

Letting Ava walk away after kissing her nearly senseless was one of the hardest things Jeremiah had done in a long time, but without knowing who'd burned his house—and exactly why—he refused to bring Ava any further into the conflict than she'd already stepped. If this incident took the usual turn of mountain warnings, within a month, maybe two, if no other "warnings" emerged, then the warning had been enough, and the clan who'd made the attack wouldn't bother him again.

But until he was sure, Ava's travels to his house, his time with her and Granny Burcham, could lead the attackers to them. Or they could get caught in the cross fire, like his pa. If he could keep her safe, even if it meant staying apart for a short while, then it was worth the distance.

He steered his wagon from the sawmill back toward the old homeplace, his timber cuts from the last few days now sleek boards for beginning the process of rebuilding the house his cousin expected to find on the property. Jeremiah had until the first week of March. Working alone while trying to keep up his job with Sid Allen promised to test the timeline, but Jeremiah couldn't have his cousin and his bride suffer for his involvement with the Creeds.

As he neared the house, the fresh scent of smoke clung to the air. He peered up the trail toward the clearing, his fingers tensing around the reins. Had the attackers returned? Why? Jeremiah had stayed to himself for almost a week, except for the visit from Ava. What else could they possibly. . . ? His breath congealed in his lungs. The barn? Wolf!

With a snap of the reins, the horse doubled his efforts and the wagon reeled into the clearing. Jeremiah's attention searched for the origin of the smoke, only to find a small campfire near the barn with a pot atop.

He took in the entire scene. Two wagons stood by the house's remains. Another pair of horses roamed the space, nipping at any existing grass. And then Jeremiah heard it, the slapping of a hammer on a nail, the deep hum of male voices, the clop of rock against rock. What was happening?

"Just in time for some hard work."

Jeremiah turned to see Elmer Williams walking toward him, his grin as wide as the sweat ring around the front of his shirt. The middle-aged man offered his massive hand. "Good to see you, boy."

"What. . .what's happening here?"

Two of Floyd Allen's boys, Claude and Victor, were finishing up the rock foundation Jeremiah had begun on the house three days before. Sheriff Webb stood by Elmer's son, holding a corner post in place as it was secured into position. Even Casper Norris appeared to supervise two Daniels boys securing the wood floor of the cabin.

"Ava spread the word that you could use a helpin' hand or two."

Air burst from his lungs. "Ava!"

"She's lined up a whole host of folks to come out and lend you a hand." Elmer chuckled and swiped at his beard. "Even Temple's volunteered to dust off his hammer and make an appearance."

Victor Allen emerged in Jeremiah's periphery, his powerfully pale blue eyes always grabbing attention first. The elder of Floyd's sons brought an easy friendliness with him, a peaceful demeanor that didn't always coincide with his father's more unpredictable temperament. "Ava sent some more salve, so I followed her orders and put it in the barn."

Jeremiah took Victor's outstretched hand, still trying to form his gratitude into words. "I'm sure she gave you detailed instructions."

"Even offered to write 'em down for me." Victor chuckled before sobering. "I'm real sorry, Jeremiah. Pa and Uncle Sid, they're hot about the whole thing and have their ears open for any news that'll give a hint to who done it."

"It's a wrongdoin' and that's the truth," Elmer interjected. "Anybody who'd spent any time at all with you or your people, Jeremiah, would've never stooped as low as this. It just ain't right."

Jeremiah drew in a deep breath, parsing his words. Elmer Williams was a good man. So was Victor Allen. But at the current moment, Jeremiah wasn't sure who to trust. . .and who to avoid. Words spread much too quickly for rash talk.

"Well, I just thank you all." The renewed gratitude pressed in on his chest and he lowered his shaking head. "Just thank you."

"It's what folks do in these parts, boy." Elmer placed his hand on Jeremiah's shoulder and gave it a good shake. "We take keer of each other, as we can. Building a cabin?" He gestured toward the new structure slowly rising a distance from the remains of the old. "We know how to do that."

Jeremiah thanked the two men again and made his rounds among the small group of volunteers until at last he came to Casper Norris, just as the man lit a cigarette. "I really appreciate you comin' out to help, Casper. I know with all that's goin' on with the Edwards boys, you and Webb likely got your hands full."

Casper glanced over at Sheriff Webb, who had moved on to another corner post. "It gave us an excuse to give the place a look-around. See if we could find any clue to who set the fire."

"And did you find anything?"

Casper tapped his cigarette, the ashes falling on some stone at his feet. "You know how it is with these clans round here. They come in, do their damage, and leave without a trace." His brown gaze came up to Jeremiah's, brow raised. "Any ideas why someone would do somethin' like this to you?"

Jeremiah rocked back on his heels, calculating his response. "I reckon my daddy could have had enemies from his time as a deputy."

"Seems a bit long for a group to hold a grudge, only to attack now."

Jeremiah met Casper's gaze head-on. "Well, I can tell you the truth, Casp. I ain't done one thing that should've brung about the burnin' of this house or the shootin' of my dog. Not one."

"Never know how the slightest toss can cause the biggest splash." Casper took another draw from his cigarette, his gaze raking over the other men, before returning to Jeremiah. "And mountain folk sure know how to nurse a grievance."

Something in Casper's countenance, his voice, put Jeremiah on edge. Did Casper know something? Was he trying to warn Jeremiah of upcoming trouble?

"Take Joe Creed's case as example." He waved his cigarette toward the charred remains of the old house. "If we're lookin' just at facts, I'd say you helpin' his mama and sister to the train depot didn't sit too well with some folks."

"And that's what you think brought this attack on?"

"What else could it be?" Casper shrugged a shoulder and took another draw. "I showed up at the Creed house the very day you left to check on the ladies, and all was just fine. Then you take the Creeds off to the train depot and come back to this?" He flicked another bit of ash onto the stones. "Here's my advice, Jeremiah. Finish up your cousin's house. Settle down with whatever girl you want, and keep usin' your skills to build houses and furniture and whatever else you want." He tipped his hat with a grin. "But leave the law to the lawmen and try to convince that gal of yours to do the same."

Chapter Fourteen

Home comes in all shapes and sizes. Round here,
it's mountain-sized with a whole lot of family tossed in for extra flavor.
Granny Burcham

Three weeks had never felt so long.
Ava blamed the kissing.

What else could it be? She'd gone three weeks without seeing Jeremiah before. Not often, but some. And, though she missed his conversations and camaraderie, she'd never ached for him like this. A deep, low longing.

Maybe kisses from the one you loved branded you in a way nothing else could. She felt. . .well. . .she felt connected to him. Her smile spread as she walked up the steps to Sid Allen's store. Belonging. Heaven and earth, when he'd wrapped her in his arms and held her against him, his lips making sure hers never got bored, she'd understood the sweetness of belonging with someone.

And besides Granny, Ava hadn't belonged with anyone else in a long time. And never like this.

Thankfully, as Jeremiah had hoped, as time passed from the Creeds' exit and the attack on Jeremiah's house, so did the tension wrapped around the entire affair. The only "talk" over the past week had been the news that Floyd Allen had been indicted on charges for rescuing prisoners in custody, assault, and maiming, filed by Pink Samuels.

Maiming?

Ava hadn't seen the entire exchange between Samuels and Floyd, but the gunfire had happened so quickly and Pink had lit out of there without one bit of trouble, she wasn't quite sure where the maiming idea came from. Floyd had been the one to have his finger shot. Nobody else fired anything.

The idea of bringing the Allens together with the Courthouse Clan under one roof, after all the current tension, well, it didn't bode well. With that thought in mind and an empty crate in hand to fill with Granny's monthly supplies, Ava crossed the threshold into the store, the familiar scent of tobacco mingled in with something new. Her smile broadened. Aha, Mr. Allen had gotten in some peppermint sticks. Granny would love a few of those.

She'd come at a time of day when the store hummed with a quiet emptiness. Early afternoon, but it was Friday. The day when Sid *usually* brought out new stock, particularly in the used clothes section. She'd sewn a few shirts and pants for Jeremiah to replace what he'd lost in the fire, but he still needed another pair of shoes. Wasn't no telling what the one pair of shoes he had looked like after the work he'd been putting in over the past three weeks.

As she knelt down beside the clothes rack, where the shoes stood on display, the back door of the shop burst open. Ava's spot behind the clothes nearly blocked her view of the men entering, but she recognized Floyd Allen's tall frame followed close by his brother, Sid.

"It ain't helpin' my cause none at all, to have that day printed in the paper." Floyd's deep voice carried through the empty room followed by the slap of paper on a counter. "The courthouse boys will use anything they can against me for this trial."

"Now, Floyd, the article paints a pretty fair picture of it all, as far as I can see. Pink looks like the coward he is, and Easter can't fire a pistol to save his life."

Article? Ava's whole body went cold, and she scooted a little farther behind the clothes rack. Surely, they weren't talking about—

"Who is this Cameron Birch, anyhow?" This from Floyd. "I don't know no Birches in these parts, but I'd like to give him a piece of my mind. He's just fuelin' the flames agin' us."

"I reckon it's a false name. The details are too good to be someone who didn't see the whole incident happen, or at least someone told the author about it with pretty detailed accuracy."

"Well, if I ever find out who this Birch fella is, I'm bound to teach him a lesson about mindin' his own business. This?" Another slap of paper sounded. "This ain't helpin' our cause, Sid. And we need all the help we can get. I got a bad feelin' about this trial. Bad feelin'."

Ava pulled the crate closer to her chest and squeezed her eyes closed. Maybe it had been a good thing the newspaper refused to publish her under her real name. She'd thought it had been such an accomplishment that they'd still taken her story, even when they'd found out she was a woman, but something in the way Floyd's words tinged with hurt gripped at Ava's confidence. Had she hurt him? Their family? She'd only reported the truth.

Half of her wanted to stay and listen to the conversation, ready to take notes for another article, but the other half fought against the idea of bringing more possible danger into her life.

"Oh Floyd, you ain't mad about the article." Sid's voice soothed out in low tones. "You've been fired up since Quesenberry left half an hour ago. What did he say that riled you?"

The room grew quiet for so long, Ava peeked from around her hiding spot. Floyd and Sid stood by the counter, a few stacked barrels blocking her full view of them. Maybe they'd started whispering.

"He came to deliver a message." Floyd's voice finally broke the silence. "Said Dexter Goad would arrange with the jury for my acquittal if I'd pledge my support for him."

Ava caught her gasp with her palm. Firstly, what audacity and completely wrong! Secondly, did the county clerk have *that* kind of power?

"You can't be serious," Sid replied.

"I told him no," came Floyd's firm reply. "I know some of them men who've been asked to join the jury, and Goad or not, I feel they'll treat me fair. If we can just get witnesses there to tell what they saw. Most of 'em know I wasn't trying to free the boys, just get them unbound. Pink could have taken them on up to Hillsville for all I cared, as long as he didn't humiliate 'em so."

"Well, while you're on bond, maybe you can rally up some of them witnesses to make sure they show up in court," Sid said. "And I'll do the same. Seems like we need to find this Cameron Birch for a testimony."

Ava jerked at the sound of Cameron Birch's name and her elbow hit the hat tree beside her. She tensed all over as two hats fell to the ground followed by a large brimmed floral confection that teetered like a poised bird on the top of the hat stand before it all crashed to the floor.

"What in the world?" Sid yelled.

Ava released a sigh and stood, crate still cradled in her arms. "I'm sorry. I didn't mean to eavesdrop." She cringed at her own admittance. "I was just over here looking for a pair of shoes to buy for Jeremiah and then you two came in and I didn't feel right about interruptin' and then—"

"I declare, Ava Burcham, you're the most trouble-findin' gal I've ever seen." Floyd shook his head and growled. "What on earth are you doin' sneakin' around and listenin' to folks' private conversations?"

Ava stumbled back a step. "No, I wasn't sneakin'. I was collecting items for Granny, and I saw the shoes and—"

"Girl, you should know better than to let Floyd get your back up." Sid laughed, his steely blue eyes sparkling. "He was pullin' your leg. Of course you weren't hiding back there like some spy to cause trouble."

"That's for the likes of this Cameron Birch character," Floyd murmured, slamming a hand down on the paper, his darker gaze holding Ava's. "Though, we'd appreciate you keepin' what you heard to yourself. Some things cause more trouble than help if spread about. Goad already has it out for us Allens."

"Of. . .of course."

"And if it's somethin' for Jeremiah, then it's on me." Sid pulled a pencil from behind his ear and made a mark on a paper he had on the counter. "That boy's done good work for me since I hired him. It's a shame he got caught in the middle of such a mess, when all he wanted to do was help out the Creed women."

"Thank you, Mr. Allen." She hated how her voice quivered ever so slightly, but with all the Cameron Birch talk, and the news about a fixed jury, well, the whole story kept getting a little crazier by the day.

"Victor said they're 'bout done with the place." Floyd relaxed his hip against the counter and tugged a comb from his shirt pocket. With careful calculation, he ran the comb through his moustache, a trademark move of his. "Talked like they might be done by week's end."

Ava blinked out of her stare at the way he carefully groomed his rather impressive moustache. "That's great news. Just in time for Jeremiah's cousin to move in with his new bride."

"Well now, where does that leave Jeremiah, I wonder?" Sid's grin crooked as if he already knew the answer to his own question.

"He's been living out of a barn for over a month. I reckon he can live out of it a little longer." Floyd clicked his tongue and replaced his comb into his pocket. "If he ain't got no family to tend, he can stay 'bout anywhere, I'd say."

"I heard tell he might just be changing the family status, Floyd."

"Zat so?" Floyd's brow crooked to match his brother's, and they both turned their attention directly to her.

Ava's face warmed by slow degrees. She'd only told her news to Granny last week; otherwise, she'd not even mentioned it to Mrs. Temple. Talking too much about it, without having seen Jeremiah since they'd made the agreement, seemed a little overzealous. Of course, overzealous would certainly have described their last meeting. Lips on lips.

Have mercy! She stuffed a plaid shirt she'd been examining into her crate and marched forward. "I think I'll take these things, Mr. Allen." Ignoring the fire in her cheeks and any further eye contact with the Allen men, she placed a slip of paper on the counter. "And the items on this list for Granny."

Sid took the paper, his brow raised with the corner of his smile.

Once she escaped the store and the cool afternoon air touched her face, Ava breathed out a long sigh. It was hard enough to go without seeing Jeremiah for so long, but adding the teasing on top of the fact that she hadn't told anyone they were actually engaged. . . ? Well, it made things a sight bit harder.

The mid-February day breezed in with some warmer temperatures and a glorious afternoon of winter sunshine. A powdering of white dusted the mountains on the horizon, providing a stark contrast against the bright cerulean sky. Her brother's eyes had been the same shade of blue. Like her daddy's. Striking. Memorable.

Ava slowed her pace, embracing the shifting memories through her mind. Granny had once told her that taking time to recall those memories was a healthy thing to do because God gave them to us as a comfort. A little opportunity to visit with those unseen but still within our hearts.

The beauty before her beckoned her heart heavenward, as if God painted the afternoon picture just to get her attention. He'd felt so far off for so long, but that may have been somewhat due to Ava having a hard time talking to Him, but if what the Good Book said was true, He'd never left her. Even when she'd thought she'd been abandoned, He'd never forsaken her. He'd sent love to her in different ways— through Granny's strength, Jeremiah's friendship, Mrs. Temple's care, and even now, in the wonders of creation. They'd become God's fingerprints in her life.

There was no place in all the world where He didn't go to touch her life, her soul.

Her heart reached out for Him, His presence. Grasping what she'd always known with more certainty. Nothing could separate her from the Father's love. Not heights or depths. Not angels or demons. Not death...or bad blood.

She belonged to Him. And He'd allowed her to *live*.

So what did He want her to do with the life He'd given her to live?

Write articles for the paper? Save the world from blockade liquor runners? Finish the book stirring in her heart? Marry Jeremiah?

Her grin tipped. Well, God surely had a sense of humor, if He'd set up sweet Jeremiah to be bound to the likes of her till death parted them. But Jeremiah seemed convinced, and if God thought to give him the notion, Ava wasn't bound to complain at all. Blessings should never come paired with complaints.

Temples' Alterations came into view among the ragged sets of trees along the roadside, and Ava felt the growing awareness of being watched. She scanned the empty road behind her then took a few more steps toward Temples'. Mr. Temple's wagon waited in its usual spot near the front of the shop. The outhouse tilted a little crooked in the back. Nothing out of the ordinary. No one within view.

With another glance behind her and a tighter grip on her crate, she stepped toward the tree-lined side entrance of the shop. She'd not made it three steps past the tree when she was grabbed from behind and spun around to meet Jeremiah face-to-face.

"What in the world are you doing, Jeremiah Sutphin?"

He tugged the crate from her arms, propped it on his hip, and, with a slight grin, slipped his free hand around her waist and pulled her toward him. "I'm kissin' my fiancée."

And he proceeded to do just that.

Once the initial shock wore off, Ava reciprocated with enough enthusiasm to have both of them breathing as if they'd run up to the top of Round Knob and back.

"You'd better stop doing that so. . .so. . .vigorously." Ava breathed out the words, remaining close to him. In fact, she'd somehow gotten her fingers fisted in his jacket to keep him within kissing distance.

"The vigor wasn't one-sided, Ava Burcham."

After the hard work and pain of the past few weeks, seeing the gleam return to his eyes nearly brought tears to hers. "What are you doin' sneakin' up on me anyhow? Aren't we supposed to be staying apart for safety's sake?"

"There ain't been no hint of trouble for weeks." His gaze moved over her face and he pushed back her hair, his thumb grazing her cheek. "I think it's safe now."

The way his touch ignited all sorts of kissing thoughts in her head seemed to say otherwise. Jeremiah must have caught the look on her face, because his grin took a rascally tilt. "You said you'd marry me."

She tugged at his jacket, smile pressing for release. "And I stand behind that decision."

"I'm awful glad to hear it." He snuck another kiss right on her grin. "How's Wolf?"

Jeremiah's expression softened with a tinge of sadness. "Improving. He's still sleeping a lot, but he actually ran the length of the yard yesterday without touching his bad leg to the ground."

"A break takes awhile to heal, but at least he's healing." She slid her hand over to his and braided their fingers together. What an oddly freeing motion. So intimate and new, yet as natural as having a conversation with him.

"I've been missin' you somethin' fierce, and this marryin' business has been takin' up a lot of space in my head."

"Mine too." And the fact she'd started sewing a wedding dress for herself proved it.

"Then what about after church on March 17th? My cousin will be all married and moved into his new place. Spring will be startin' in the mountains. We can—"

"Three weeks?"

He squeezed her hand. "Three weeks."

"But where would we live in just three weeks' time? You don't have no extra minutes to find a place for us and finish one for your cousin too?"

"If you don't mind helping me complete a little project I've been workin' on. . ." He tilted his head, a glimmer in his eyes. "Then I can provide us a place to live."

"How on earth have you been able to figure out a place to live while you've been workin' on your cousin's house?"

His gaze darkened and he lowered his forehead to hers, his lips drawing temptingly close. "Oh Ava, don't underestimate the miracles a man can work when he loves a woman."

❧

Jeremiah guided Sally down Main Street, Hillsville, toward the jeweler's. He'd kept careful inventory of his parents' heirlooms for years, and with a trip to the cellar of his new place, he'd dug through the crates of their belongings to find a simple necklace of his mother's. It had been her pride and joy. The most precious gift his father had given her.

Simple in its presentation, the single pearl held two diamonds on either side. Mama had told him she'd seen it in a storefront shop one time and that very next Christmas, Daddy delivered it to her along with a half-dozen hothouse roses. She'd worn it every day. "As constant as your daddy's love for me," she'd said.

Jeremiah couldn't think of a sweeter promise to give his bride. If he could offer her something as constant as his parents had, something she didn't have the history to experience, then perhaps he could diminish those fears she carried around. Love did that. Or so he'd always thought. And the Bible confirmed the notion. *Perfect love casts out fear.*

Jeremiah didn't place any claim on loving perfectly, but with God's help, he could try to love Ava well. He took his time hitching his horse and making sure the necklace rested securely in the inner pocket of his jacket before starting down the street toward the jeweler's. A loud pop exploded from up ahead. Near the courthouse. Jeremiah looked back at his horse, whose ears perked high. She stomped her foot with a restless tug against the knotted reins.

"It's all right, old girl." At least Jeremiah hoped so.

The popping sounded again. Was that gunfire? Jeremiah increased his pace up the street away from the jeweler's toward the courthouse, only to meet Dr. Nuckolls and Sheriff Webb coming from that very direction.

"Jeremiah." Webb offered his hand, his newly minted silver badge glimmering against his suit coat. "What brings you into town?"

Jeremiah hesitated on a confession, the news unvoiced yet. But why not? They'd chosen a date. He'd talked to the preacher. Everything was set. "Well, as a matter of fact." He cleared his throat and worked out the words for the first time. "I'm on my way to the jewelry store to fix up a ring for my bride-to-be."

"You don't say." Webb laughed and clapped his hand on Jeremiah's shoulder. "It's 'bout time, boy. Who's the lucky lady?"

Jeremiah couldn't tame his grin from broadening, but before he could answer, Sheriff Webb's laugh broke through.

"I think I know this one. It wouldn't happen to be a troublemaking seamstress, now would it?"

"Ava Burcham?" Dr. Nuckolls's chuckle joined in. "Well, it's about time, for sure. You two've been thick as thieves for ages."

"You remember them sneakin' up to the top of the Elliott Hotel to do some science experiment 'bout gravity the new teacher had told 'em to do?"

Webb's reminder of his and Ava's ninth-grade challenge to wrap an egg and then drop it from various heights without breaking it brought a grin.

"Is that the time you broke your wrist?" Doc Nuckolls shook his thick head of hair.

Of course, the doc would remember! But how could Jeremiah have known that the hotel owner would have such a fit over finding splattered egg against the side of his building? If Jeremiah had been looking where he was going as he ran away from the proprietor, he'd likely never have broken his wrist. Jeremiah allowed the men's laughter to dissipate before answering. "I imagine we'll have plenty of adventure in our future together too, though I'm hopin' for fewer broken bones and splattered eggs."

"Better you than me, boy." The sheriff squeezed his shoulder again just as the popping sounds commenced. "She's a spitfire, and make no mistake."

"I'm glad for some good news after all the bad that's happened to you lately, Jeremiah," Doc added. "Plus all that's happened with Joe, and then the entire Allen mess."

The gunfire crackled again, but neither man seemed to notice.

"Speakin' of Joe Creed. . ." Webb sobered, casting a glance around them. "I've been studyin' some on your thoughts, Jeremiah, and discussed a bit with Doc here. There are some questions he posed and some reminiscences I've made over the situation that have me, well. . ." His voice trailed off and a look passed between the two men. "Would you mind stopping by the jail after your marryin' business and giving me a full accounting of your dealings with the Creeds?"

"Of course." The gunfire continued, pulling Jeremiah's attention back up the hill. "What's goin' on at the courthouse?"

"Goad and Foster are showin' off their new guns. Target practice, it seems," Doc answered with a grimace. "Rumor has it, they're worked up about Floyd's trial. Expectin' trouble."

"But the Allens wouldn't cause trouble in the courtroom, surely."

"I don't know." Webb rubbed the back of his neck and sighed. "They've gotten out of most of their court cases by sheer luck, knowin' the right folks, or, from what some folks say, intimidatin' the witnesses."

"Now, Lew, there ain't no proof of the intimidation, though Floyd's temper brings a bit of bite with it, to be sure." Doc raised a brow in mild reprimand to his friend and turned back to Jeremiah. "But the fact that Floyd Allen has had about as many trials as anybody else in this court and not spent one day in jail? Either lots of folks are out to get him, or he knows how to work the system."

"And with all the work the law's done lately to try and end lawlessness, well, Judge Massie, the one over Floyd's trial, wants to do things the right way. Set a precedent that the law needs to be respected."

"But target practice?" Jeremiah waved toward the direction of the courthouse. "Seems to me like they're hopin' for a storm."

Lew breathed out a sigh and met Jeremiah's gaze. "You've lived long enough round here, boy, to know it's important to be prepared for storms of every variety."

Chapter Fifteen

A quick temper and trigger finger makes for some bad company.
Granddaddy Sutphin

J eremiah?"

He froze on his walk down Main Street and gave a slow turn toward Ava. He looked mighty fine in the new jacket she'd made for him to wear for their wedding. A style as up-to-date as any of the well-to-do in the area. Sunday was only a few days away and then. . . well, then he'd be wearing that jacket for her benefit as her groom.

She grinned and increased her pace toward him. The cloudy and cold day brushed a dampness against her cheeks as she approached, but, thankfully, the rain had stopped for the two-hour ride into town.

Had Jeremiah been called as a witness to Floyd Allen's trial too? Well, if he walked in all spruced up like that, he'd likely impress even the county commissioner, who was known for his style.

Jeremiah's expression didn't reflect his usual greeting. In fact, he frowned and shifted his attention away from hers. Ava walked past the courthouse steps to meet him at the corner, near a large locust tree that shaded the grassy knoll where the courthouse stood elevated above the rest of the surrounding buildings. Come to think of it, if he'd been on his way to the courthouse, why was he walking away from it? And dressed in such style as he was, he'd not come to purchase work supplies.

"I didn't know you'd be in town today." She drew closer, his expression growing a little more tense as she approached. "Are you testifying too?"

His attention flipped to her face. "You're testifying?"

"It came as a surprise to me too. Got served papers just yesterday."

He cleared his throat and looked back behind him toward the shops. Why was he all fidgety? Like he was hiding something? "So, are you testifying?"

"No. I've not been asked yet."

Her eyes narrowed as he looked away again. "What're you hidin', Jeremiah Sutphin?"

His gaze swung back to hers, wide and caught. "Hidin'? What would make you think somethin' like that? I have a few errands to run in town, is all."

"Dressed like you're goin' to a wedding?" She gestured toward his getup. "And actin' as skittish as a turkey in November."

"Well." He cleared his throat. "Then I planned to peek in on the trial. Nothin' wrong with cleanin' up for court."

A bell rang from the courthouse, an alert court was back in session after the dinner break.

"You'd better hurry along, Miss Burcham." The sparkle came back to his eyes along with his rascally smile. "You've been summoned."

"Don't think this gets you off the hook. I know you're up to something."

He tipped his hat and took a few more steps away from her, taggin' on a wink. "It's all right to not know everything, Ava. Just remember that."

She rolled her eyes at the ridiculous man and made her way up the steps of the courthouse, casting a glance down the street once more, without catching another glimpse of him. Oh where had he gone? The shoe shop? A restaurant? She shook off the curiosity and finished the climb up the steps to the second floor of the building where the courtroom stood.

She'd never been inside a courtroom before, and the area looked smaller than she'd imagined. Two large windows on either side of the room, and directly in the middle, raised on a stage, stood the judge's area. His seat had its own fencing of matching oak surrounding it. A similar fence-like area in the center of the room caged in some folks Ava recognized. Floyd Allen and his lawyers. And Mr. Foster, the Commonwealth attorney. Dexter Goad sat to the right, gussied up in the finest suit Ava had ever seen. Sheriff Webb sat just in front of Mr. Goad, with several of the deputies poised or seated behind him.

A small group of men entered from a door on the far right of the room and took their seats in chairs running in front of the judge's seat, facing the galley. From a discussion with Granny about how a court hearing worked, Ava guessed they were the jury. They looked a little tired from already spending several hours listening to testimonies. At least, this late in the afternoon, Ava imagined the end wasn't too far off.

Ava took a seat on one of the long benches, attempting to get as near to one of the potbelly stoves as she could. The dampness in the air paired with the long ride left a deep chill over her skin, so she pulled her cape more tightly around herself just as another door on the back wall opened.

Judge Massie entered, his black gown flowing around him. His keen gaze took inventory of the room. He had a kind face, soft gray eyes, and an open expression. Granny always said there was a lot to appreciate in a first impression, especially under strain and stress.

After going through all the preliminaries, witnesses were called forward to testify.

Walter Hill. Posey Banks. The other deputy, Easter, who'd been traveling with Pink Samuels up the mountain with the Edwards boys. He stated that they released the Edwards boys to Floyd because the two deputies had been outnumbered by all the Allen clan. His words proved, to Ava's mind, that Floyd hadn't forcibly taken the boys from the deputies.

Of course, the Allens had outnumbered the deputies, since the lawmen had chosen to take the Edwards boys on the road that passed more than one Allen residence. She wondered now if shoving the boys' capture in the Allens' faces was worth it to Pink.

A couple of the Allens testified before Ava was called, but most everyone's responses had a similar theme—a truth even Floyd admitted to without reserve. Assault, for his hitting Pink Samuels. The judge held Pink in contempt for not showing up for the trial as a key witness, but each new testimony, prosecution or defense, seemed to point to the same conclusion: Floyd had assaulted Pink Samuels and, despite his intentions, he'd interfered with prisoners in custody, causing an obstruction of justice.

It was just the facts.

And Ava became one of the voices to confirm Floyd's interference.

Thankfully, she didn't see how and where Floyd had hit Deputy Pink Samuels, so she didn't have to attest to the assault part of the case, but blocking the road and taking Samuels's gun was certainly encumbering the lawman's work. Though Ava made sure to relate that one of the deputies had fired at Floyd, who didn't have his gun drawn, and that both lawmen ran off, leaving the prisoners sitting in the buggy without any guards.

Ava had gone on to add, "Of course, Floyd Allen cuts an intimidating figure when he's hot, so I don't blame a soul for runnin' off. Especially if he's fierce enough to walk right up to Samuels and take his gun away from him."

"Fierce, or crazy," someone shouted from the galley, which caused a few of the folks in court to chuckle. The hardened expression on Floyd's face eased a little as he watched her. Maybe he knew she didn't want to cause harm to anyone, but someone had to tell the truth. There were some folks who gave accounts of the situation that seemed as unbelievable as a fairy story. One even said the Allens unhitched Pink's wagon and pushed it off a cliff.

Mountain men may be hardheaded and sometimes hot-tempered, but they were mighty efficient. None of them would have wasted time to find a cliff to dispose of the wagon, let alone destroyed a perfectly good vehicle.

"Order! Order in the court." Judge Massie's gavel beat a reverberating click through the room, and then he turned to Ava. "Did Mr. Allen's behavior frighten you, Miss Burcham?"

"Not his behavior, sir. But I get nervous when there's loose gunfire, as any smart person should, I think."

His smile softened beneath his white moustache. "Smart, indeed."

She went back to her seat, and after a few more testimonies, the lawyers presented their closing arguments. Though Floyd's lawyer waxed eloquently about Floyd's intentions to free his nephews from their bonds but not police custody, the evidence appeared too solid to deny a guilty verdict of some sort. Commonwealth attorney Foster gave an equally articulate closing argument, taking a few jabs at the court's need to rid Carroll County of the mob violence endemic throughout its rural areas and encouraging the jury to bravely make the right and honorable verdict.

Yet, when the jury returned after a brief respite, they'd not come to a conclusion, so Judge Massie adjourned court for the day and asked all to reconvene in the morning at eight o'clock.

"You think anyone's gonna take stock of your testimony, Ava Burcham?"

Ava looked to her right where Keen Gentry stood, lurking in his usual way. "As much as anyone else's, I suppose." She held his gaze, refusing to cower to his height or vulgar expression.

"They're all just bidin' time till you start actin' like who you really are. What's in your blood." His sneer twisted beneath his dark moustache, and Ava pinched her gloved hands together to keep from adjusting her expression.

"Why do you feel like you need to speak to me at all, Keen, especially when you ain't got nothin' of use to say?"

He leered closer. Ava readied her fist.

"No woman humiliates me. I won't abide it."

"So you're gonna try to intimidate me with your lies."

"Naw, just makin' sure you recognize what everybody else already knows." His stare never left hers as he tipped his hat. "You can't get away from your past, not when it's part of your blood."

Air had closed off in her throat for a response, so she merely glared at the vicious man and turned away, her gaze meeting Jeremiah's across the crowded courtroom. Would her past always wait in the shadows of her present? Was God truly big enough to wipe away the bloodstains haunting her future? As Jeremiah marched toward her, his smile dissolving as he approached, she couldn't fight the niggling doubt of the what-ifs plaguing hope into extinction.

Could she trust God completely?

⌇

She'd almost caught him red-handed.

Jeremiah fiddled with the ring in his pocket as the court session came to a close, his grin spreading at the idea of sliding it on Ava's finger as a surprise for their wedding day. Thankfully, he only had a few short days to wait, because, knowing Ava, she'd question him into a confession about his odd behavior, and he wasn't sure how long he could hold out before spilling the truth.

He hadn't been inside a courtroom since the trial over his daddy's death. A useless case for any real answers, since no one could prove who'd fired the shots that took his father's life. He'd been hit by four bullets. Between two feuding families. And no one planned to share any information to frame their own.

As the court adjourned, Jeremiah found Ava in the crowd. Keen Gentry leaned close to her, and whatever he said slipped the smile right off Ava's face. Jeremiah's fingers fisted around the ring in his pocket and he started forward. Keen must have noticed his approach, because he slipped away from Ava and pressed through the crowd toward Jeremiah.

Keen held on to Jeremiah's gaze, his glare accompanied with a snarl curling beneath his moustache. Jeremiah didn't so much as flinch. Keen had meanness on his side, but Jeremiah had two inches, a quick mind, and a pretty good track record with a pistol. With an intentional bump of his shoulder against Jeremiah's, Keen kept going, exiting the room.

Ava met him in the middle of the galley aisle, her face pale.

"What is it?"

"Nothing important." She attempted to walk past him, but he caught her arm in a gentle hold.

"Ava?"

"Let's go for a walk." Her upturned face, her expression, pleaded. "What do you say?"

With a nod, he linked her arm through his and started toward the door, just as Floyd's lawyer met them.

"Jeremiah, you got a minute?"

Jeremiah sent a look to Ava, who offered a slight nod.

"What can I do for you, sir?"

Bolen, a massive man, bent his head and rested the folder in his arms against his hip. "From the looks of things, Floyd ain't gonna find a favorable verdict tomorrow. I'm looking for some more witnesses to offer to Judge Massie so we can show Floyd didn't have any intention of freeing his nephews. Would you be willing to testify as a character witness, seein' that you've known the Allens so long and your daddy was friends with them?"

"Yes, sir, if you think I can help."

Bolen released a sigh. "Any honest testimony to the truth of what happened should be a help to us."

With that, the man exited the courtroom, and Jeremiah followed with Ava's arm linked through his. Like they belonged. He grinned. And rightly so. They made it down the steps before he spoke. "Are you plannin' to stay in town tonight?"

She nodded, keeping her attention forward. "I booked a room at the hotel 'cause I figured I wouldn't be leavin' town until too late to get back to the Temples'."

"Which hotel?"

"The Thornton."

"Same as me." He turned their steps in the direction of the white-painted, three-story hotel standing right beside the courthouse. "Maybe we can talk in the sitting room and out of the cold?"

Her smile quivered to life, and he moved them to the hotel, finding a small table for two situated near one of the large fireplaces in the grand place. Jeremiah would have stayed at the Elliott House, which would have been cheaper, but it had no vacancies. Likely due to all the curiosity about Floyd Allen's trial.

Once they'd gotten settled and after a little prodding, Ava shared about the conversation with Keen. The old accusations. His dislike for her. Keen had a tendency to hold a grudge, but why did he single out Ava? Just because of the slap she'd given him at the Combs' place? Something seemed off about it all. Keen was at least ten years older than Ava, probably more, and he'd moved into Carroll County years ago from some other place. Jeremiah's pa had told Jeremiah he thought Keen was outrunning the law when he came across the state line. That seemed to happen a lot in these parts.

"You know he's just trying to get inside your head and make you afraid, don't you?"

She nodded, her gaze coming up to his. "But I can't help feeling—wondering if he's right, Jeremiah. What if I become like her?" Her eyes shone with waiting tears. "What if you're stuck with me and I start goin' crazy?"

He took her hand for every guest in the hotel to see, hoping his certainty might rub off on her thinking a little. "Here's what I know. God made you. Body, mind, and soul. You claim to know Him, ain't that right?"

She nodded.

"Well, that don't take away sickness or fear, but the more we remember whose we are, the more equipped we are to handle whatever comes." He squeezed her fingers. "*Whatever* comes."

"But I don't want you to have to live like that."

"Ava, stop." He held her gaze. "You are strong. Sound. Bullheaded sometimes, but I can live with that."

She attempted to pull her hand away, her lips twitching ever so slightly.

"Remember where you've come from."

"That's what I'm worried about."

"No, not your mama. People stronger than her."

Her brows crinkled into confusion. "What do you mean?"

"Besides your Granny Burcham bein' one of the soundest minds in the world, *and* the fact God made you to be who you are. The woman I plan to marry." He punctuated his words with another squeeze to her hand. "But also think about this. Your daddy hid you so you could live. Your brother jumped in front of you and took that bullet so you could *live*. Don't waste the lives they gave up for you by second-guessing every minute of your own. They wanted you to live, Ava. So *live* with joy and freedom and. . ." He brushed a thumb across her cheek. "Love."

She sniffled and offered him a semblance of a smile. "I want to live like that."

"Then be brave enough." He squeezed her fingers. "Let's be brave enough together."

❧

Jeremiah waited by the front door of the hotel and checked his pocket watch. Seven thirty. Already, he'd noticed people filing up the steps, passing the white columns to the second floor of the courthouse, likely getting their seats as early as possible.

Out of his periphery, he caught sight of Judge Massie walking toward the doors, Webb at his side, hints of the conversation making it to Jeremiah.

"We don't need to disarm everybody, Lew. Floyd Allen promised me he'd take whatever verdict the jury came to, and I plan to hold him to his word." The judge stopped to adjust his tie in a mirror by the door. "Besides, trying to disarm everyone is likely to cause more trouble than help, from the crowd we're expecting today."

"There's been things going on lately, Thornton. Allens, Creeds, Daniels..." Webb placed his hands on his hips, the movement revealing a holster with a .32-caliber Colt secured to Webb's side. "Somethin' feels off today."

"We got to trust the law to do its work, Lew." Judge Massie patted Webb on the shoulder and continued out the door of the hotel toward the courthouse. Webb started to follow and then caught sight of Jeremiah.

"I saw you in the courtroom yesterday and was hopin' to get a chance to talk with you."

"Yes, sir?"

"I don't have time to talk about it right now." Webb sent a look around them, taking in the room, and then leaned closer to Jeremiah, his voice quieter. "I've uncovered a few things about the Creed case. It seems to be linked to Solomon Dunn's death. And maybe a few other older cases. I can't be sure. But your concerns were right."

Solomon Dunn? The man killed around the same time as Joe Creed? "Do you have any idea who's involved?"

The sheriff gave the room another look. "I have a few ideas, but it's not safe to talk about it here."

A chill tiptoed up Jeremiah's spine that had nothing to do with the cool air from the doorway. "Want me to meet you at the jailhouse after court?"

"Naw." Webb shook his head. "The jail ain't safe either. Not for this."

The jail wasn't safe? Did they have some prisoners housed there associated with Joe Creed's death or dealings?

Suddenly, the sheriff stood a bit taller and tugged at the lapel of his brown suit jacket. "I'm in need of some new shoes."

"New shoes?" What was he talking about?

Webb's stare never left Jeremiah's, boring deep. "That's right. I plan to go over to Murphy's right after court and find me a new pair. I'll likely be there awhile, lookin'."

The intention in his expression took root. "I was planning on lookin' for some myself," Jeremiah replied. "Maybe we can catch up a little more then."

Sheriff Webb grinned and offered a curt nod. "Till then."

Ava arrived only a few minutes later, her hair tied up in a simple bun, her smile more brilliant than the evening before. "You seem better this morning."

She linked her arm through the one he offered. "I spent the evenin' counting my blessings and remindin' myself of a wise man's words."

He squinted down at her, trying to stave off the foreboding the conversation with Webb left behind. "You're a very smart woman."

"I don't reckon we need to be in a hurry. From what I remember from my daddy's case, the jury will still need time to deliberate this mornin'. Have you had breakfast?"

They enjoyed biscuits and gravy with a side of eggs, keeping the discussion away from the Creeds. Jeremiah didn't want to contemplate what Webb had discovered until he absolutely had to.

When they finally arrived in the courtroom, they barely found a place to stand for the sheer number of people crammed into the galley area. At least two hundred and fifty. Maybe more. The scent of tobacco, sweat, and wool permeated the space as they wedged through the crowd to find a standing spot against the back wall, passing Sid Allen, who was in discussion with someone. He nodded as Jeremiah passed.

Their spot in the back afforded a fairly decent view of the space. Floyd Allen was in deep conversation with his two lawyers, looking professional in a black suit jacket covering his gray sweater. Judge Massie sat in his large leather chair, head bent over the desk as he went through some papers.

"He give them jurors a good talkin' to before they was sent back to deliberate." Elmer Williams shoved the man beside Jeremiah aside and took his place. "Told them to stay true to the law of Virginia, regardless of their feelin's about Floyd Allen, good or bad."

Jeremiah offered his hand to the older man. "From the sound of yesterday's testimonies, I don't see how they can do much else but find him guilty."

Elmer nodded toward Ava and rubbed his chin. "I reckon so, but old Floyd ain't gonna like it none." He shook his head. "He's always left this courtroom a free man."

"I suppose if he told his nephews to take their sentences like men, he'll have to do the same." Ava pressed close to Jeremiah's side. He grinned. He liked having her close. The very idea of seeing her every day—and night—of the week nearly had him moving the wedding date up to tomorrow. But he only needed to wait three more days. Only three.

"How'd your cousin's weddin' go?" This from Wesley Edwards, who peered around Elmer, his easy smile in full swing. "Mama said it was the talk of Sunday dinner."

"Ellis sure did put in the money for it," Jeremiah responded. "I ain't never seen such a sight. It's a shame you missed it." He nodded toward the boy. "You must have just got out of jail?"

"Yep, sure did. Just in time for *your* weddin', from what I hear?"

He wiggled his brows at Ava, and she closed her eyes in mock exasperation. "Nobody can keep secrets around here."

"Now why would you want to keep a weddin' a secret?" Wesley laughed. "Unless you're embarrassed to marry Jeremiah Sutphin."

"I ain't embarrassed one bit." Ava's marble eyes took on a glint of fire. "I just don't want a crowd oohin' and aahin' over everything. That's all. Some folks don't have to have an audience, Wesley Edwards."

Wesley tipped his head back in a hearty laugh.

"How'd the house turn out?" This from Elmer. "I reckon you got it all finished up for your cousin?"

"Sure did. And it's ten times better than the house before, so there's some silver linin' in the middle of all the trouble."

"There you go, boy." Elmer tipped his head toward Jeremiah. "You're so much like your daddy with them silver linings."

The compliment pressed through Jeremiah with the warmth of a bittersweet embrace, and his fingers reached for the ring housed safely within his pocket. Those silver-lining thoughts had done him a heap of good recently.

A knock sounded through the muffling of voices, drawing Jeremiah's attention to the front of the room. Sheriff Lew Webb opened a door to the right, behind the judge, and in walked the jurymen, taking their seats along the front of the room, just below Judge Massie.

The cry of a baby pierced the sudden quiet, followed quickly by a woman's shushing response. A strange hush fell over the room. Judge Massie looked over the crowd and then focused on a man at the farthest end of the jury's row.

"Has the jury reached a verdict?"

The jury foreman stood, paper in hand. "We have, Judge."

Lew walked over and took the paper from the foreman then handed it to Dexter Goad, the county clerk. A group of deputies sat just behind Dexter Goad's place at the bar. A few Jeremiah recognized, but Webb had brought on some others, and of course, Casper Norris sat among them. Their posture tense, alert.

Why? Did they really believe Floyd was crazy enough to cause violence in a courthouse? Out in rural Fancy Gap was one thing. Here in the middle of town with tons of folks watching? Another.

"Will the defendant please rise?" the judge announced, his expression unreadable as he turned to Floyd.

Quiet shrouded the room. Everyone waited in poised expectation.

Floyd stood, with his lawyer joining him.

Massie nodded for Goad to continue.

" 'We, the jury, find the defendant, Floyd Allen, guilty as charged in the indictment and fix his punishment as confinement in the penitentiary of this state for one year.' "

A gasp sounded in the crowd.

"Is that your verdict, gentlemen?" Goad addressed the jury.

They answered with unanimous nods. Goad turned and placed the slip of paper in the pigeonhole of his desk.

Floyd stared at Goad, as if in some kind of trance. Had he heard the county clerk's words?

"We'd like to request a new trial due to new evidence, Judge."

Bolen shuffled a few steps forward. "I can file affidavits to support this motion, if it's amenable to you."

"Very well." Massie shifted through some papers on his desk. "When can you be ready to argue the motion?"

"I think we can have our witnesses here by tomorrow morning," came Bolen's reply.

"We will set it to be argued in the morning." Massie turned as if to talk to Goad, but Bolen recalled his attention.

"Will Your Honor allow Mr. Allen bail pending this motion?"

Massie shifted his attention from Floyd to Bolen to a few other faces in the room. The silence swelled. A man coughed. A woman sniffled.

"I can't grant bail after the defendant has been found guilty and convicted." Massie spoke with deliberation, attention focused on Floyd, as if he wanted the defendant to understand the point of law and find some hope in it. "If an appeal is granted, I will bail him pending the appeal."

"We can pay whatever bond you think is necessary," Bolen continued.

"I can't do that, sir."

"The judge preceding you allowed for those occasions, Your Honor." Floyd's co-counsel, Tipton, stood. "It's not uncommon around here."

His statement didn't go over well with Judge Massie, whose lips firmed into a frown. He drew in an audible breath. "Be that as it may, it is not the custom in Virginia, or with me."

"In that case, Mr. Allen would like to speak with one of his boys to make arrangements for tomorrow, Your Honor." Floyd's lawyer gestured toward the back of the room where Floyd's sons sat, and Judge Massie nodded his agreement.

Bolen beckoned the boys forward, but Victor was talking to a man beside him, so his younger brother, Claude, approached the front of the room alone. "What's happening?" Ava leaned close, her whisper tickling Jeremiah's cheek. "Ain't Floyd been found guilty?"

"Yes, but his lawyer is saying they have new evidence that wasn't presented yesterday that might help Floyd's case." He nodded to where Claude and Floyd were whispering together, heads nearly touching.

"I imagine Floyd's givin' Claude details on who to seek out. They've already approached me about it."

"So we'll have to be here again tomorrow?" Her gaze fastened on his, so soft and appealing.

"Well, *you* don't have to stay. You've already testified."

Her lips crooked up on one side. "I can afford one more night sleeping in a fancy hotel, I think." She winked. "I've sold two dresses this week."

His words pressed low. "Have you now?"

"And I think I should spend some time tryin' to find a gift for this man I'm marryin' on Sunday."

His grin stretched as wide as the swell of his chest, and he nearly breached the gap between them to taste her smile. My, how he loved her. "I think your man's already gettin' everything he wants on Sunday."

Her gaze roamed his face, her gentle caress touching him deeper than her lips ever could. "I love you a bushel and a peck, Jeremiah Sutphin."

He chuckled at the old sayin', but the sentiment dipped all the way to his soul. She loved him. She'd shown it for months, but the words paired with the actions sent his pulse into a ready response. He turned back to the room, his grin nigh near impenetrable.

"Is there anything else you can do with your case today?" Massie steadied his attention on Floyd's lawyer, his voice hushing the murmurs of the crowd.

"No, sir."

Massie turned to Webb. "Then, Sheriff, take charge of the prisoner."

Sheriff Webb nodded to the judge and took slow steps across the courtroom toward the defendant when suddenly Floyd Allen erupted from his seat, the chair legs slamming against the floor. Ava jumped at Jeremiah's side and wrapped her hands around his arm.

Floyd reached for the bottom left of his sweater, as if searching for something, and everything seemed to happen at once.

Sheriff Webb shouted out toward one of his deputies. "Take him."

The other deputies stood from their seats, almost in unison, except for Casper Norris, who was already on his feet.

Floyd finally stopped messing with his sweater and straightened, his dark eyes staring ahead, not at Webb as much as beyond. "Gentlemen, I ain't a-goin."

A gunshot sounded, followed immediately by another.

And then the entire room flared into chaos.

Chapter Sixteen

Wounded hearts beat a more cautious rhythm, but a steadier beat.
Granny Burcham

A va may not have understood everything going on in the court-room, but she knew the sound of gunfire. Two pops in quick succession, both from the front of the room, followed by another much closer to where she stood.

Everything slowed down.

Ava rose, and Jeremiah stepped in front of her. Dexter Goad stood poised as if a statue, smoke rising from the Colt in his hands, and Floyd Allen dropped to the floor. Judge Massie slumped in his chair.

Casper Norris shifted in her periphery. Another pop.

Someone else fell. Who was it? Foster? The sheriff?

Claude Allen's pistol was already raised and smoking.

This isn't happening.

And then shots exploded in all directions.

She stared a moment, mesmerized, shocked. Her mind not making sense with the actual events happening before her, like she'd awakened from a dream but still wasn't lucid.

She blinked as a shot zipped past her head and split into the wall.

Jeremiah pulled Ava to the ground beside him, placing a protective arm around her, but from over his shoulder, she saw Sid Allen joining Claude in returning fire toward the front of the room with plenty of gunfire from the front responding.

People screamed. Smoke branched throughout the room, flashing like muted lightning from the dozens of shots. And the terrible dream cleared into a nightmarish reality.

They were in the middle of a shoot-out.

A woman holding a little baby fell to the ground near them, and Jeremiah crawled forward to help her. In a second, the chaotic crowd swarmed around. To keep from being trampled, Ava pushed herself off the floor and started for the door, shouts and movements in her periphery drawing her attention to the front of the room.

Judge Massie's chair sat empty, a dark mass on the floor nearby alerting Ava to his whereabouts. William Foster ran the length of the bar and was mowed down by bullets, falling by painfully slow degrees near where several other bodies lay. From the front of the room, Goad continued a gun battle with Sid and Claude Allen, while several of the deputies backed up his assault.

And then the smoke, like a heavy mountain fog, invaded her vision, leaving nothing but the noises of gunfire and screams from all sides. She moved with the throng as they propelled her toward the door. A man jumped out of one of the nearby windows. Another bullet zoomed too close. Wood split on one of the benches she passed. Where was Jeremiah?

Smoke coated her breaths, burning her eyes. Bullets continued to escape even outside, following her down the courthouse steps and onto the front lawn. She bent low, looking for a safe place to hide, drawing in a breath of the cold air as she followed the crowd. Men and women ran past, disappearing down the muddy street or into nearby shops. She made it across the street, near the alley that led to the jailhouse, affording a little distance between her and the gunfire, but not much. Another bullet, from the direction of Claude Allen as he ran from the scene, appeared to be aimed at no one in particular. Wild fear or fury at this point, she reckoned. She bent low, looking for a safe place to hide among the nervous horses and empty buggies, but not too far that she couldn't run to Jeremiah's or someone else's aid if needed.

People continued to spill from the courthouse as gunfire popped through the morning air. Victor Allen ran up to his brother, his hat pressed between his hands, almost pleading. What was he doing? Trying to get his brother to listen? To stop?

She studied a small crowd, mostly jurymen, running from the courthouse and back toward the bank, gunfire following them. One of the retreating men bumped into Ava as he rushed forward, sending her spiraling backward onto the muddy street. She pushed up from the ground, slipping from the slushy mess, when strong arms came up around her.

She looked up, air bursting from her lips in a surge of relief. "Jeremiah!"

He steadied her with his hands to her shoulders, glancing over her face and body before scanning their surroundings. "We need to get away from here."

"How did this happen?" Her question froze in puffs of air.

A shout pulled their attention back to the courthouse, where Floyd Allen limped down the stairway, firing at someone behind him. A body toppled down the stairs. People scattered like startled birds, screaming as they ran and looking for cover in every direction. Sid joined Floyd, with Wesley Edwards nearby, both still firing behind and before them. It was madness.

Another bullet sounded off its high-pitched zoom by Ava's head, as an echo of gunfire resounded from the courthouse stairwell. Floyd buckled to the ground again, but Sid helped him up, continuing to fire behind him until Dexter Goad surfaced from the shadows of the stairwell. He held the side of his face but continued firing, their gun battle growing closer.

Without warning, Jeremiah gripped Ava by the waist and hoisted her into a nearby wagon.

"What are you doing?"

"Move as far back into the wagon as you can." He gave her a little nudge. "At least the wood is somethin' to protect you. I'll get the reins."

As if in response, wood splintered at the impact of another bullet along the side of the wagon nearby, causing the horses to scuttle in a nervous dance. Jeremiah rounded the back of the wagon bed, but he had just turned the corner when he jerked straight and reached for his upper chest. His eyes widened and fastened on Ava's, a mingling of shock and confusion crossing his features.

"Jeremiah?"

He blinked and stumbled forward a step. A faint stream of red spread beneath the fingers he clutched against his white shirt and he shook his head, as if trying to decipher the problem.

No! Breath whooshed from Ava's lungs in one word. "Jeremiah!"

She pushed up to her knees, attempting to get to him, but the horses reared so violently, the motion sent her reeling backward. Her head hit the wagon's rim, and she slumped onto the wagon bed. As darkness clouded her vision, her last sight was Jeremiah stumbling to the muddy ground, his hand to his chest, his gaze holding hers.

There was nothing Jeremiah could do. The gunfire sent the horses into a panic, and in one timeless instant, Ava jolted back against the wagon, slamming into the side, and the horses raced in wild abandon down the street. The immediate shock of the wound to his chest weakened him to his knees and he blinked against the pain. He had to get to her. But his legs refused to comply. How could his mind know what needed to happen and his body fail to respond?

Floyd and Sid Allen, along with a few of the other boys, ran down the alley just beyond him, untying their horses mounted there. Jeremiah pushed himself up from his crouched position and groaned as pain shot through his left shoulder and down his arm.

"Can you mount?"

In answer to Sid's question, Floyd fell off his horse. "I can't, boys. I'm gonna die here. Go on."

"I'm stayin' with you, Pa." Victor dismounted and ran to his father's side, helping him to a more upright sitting position.

"Why'd you say you wouldn't go with the sheriff, Floyd?" Sid asked. Jeremiah craned his neck to hear, trying to hold on to the side of a deserted wagon to bring himself to a stand.

"It was all a joke betwixt the lot of them. Dexter Goad winked at the sheriff. I saw it with my own two eyes." Floyd's voice broke as he winced to a stand, supported by Victor. "I couldn't abide goin' with 'em then. I just couldn't. Dexter already had his gun out. He was waitin' for his chance all along."

"We need to get out of here," came the call from one of the other boys.

The world started getting fuzzy. Jeremiah's vision swarmed as Sid reached down to say something else to his brother before joining the rest of the group. Jeremiah turned away and took a few steps toward the drugstore. He had to get help. Had to find Ava.

The buildings swayed. Or was that him? With a last push, he reached the door of the drugstore and collapsed.

Chapter Seventeen

*Hope ain't a sit-back sort of thing. Oh no, sometimes you have to
hold on to it so tight, it exhausts you to your bones, and sometimes
you have to pursue it like a hound on a scent. That's the
only way to really know what it's all about.*
Granny Burcham

Ava jostled awake, the steady rocking of the wagon tempting to
pull her heavy eyelids closed. First, she noticed the overcast sky
above, shifting clouds in various shades of gray, and next came a throbbing ache from the side of her head, just behind her right ear.

Where was she? She forced her eyes open wider, the wagon sides
giving off no clues to her surroundings. She turned to look out the
back. Open fields spanned on one side of a muddy, narrow road while
a forest lined the other, as the wagon tilted from its uphill climb. That
didn't give her many clues. She pushed up to a sitting position with
a groan, the ache intensifying in her head, and the tug of her satchel
against her shoulder inciting an uncomfortable throb in her neck. Her
hand moved to the source of the pain at the side of her head only to
meet some damp, sticky consistency. Blood?

Memories began a sluggish resurrection.

The courthouse? Gunfire. Her eyes flew wide. Jeremiah!

She blinked against the offending light, trying to press through
the gray, and peered around the pair of horses pulling the wagon. A
small clapboard house sat at the top of a hill, nearly camouflaged by
the surrounding forest and shadow. The horses must have found their
way home. But *whose* home? Once she sorted that out, she could get
back to finding Jeremiah.

Her stomach curled with a mixture of pain-induced nausea and
the idea of seeing Jeremiah shot. He would be all right. *Lord, please, let
him be all right.*

The horses made their way to an adjacent barn, as if an invisible driver guided them inside, and once they came to a stop, Ava slid to the edge of the wagon. The scent of hay and animals nearly overpowered her, and the world weaved a little as her feet touched the ground, nearly inspiring her to lose her mighty fine hotel breakfast.

That'd be a waste for sure.

She braced her palm against the wagon to steady her steps and glanced around the barn. Large enough for two horses and a milking cow, but the surroundings gave no other hints to her location.

"I heard somethin' come up the road, I tell ya."

The unfamiliar male voice carried from outside. A young voice. Ava froze. Who was he? Safe?

"Sounded like a wagon. With all that's happened at the courthouse, we can't be too careful."

Ava scanned the barn for a hiding place, wrestling against a bout of nausea her movements inspired. A large tackle box near the wall offered a sliver of space behind, shadowed by the stall. She steadied her way to the spot and slid into place.

"Lookie here!" a male voice called, the tone resounding off the inside of the barn. "They found their way home."

Ava pulled her foot in as tightly as she could, its tip barely hidden by the edge of the box.

"We ain't got time to ponder over your horses, Martin. We got to figure out what to do."

She searched her muddled brain for the owner of that second voice. Familiar.

"I told ya. When I left the court, I saw the sheriff down. I'm sure of it. Shot more times than I can count. That's all Gopher wanted."

"He would've liked to get Goad too, but at least there's the sheriff."

The sheriff? Ava's palm came up to catch her gasp. Sheriff Webb was dead?

"Did you hear somethin'?" From the familiar voice.

The feet shuffled so close, the boots of one of the men came into view. "Don't go gettin' skeered off now. We got away from that courthouse lickety-split. Ain't nobody can pin anything on us as far as I can tell. Mooney's inside the house, and Zeb and Luther'll be here in no time."

A thump sounded.

"Hey, what'd ya hit me for?"

"Because you're talkin' sloppy. We ain't safe until all this is cleared up and nobody else knows what all happened with Creed. Plus, we got to make sure nobody can trace nothin' back to us. And we ain't safe till *everybody's* back here and accounted for."

What was going on? These men had something to do with Sheriff Webb's death? And Creed? Did they mean Joe?

One was named Martin. Which didn't help at all, because she knew quite a few Martins. Another was Mooney. There was only one. Mooney Childers, but he didn't seem the sort to get caught up in something like this. Of course, she'd thought that about Joe too. Maybe all the moonshining business wasn't as cut-and-dried as she'd thought.

The sound of a horse's hooves beat nearby.

"It's Zeb."

"We gotta git out of here, boys," came a new voice. Zeb. "Two of the deputies followed me as far as the crossroads and then I lost 'em, but they got Luther, and he'll squeal like a pig if they hurt him bad enough."

Quiet for what seemed like forever. Ava peeked around the tackle box. Two of the men were turned away from her in the barn door and the other, Zeb, was dismounting. She slid her head back before his feet hit the ground. She didn't know him.

"We ain't runnin' if we don't have to," the more familiar voice said.

"But if Luther tells them what he knows, it won't matter 'bout the Allens. The deputies will be after us in no time."

"Not if we get to Luther first." The familiar voice took such a dark turn, Ava shivered. "They're gonna be too busy carin' for the mess at the courthouse to ask too many questions of their prisoners today, so this is our best chance."

"Chance?" Martin repeated. "You think we can get Luther away from the law?"

"I wasn't plannin' on getting him out, only makin' him silent."

"You mean. . . ?"

Ava understood at the same time as Martin, evidently, because she pressed her palm more tightly over her mouth to keep her breaths silent.

"Maybe there's a chance to free him," Zeb offered. "Come nightfall, I reckon you could get in and out pretty as you please, since most of the folks is gonna be tendin' the wounded and, as far as I can tell, the Allens have run off."

"Then, Zeb, you go take care of Luther."

Silence followed.

"But. . .but it's Luther."

"I don't care who it is. If he's gonna give us all up, then we gotta make sure he can't talk."

More silence. Then a click. A gun.

"Martin ain't got the spine or practice for it. I need to stay here and sort out our escape plan in case you don't come back or Luther betrays us before you can get to him. So that leaves you."

"But he'll be in jail," Zeb replied, his voice tight.

"You know who to talk to in the jail. He'll help you out."

The voices lowered, distanced, and Ava leaned her head back against the wood, attempting to process everything she'd heard and the unsaid things in between. Sheriff Webb was dead, most likely killed by one of the men standing outside this barn. Some plan, even darker than killing the sheriff, seemed to be in the works among the men, and one of them was going back to the jail to "take care of Luther."

Her head throbbed and all she wanted to do was give in to the pull of sleep, but she had to get back to town. Had to warn the deputies about this plan. Find Jeremiah.

She waited what seemed like forever. A running horse disappeared down the road, presumably Zeb leaving for town. If she could just get to a road, she'd sort out where she was and how to get back to Hillsville.

Eyeing the pair of horses, she carefully slipped from her hiding spot, staying close to the ground. Her stomach roiled against her movements, a little less than it had before, but she kept her approach slow. After another glance to the door, she slid over to the nearest horse and began unhitching his harness from the wagon. He made some low noises, likely unhappy at having his rest interrupted, but Ava coaxed him away from his companion, keeping his body as a shield between her and the barn door. If she could just get onto the path, she had a chance at outrunning the men. She had to try. Luther, whoever he was, and possibly even more folks, depended on it.

She grimaced up at the sleek, black stallion and sighed. Not a saddle in sight. She hadn't ridden a horse in years, and never bareback, but how different from riding her mule could it be? Besides a lot taller. And certainly faster.

With another glance to the door, she led the horse to a bench near the entrance of the barn, her catapult for mounting the steed. He shuffled nervously and sniffed, reluctant to follow her guidance, but she gave him a strong tug for obedience, careful to keep silent.

She braced her hand against a nearby pole and prayed the jolt from the bench to the horse wouldn't lead to an immediate bout of vomiting.

"Well, well, what do we have here?"

A frigid grip tightened her stomach. The familiar voice bled into a dangerous clarity. She rushed to jump onto the bench, but a strong hand caught her arm before she made it. He spun her around, nearly sending her back to the ground in a dizzying heap, and she came face-to-face with Keen Gentry.

"Looks like you've made a wrong turn, Miss Burcham, and this time, you ain't got anybody around to protect you."

Faint light filtered through Jeremiah's closed eyes as he rallied into consciousness. He drew in a deep breath, inciting a dull ache in the left upper side of his chest. With a groan, he reached for his shoulder, but a surge of weakness paused his attempt, inciting another groan. What had happened?

He strained his eyes open and looked around the well-situated room. Not his own. But familiar. The window afforded a darkening view of some of the Main Street shops of Hillsville. He blinked back to the room. Was he in the Thornton Hotel? Why? At night? A faint glimpse of the edge of the courthouse came into view out the window and Jeremiah stirred fully awake.

Ava!

He commanded his legs to the floor, but they barely moved beneath the light blanket covering him from the chest down. A second attempt proved as useless and sapped him of the little strength he'd conjured. He collapsed back against the pillows, offering a prayer for help. For Ava.

"I'm glad to see you're awake, Mr. Sutphin." Dr. Nuckolls walked through the door, his solemn expression made all the more grim by the shadows beneath his eyes. "The sooner you can get some nutrients into your system, the faster you'll be up on your feet."

"I. . .I have to get out of here, Doctor. Ava. . .Ava—"

"That fiancée of yours will have to come to you, boy. You've lost enough blood to keep you in bed for—"

"Ava's in trouble. She was in the back of a runaway wagon after the shootin' and—"

"Then she was safer than other folks." Doc Nuckolls stepped closer, examining Jeremiah's bandages. "A bullet made a clean pass through your left shoulder. Caused a lot of blood loss but should heal well."

"She fell in the wagon on the way out. Hit her head. There ain't no tellin' where she is now, but—" He tried to move again, making a little more motion in his legs than he had before. Promising. "I have to try to get to her."

Doc's hand pressed against Jeremiah's chest, holding him in place with more strength than Jeremiah would have thought possible. Of course, the overall weakness in his body likely helped matters.

"I'm afraid we'll have to wait awhile to look for Ava."

Jeremiah focused on the doctor, his whole body coming to alert. "What?"

With a large sigh, Doc Nuckolls shook his head and took a seat in the chair near the bed. "Sheriff Webb, Judge Massie, and Foster are all dead, Jeremiah."

Air pushed from Jeremiah's lungs in a rush. No! "Sheriff Webb?"

"Likely one of the first to die." Doc scratched his head, his words weighted, slow. "Poor man was shot no less than five times, and most of those from behind. I suppose he got caught in the cross fire."

Jeremiah strained to recall anything from the shooting. Who had been behind Webb? Goad? Yes. And the deputies. Anyone else?

"Goad's sent a wire to the governor for help. Some detectives are on their way with a plan to search out every man involved in this shooting until they're either found or killed in the process, from what I hear. The whole town's on edge."

"Who are they afraid of? The detectives?"

Doc's hard-pressed lips crooked slightly. "You don't know? Who do you think they'd be afraid was going to come back and finish the job?"

Jeremiah sifted his memories for an answer but came up with nothing.

"The Allens. People think they'll come back for vengeance on their kin or out of pure spite."

"They're not those kinds of folks, Doc. Surely you know that."

"You're not gonna have many folks in town believe you on that, Jeremiah. Floyd Allen was on trial today, and the Allens took out three law officials and tried their best to get rid of Dexter Goad."

"From what I saw, he was doing his fair share of shootin' too."

Doc nodded. "And it's a miracle he survived. We found more than ten gunshot holes in his clothes, and only one got him on the cheek, but the fact still remains, the Allens killed court officials. Or that's how folks see it."

This was unbelievable. Of course, the Allens had done wrong by shooting the lawmen, but even though Floyd had a hair-trigger temper, he didn't seem the type to have planned something like this. And from the chaos in the courtroom yesterday, how could anyone prove who shot who?

Jeremiah squeezed his eyes closed. "Who else is dead?"

"One of the jurors, and there are several wounded." Doc rubbed a hand over his face. "In fact, Floyd's pretty shot up himself. In one of the front rooms of the hotel. Victor's with him. Good boy. But the rest have skipped town, and despite folks' fears, I don't expect them back unless someone brings them back, except Jack Allen. He came up to visit his brother, thinking Floyd is dying."

"Is he?"

Doc shrugged a shoulder. "That man's survived more wounds than most folks, so I'm not going to hedge a guess."

"Did Jack cause trouble when he came?"

"Not a bit. Came in, saw his brother for about an hour, and then left."

Jeremiah attempted to move his foot. A little better. Then his left arm, but the soreness throbbed so badly his head began to ache. He had to find Ava. "So Floyd's under arrest?"

"Nobody's under arrest as of yet, though some men asked me about taking him to the jail. He's in no condition to be moved yet, so I told them to let him be for the night." Doc stood and rubbed his palms together before giving Jeremiah's bandages another look.

A light flickered to life from the window, goldish red.

"What in the world?" Doc Nuckolls walked over to the window and peered out. "Well, looks like the new deputies are camped out in the street and across the road, likely keeping their eye on Floyd and any ambush they expect to happen."

"Deputies?" Jeremiah's eyes had grown heavy again, despite fighting the pull. He'd barely moved a few muscles, but everything had grown increasingly weak.

"About thirty men were rounded up and deputized this afternoon in order to prepare for the worst."

"I. . .I need to talk to them." Jeremiah sat up straighter, drawing his mind from its sluggishness. "They can help us find Ava."

"The detectives will be here shortly, and they've got quite a reputation. I reckon they'll engage in a manhunt." Doc Nuckolls turned from the window, his gaze softening as he held Jeremiah's attention. "You want to find Ava?"

"Yes." His response sounded far away and not part of his own body.

"Then rest and nutrition is what you need, and I'll mention it to the detectives when they get here." The doctor's voice distanced as Jeremiah's eyes fell closed. "The Lord knows the last thing we need is another senseless death related to this tragedy. Hopefully, we'll find Ava."

As sleep overcame his thoughts, Jeremiah kept repeating the prayer. *Keep Ava safe. Please, keep her safe.*

Chapter Eighteen

Always keep an eye open for the trouble, boy.
Both, if you can spare 'em.
Granddaddy Sutphin

A va struggled against the ropes wrapped around her chest and arms strapping her to the uncomfortable ladder-back chair. Apart from sneering like the villain he was, Keen had marched her to the little cabin, tied her up, and threatened Mooney and Martin on their lives if they so much as loosened the bonds while he was gone.

And then, with nightfall shadowing the skyline, he'd ridden off without another word.

"Stop lookin' that way at me, Ava Burcham. You got yourself into this mess." Mooney turned his chair away from her, his pale eyes glancing in the corner where she sat too far away from the fire to get much use out of it.

"What have you got yourself caught up in, Mooney? With Keen Gentry?" Her head tempted to droop from need for sleep, but as long as he was talking she could try for help. . .or information. "You're smarter than that."

"Be quiet, Ava. We ain't supposed to talk to you." This from Martin, who paused long enough in his pacing to send Ava a glare. He'd nearly paced a hole in the floor from the front window to the back door of the small space.

"Well, you are right now, aren't you?"

He sneered and resumed his pacing.

"You don't know nothin' about it," Mooney grumbled from his spot, keeping his back to her. "Nothin'."

"Then justify yourself so I won't think you're a flippin' fool." Though she doubted he could change her current opinion of him. "I can't imagine what your mama thinks of you—"

He shot up so fast his chair toppled over and crashed against the

186

floor. "Don't you dare act like you know anything about my mama. She would be dead if it wasn't for the likes of Keen and his folks."

Ava stared up at him, refusing to allow her expression to change as he loomed closer, his fiery hair glowing bright orange with the firelight behind him.

"I'm sorry, Mooney. I'd've done about anything to have saved my daddy."

The sudden flare in his eyes died and he stepped back, opening and closing his fists at his sides. "Once this is all done, you'll see. No one else need be hurt now that the whole world's after the Allens and we can get on with our business."

"Shut up, Mooney." Martin hit the man in the arm. "Don't say nothin' else. I want to get back to the job and my family without spendin' any more days in Keen's stinkin' cabin than I have to. We ain't seen a cent of what we was promised, and I'm ready to just get out of here while I can."

"Keen seems like the sort who'd just let you get out of this real easy, don't he? All nice and forgivin'." Ava raised a brow, her well-placed comment working its wonders as Martin tensed anew.

"Shut up." The back of his hand hit her cheek, rocking her head and reigniting the sharp pain behind her ear. Her vision darkened.

"What'd you do that for?" Mooney pushed Martin away.

Ava attempted to hold on to consciousness, to fight against the throbbing darkness invading all sides of her view, but she failed.

The fire's glow barely made a dent in the predawn darkness as Ava opened her eyes and reoriented herself to the filthy cabin's surroundings. Mooney's head bent in a crooked way, hinting that he was asleep, but Martin stood with his arm resting on the mantel, staring down into the dying embers. Everything gave off a blurry hue. How had she gotten here?

She grasped for memories like they swam in water, slippery to the touch.

The wagon. The shoot-out. Jeremiah!

She tried to stand up and go for the door but couldn't move. Ropes wrapped around her chest. Right. Keen had tied her up.

The pain in her head almost closed off her vision again, but she pressed her eyes closed and took a deep breath to keep her pulse from increasing and pumping like clanging pots between her ears. When she opened her eyes again, the faint morning light, barely visible, filtered through the window. Her breath caught. The light took a human form, grasping fingers reaching out for her, bony and thin, like her mother's.

A scream lodged in her throat. She closed her eyes and plunged her prayers through the fear and the pain, desperately attempting to refocus her thoughts. Through Christ she had a sound mind. His blood changed her bad blood to wholesome. *The Lord your God is in your midst. Here. And greater than your fear.*

When she opened her eyes again, the light had transformed into a dust cloud lit by gray morning with a touch of golden embers mixed into it, giving it an otherworldly glow. Nothing else.

The taste of blood salted her lips. She caught her slipping thoughts and barely recalled Martin hitting her. She glared at his grim profile from her spot in the corner. If she got free, she'd give him a reciprocal pat or two and see how he liked it.

The sound of approaching hooves drew Martin to the window, the sudden movement waking Mooney.

"It's Keen."

"Zeb with him?" Mooney stood from his seat and crossed to the window.

Martin shook his head. "I don't see him."

Ava ordered her mind to focus, to process the words. Only Keen. If he'd gone to find Zeb, then something must have happened to alter those plans. Ava forced her breaths calm, to keep her thoughts ordered.

Mooney opened the door before Keen reached it, allowing the man to saunter in, cigarette clenched between his teeth. He scanned the room, finally leveling his gaze on Ava before turning back to Martin and Mooney. "We need to get out of here. Now. And we'll take to the brush."

"What's happened?" Martin came forward, looking out the open door. "Did Zeb get caught? Is he comin'?"

"Zeb got Luther free from jail. Met 'em on the way into Hillsville." Keen removed his cigarette and tapped it, spraying ash to the floor. "We had a disagreement. He drew on me and I had to shoot him. Luther too."

A croak of a sound emerged from Martin and he looked away toward the fire. "You killed Zeb Daniels."

"Self-defense." Keen tossed the cigarette to the ground and smashed it with his foot. "Unfortunately, somehow Zeb's family got wind of the trouble."

"The Daniels?" Mooney jerked his attention to the window. "Keen, if they find out we've been skimmin' from the top, they'll—"

"Zeb's already made sure to tell 'em, I reckon. I shoulda never trusted a Daniels." Keen crossed the room, his gaze fixed on Ava. "They'll be on us within the hour if we don't get to the brush. Horses ain't no use there, so we'll have a chance."

"After all we've done." Martin's voice rose an octave. "We're gonna leave with nothin'?"

"You'll be lucky to leave with your life, Martin, if we can get across the state line. Once things calm down, you can come back."

Mooney started gathering up supplies, but Martin stepped to Keen's side. "You're sure they're lookin' for all of us, or just you?"

Keen turned faster than lightning and grabbed Martin by the collar. "I can make sure you never come back home, boy. You hear?" He shoved Martin back and gestured with his chin. "Get supplies."

"Where're we gonna go?" Mooney asked from across the room, dousing the fire with his coffee.

Keen knelt down to Ava's eye level. "We'll go to this abandoned house I know 'bout. Far off the path. Then we'll make plans."

"And what about Ava?"

Keen studied her, and despite the stifling pain begging her eyes closed, she glared back. He tugged the cigarette from his mouth and released a cloud of smoke with his smile. "We're takin' her with us for now, as insurance to the state line. The Daniels had a soft spot for the Burchams, if I recall." He tapped his cigarette then wedged it back between his teeth, eyes glimmering with serpentine interest. "It's a good thing you're useful, Miss Burcham. For now, anyway."

If eating meant Jeremiah healed faster, then he should be ready to leave by sundown. He'd consumed enough at breakfast to raise the brows of the maid who cleaned up after him and even asked for seconds at lunch, much to Doc's amusement.

After another nap, he made his way out of his room, grateful to be housed on the first floor. The hotel buzzed with activity. Openly armed men stood in the parlor of the hotel, evidently gathering for something. What had Doc called them? The Baldwin-Felts Detective Agency? Jeremiah couldn't remember ever seeing a detective before, even with his father's line of work, but, boy, did he get a chance to see them now.

Dozens of them.

Some of the locals mingled in with the new crowd, but it was easy to spot the difference. Besides the large silver badge of a star on the outside of each man's jacket, bowler hats, pristine fedoras, and high-class duds set them apart from most of the town folks in their simple slacks and dress shirts. An occasional vest here and there.

Tom Hall, the hotel owner, caught sight of Jeremiah from across the room and walked over to greet him. "Well, looks like you've found your feet, boy."

"Thank you for your hospitality, Mr. Hall. I'm hoping to be strong enough to leave in the morning."

Tom chuckled and attempted to cover his smile with his hand. "Doc told me you were set on finding your gal, but I wouldn't worry too much. If she's smart, she's gone on to her granny's, away from all this." He waved a hand toward the gathering. "Though I don't mind it none for business."

"I'd say not."

"Everybody's all excited right now because the detectives just arrested Floyd and are getting ready to move him and Victor to the jailhouse for safekeeping until he can travel on to Roanoke."

Jeremiah searched the space for any sign of Floyd or Victor. "Victor? Why Victor?"

"He's an Allen, I reckon." Tom shrugged a shoulder. "Several folks have told the detectives 'bout Victor's gentle-tempered ways, but there's a bloodlust in every corner of town, so I can't imagine anyone listenin' to reason just yet, but hopefully reason'll show up eventually."

With prejudice and fury on the upswing, Jeremiah reckoned a visit from reason might be a long time coming.

"And folks is showing up from all over," Hall continued. "Didn't take long for word to spread. I heard tell the *Roanoke Times* has already featured an article on the 'massacre' as it's being called."

Jeremiah winced at the word. Massacre. But from what he'd seen inside the courtroom yesterday? The incessant gunfire. Men falling like trees. The screams and rush to leave, regardless of who was trampled or fallen? Perhaps the gun smoke obscuring the scene had been a mercy to more folks than him. And maybe it protected a few too.

As Jeremiah took another sweep of the room, he caught sight of a man staring at him. The light-haired man, graying at the temples, carried an air of authority about him, almost severity. His angled, strong face matched the aura, and he held Jeremiah's attention with stern dark eyes, almost as if he was attempting to read Jeremiah's thoughts.

The man started moving across the room toward Jeremiah, his face softening into a smile as he closed in. He turned to Mr. Hall first, offering a nod. "Mr. Hall."

"Mr. Baldwin." Hall's smile tensed ever so slightly, and he turned to Jeremiah. "Jeremiah Sutphin, this is William Baldwin of the Baldwin-Felts Agency. He'd asked to have a word with you earlier this mornin', but I didn't want to interfere with your healing rest."

Jeremiah took Baldwin's hand. "Nice to meet you, sir."

"We're collecting as much information about the Allens and the courthouse gunfight as we can." The man gestured with his chin back toward Jeremiah's room. "Do you have a few minutes we could get your statement? Deputy Norris said you may have more insight on the Allens, since you worked for Sid Allen. Isn't that right?"

Jeremiah sent a look to Hall, who exited the conversation with a slight bow of his head.

"It is. I've worked for him over the past six months and been acquainted with his family most of my life."

"And your father was a lawman, I understand?"

"Yes, sir. For fifteen years."

Jeremiah turned to a movement in his periphery, and Casper Norris approached, hand out and smile at the ready. "Glad to see you're up and moving, Jeremiah. I heard you had a rough time of it."

"Getting better every hour."

Casper nodded, his grin growing. "Good to hear. I suppose the Allens had all sorts of unsuspecting enemies they were hoping to take out."

Jeremiah flinched at the implication. "I don't think any of the Allens shot in my direction, Casp." He studied his friend. "I think my enemies have already doled out their vengeance on me by burning my cabin."

"Norris is going to join us for our conversation, Mr. Sutphin, if you don't mind." Baldwin opened his palm for Jeremiah to lead the way to his room.

Jeremiah took one of the chairs in the room while Mr. Baldwin took the other. Casper chose to stand, keeping his attention mostly focused on the window.

"I asked Mr. Norris to come along since you two know each other and he can fill in any information I may miss in my inquiry." Baldwin drew a notepad and pen from his pocket. "Would you mind going over your observations from yesterday's gunfight, starting with your entrance to the courthouse, until I ask you to stop."

Jeremiah relayed everything he could in as much detail as possible, leaving out the teasing conversations he'd had with Ava. Just the thought of her squeezed pain through his chest. Where was she? He knew people could die from head injuries. Was she lying somewhere in the rain, unconscious and bleeding?

"And you have no guess as to who fired the first shot?"

"No, sir," Jeremiah answered. "I thought it came from the front of the courtroom somewhere, and I saw Floyd fall to the ground after the second one."

Baldwin asked a few more questions, mostly about Jeremiah's thoughts about the Allens, to which Jeremiah spoke truthfully that, though hot-tempered at times, they'd always been good to him.

"We're heading out to Sid Allen's house in the morning." Baldwin raised his brow, watching Jeremiah's face. "How should we prepare? Any secret passages? Underground forts? Do you think his clan will be in wait for us?"

"Excuse me?"

"We've heard the Allens had all sorts of preparation in place for this day, and you seem the honest sort who'd help prepare us."

"I don't know who's been joshin' you, Mr. Baldwin, but Sid Allen only spent extra money on fancy things for his house, not forts and the like." He grinned at the idea. "I've heard folks speculate about secret passages, but I've been all over that house and never seen one. As far as layin' in wait? It's my thought that if any of the Allens really wanted to find you, they'd come lookin', not waitin'."

The slightest movement twitched in Mr. Baldwin's jaw, and he made to rise.

"Wait, sir, I could use your help with somethin', if you would."

Mr. Baldwin relaxed back in the chair and tucked his notepad into his jacket pocket.

"My fiancée, Ava Burcham, disappeared yesterday after the shooting, in a runaway wagon. I ain't seen or heard of her since."

"Mr. Sutphin, our agency doesn't deal in domestic matters."

"No." Jeremiah paused the man's rise with a hand to his arm. "It ain't like that. Somethin's wrong. She would've come back by now, because she saw me get shot."

Baldwin's brow raised. "Do you think there's foul play? Kidnapping? Would the Allens have taken her as ransom?"

Jeremiah blinked at the strange turn of conversation. "No. I don't think she's been kidnapped, and I'm certain none of the Allens would have done it, if she was."

"Ah." Mr. Baldwin sighed and stood, shaking his head. "Well, you know how womenfolk can be after such a tragedy. She's likely too terrified to come back into town and is waiting until the law takes things in hand."

Clearly, Mr. Baldwin wasn't familiar with mountain women. . .and especially Ava Burcham.

"Not this woman."

"I am sorry for your plight, Mr. Sutphin." He hooked his hands around the lapel of his jacket, and Jeremiah stood to match his height. "But we can't go scouring the county for every missing lady, especially with all the people who've dispersed after such a tragedy as happened yesterday. I do hope you find her soon."

Jeremiah suppressed a growl. "I plan to do just that first thing in the morning. I need to hire a horse and buggy, pick up my dog, and I'll search the entire county, if I have to."

"What?" Casper's shocked laugh pulled Jeremiah's attention to the window. "You mean that dog of yours is still alive?"

"He had to put in a hard fight for it, but he's alive and with my cousin until I can get to him."

Casper shook his head, taking a few steps across the room, closer to Jeremiah. "Wasn't he shot three times, at least? That's some kind of dog."

"Well, he's strong and smart." Jeremiah nodded toward Mr. Baldwin. "Best tracker I've ever had."

The detective tilted his head, gaze focused back on Jeremiah's face. "Well, we might take you up on a good tracker if you and your dog are fit enough for joining our men."

"I appreciate your work, sir, but I ain't interested in a manhunt." He almost grinned. "I'm only interested in hunting after a very particular woman."

Mr. Baldwin's lips tilted ever so slightly, as if he readied a comment he didn't voice. "Well, if you change your mind, we could use all the able bodies and those familiar with the mountains that we can get." He offered his hand and Jeremiah took it. "Good day, Mr. Sutphin."

Casper lingered for a moment, giving Jeremiah the oddest look. "You sure you're fit for travel tomorrow?"

"Whether I am or not, I have to go. I know something's wrong. I have to find her."

Casper released a chuckle and shook his head as he left the room.

It wasn't until an hour later, as Jeremiah played over the conversation with Baldwin, that Casper's statement came back to mind with an unsettling nudge. Jeremiah had no recollection of telling anyone about Wolf's particular wounds, except Ava. How could he have known about the number of times Wolf was shot?

A sudden weight fell over Jeremiah's shoulders. Unless Casper Norris was there when it happened.

Chapter Nineteen

God ain't sittin' up in heaven watchin' a show down here on earth.
He don't mind gettin' His hands dirty. Else, He'd never sent the Savior.
Granny Burcham

R ain dogged every path they took through the forest, rerouting Keen's plans and slowing their pace to wherever the horrible man planned to hole up for a few days. Ava searched for landmarks, occasionally noticing a mountain peak or cliff side she thought she recognized, but they never walked high enough for her to ground herself in the landscape.

During one of their stops near an overflowing creek, she had time to wash the dried blood off the side of her head, but her clothes hung damp and gritty against her body, weighing down her already exhausted stride. The ropes tied around her wrists didn't help much either, especially with Keen pulling her along over all sorts of rough, soggy terrain. At some points the ground had become so soft, they sank to their ankles in the mud.

Mooney and Keen talked the most of the three men, though no one spoke a great deal. The impassable paths and constant rain dulled any real desire for doing much more than putting one foot in front of the other. Martin brought up the rear, sulking.

At least her mind felt a little clearer than earlier in the morning. Maybe the mountain air helped, but also she'd found some willow bark and peppermint in her satchel. Alternating between chewing on the two not only helped ease a little of her hunger but curbed the headache and residual nausea. She did sneak a few bites of the jerky she had in her satchel when the menfolk gave her some privacy to relieve herself.

The dark clouds had hastened the evening shadows when they finally came to a path Ava recognized. The mountain trail which led up to her granny's. It had taken them almost an entire day to walk five or six miles. Her body sagged against the weariness. Her wrists burned from the rope's irritation. Exhaustion and hunger likely aggravated her head injury's symptoms, because her dizziness had grown a little worse the farther they trekked. Why were they on this mountain trail? Did Keen mean to go to Granny's house?

"This way. We're almost there."

They took the new trail Ava had seen over her last few visits to Granny's. As darkness crept closer, the trees fell away to reveal one of the prettiest houses Ava had ever seen. Brick. She loved brick. A front porch lined the entire front like an invitation to rest a spell.

How had she not known about this house hidden away so close to Granny's?

"I saw it when I was out on one of my runs a few weeks back. Passed it several times after, and it looks like whoever's been working on it abandoned it for now." Keen wiped a hand across his face and gestured toward the door. "I'll see that it's empty and then we'll make camp here for the night. Maybe two."

Rain pelted down at a harder pace, so Keen jerked her up on the porch and handed the rope to Mooney before marching through the front door as if he owned the place.

"Who on earth would build such a fine house away back here off the road?" Martin walked the length of the porch, the peppering of rain competing with his words. "Whose do you figure it is?"

"Somebody who's either too rich to need it or too dumb to protect it, if you ask me." Mooney leaned his head back against the brick of the house and closed his eyes, the rope slack in his hands.

She could run. The rain fell in torrents and the night grew closer. Colder.

"It's all clear." Keen burst from the house, and Mooney tightened his grip on the rope. "There are some canned goods and dried meat but not much else. No weapons or tools. Get a fire started, Martin. Mooney, tie Miss Burcham somewhere and then we'll warm up some of those beans."

Mooney tugged her forward, and despite the ropes, she welcomed the shelter and the wooden chair. Keen lit a single lantern, illuminating the one large sitting room. There were two doorways connected to the main room which seemed to lead into other rooms, and a partially finished staircase disappeared into darkness above. Who had built this?

The intricate carvings on the back of the chairs looked familiar. Had she seen some for sale in the Allens' store?

"Here." Mooney pulled up a chair in front of her and took a seat then loosened her bonds. "You can't eat if you're tied up." His gaze locked with hers, voice dropping to a whisper. "But don't think about trying to escape, Ava. Keen's a good shot."

She dipped her chin in acknowledgment of his warning then took the can of beans he offered. Mooney moved back to the fire, and Ava dipped her fingers into the can to scoop up the contents. Beans had never tasted so good.

Martin paced from window to window. Keen stood by the open door, cigarette in hand, staring out into the rain.

From what she'd been able to piece together, Zeb Daniels had told his family about Keen's orders to kill Luther. When Keen went in search of Zeb, and Zeb had rescued Luther instead of killing him, an argument turned into Keen accomplishing the job Zeb should have done. Then Keen killed Zeb too, inciting the fury of the Daniels clan and destroying whatever business plan Keen had worked to accomplish. So not only was there a posse from town out to arrest anyone involved in the courthouse shooting, but Keen had the Daniels clan after him too.

And if he got too desperate, he'd become unpredictable. She knew exactly what that looked like. She needed to find a way to escape before the noose of revenge or justice began to tighten around Keen.

"I'll keep first watch," Keen announced, pulling from his place at the door and turning to the room. "Mooney, put Miss Burcham in that back room and move the chest against the door, so you can rest and she can't escape." His dark gaze found hers. "I'll be on the porch right near the window to that room, should you get any crazy ideas about escapin'."

Mooney followed the orders, and Ava found herself in a dark room with a bed, side table, and chest of drawers in the sizable space. The men kept the lantern in the larger room, so she only had the sliver of light from beneath the door to recognize the outlines of furniture. Keen's cigarette lit a faint glow just outside the window on the other side of the wall from the bed.

Ava pulled her heavy, damp skirts forward, the bed calling her to rest, but she couldn't soil some stranger's fine bed with her filthy clothes. A little searching in the chest of drawers revealed a pair of trousers and a long shirt, or at least that's what the items felt like. Soft. Clean. With the sweet scent of fresh-cut wood. Tears nearly blinded her. *Oh Lord, please let Jeremiah be safe. Alive.*

She slipped to the farthest corner of the room, using the chest of drawers as a shelter from Keen's window view, even though she doubted he could see much of her in the dark, and quickly changed into the clothes, using her underdress to wipe away some of the mud from her body. The feel of the dry clothes against her damp skin nearly resurrected new tears. With a stumble, she fell against the bed, consumed almost immediately by the tow of sleep and the sweet scent of leather.

Dawn brought another gray and rainy morning, but at least Ava could make out her surroundings a little better. She sat up on the bed and stretched, only to groan from her sore muscles. The furniture in this room had the same hints of design in them. The drawers in the chest of drawers and side table. A little vanity she hadn't noticed before stood in the corner, complete with a delicate mirror attached.

She looked down at the colorful quilt covering her, its shapes and hues still dull from the morning light, but she could see some of the nearest patterns. A rosebud square. A plain green one. A fishing pole—

Wait. She pulled the quilt close to her face to examine the squares. One by one the evidence fell into place. The tree patch. One of Wolf.

She re-examined the furniture surrounding her and touched the man's shirt she wore, the truth emerging. This was Jeremiah's house. And, if he was able, he'd come back to this place at some point.

The quilt pinched beneath her fists. She had to find a way to let him know where she was.

By noon on Saturday, Dr. Nuckolls gave a reluctant go-ahead for Jeremiah to leave his care. Jeremiah figured the doctor didn't have much choice, as Jeremiah had plans to leave regardless of his approval or not. A fatigue still hung over his body, but if he had enough strength to hang on to a horse, that's all he needed to start his search.

He returned his room key to the hotel desk and gave the attendant enough money to cover the clean shirt Hall had purchased to replace Jeremiah's bloody one, as well as some of the cost for the room, though he hadn't brought enough with him to meet the entire fee. A few people stood around in the parlor of the hotel, most faces unfamiliar. He'd heard folks had started arriving from all around once word spread about the shooting. Doc even said there was a man who'd ridden up from Charlotte and another from Atlanta. Why on earth would this tragedy from their little town be interesting to folks in the city? And so far away?

"Excuse me."

Jeremiah turned toward the voice just as he reached the front door of the hotel. A man about his age but dressed to the nines, and then some, approached and offered his hand. His fedora tipped in the way most of the city folks wore it—fashionable, as some had said—and his brown suit matched the hat in an uncanny sort of way.

"I'm Carter Elliott, reporter for the *Roanoke Times*. Were you in the courthouse Thursday morning when the shooting happened?"

"I was."

The man's lips tilted into a grin, as if he'd won a prize. Jeremiah wasn't too sure he liked bein' the prize. "Would you mind answering a few questions for me?"

"If you can ask them while I walk." Jeremiah stepped out the door.

"Yes, of course." Mr. Elliott followed on Jeremiah's heels. "Is it true the Allen clan all pulled their weapons and started firing as soon as the verdict was handed out?"

Jeremiah blinked and hesitated in his steps. "Who told you that?"

"I've heard it from others, and I've interviewed at least fifteen people this morning."

"No, there was one gunshot and then a quick second, as far as I recall. And it seemed there was a healthy dose of gunfire from all sorts of folks in the room. Not just the Allens."

Jeremiah nodded at Pink Samuels as he passed him on the road, the man no worse for wear and likely happy as a lark at the Allens' current trouble.

"Had you heard rumors about their plans? To shoot up the courthouse all along?"

"No. In fact, if the Allens had made plans to do such a thing, I imagine they'd've been a lot more prepared for the shooting than it looks like they was."

"So they're violent folks?"

Jeremiah paused at the other side of the street and turned to the reporter. "Mr. Elliott, I can't know what was in the mind of anyone in the courthouse except my own. About half the folks in this county are prone to tempers if pushed hard enough, and I reckon Floyd Allen's flared bright enough to light up a Christmas tree when provoked, but as far as the awful events that happened at the courthouse?" He shook his head. "That just don't seem like somethin' the Allens would plan to do."

"So you know them? Well?"

Jeremiah started walking again, turning toward the livery. "Most of my life."

"And are you leaving town?"

"I am."

"By yourself?" The man's voice slid into a higher pitch.

Jeremiah squinted over at him. "That's what I'm hopin'."

"Aren't you afraid you'll get attacked by them?"

The itch to laugh tickled the back of his throat. Is that what people thought? Really? "No, I ain't."

"And do you think they're hiding out at Devil's Den like some folks have said?"

This brought Jeremiah to a halt again, right in front of the livery. "Devil's Den?"

"Some people have reported there's a large cave system in the rocks of that mountain where people can disappear for days or weeks, if they want to."

Jeremiah barely tamed his smile. "Well, I've been to Devil's Den a few times, and I ain't never seen a cave system, nor much a cave at all. There's a nice covered outcropping and a pretty view, but, Mr. Elliott . . ." Jeremiah faced the man. "If that's what the posse or the newsfolks have been told, then I think there's a little more shine on your rock than treasure. Excuse me."

He doffed his hat and stepped into the livery, hoping his horse hadn't been "borrowed" by some of the posse for their southward ride to investigate Sid's house. Thankfully, his faithful horse waited for him.

As he brought Sally out of the livery stable and readied to pay for the service, someone called his name.

Jeremiah's shoulders sagged with a bout of frustration. Would he never get out of town?

He turned to find County Commissioner Dexter Goad approaching at a clipped pace. He wore his usual bowler, and his long-tailed coat billowed out behind him as he walked. A bandage on his cheek and around his neck marked where a bullet had entered one side and exited the other. The wound failed to slow the man down at all.

"I'm glad I caught you before you headed out."

"Commissioner." Jeremiah nodded an impatient welcome. With a break in the weather, he needed to get on the road. "I'm glad to see you're healing well."

Goad pressed a hand to his cheek and dipped his chin, his face sobering. "I was one of the lucky ones. We've had quite the hit this week, Jeremiah."

Jeremiah could feel the odd mixture of loss and energy zipping through the air. The buzz of strangers searching for gossip or an adventure. The reserve of some locals and the readiness of others to share a story. "We have, which is why I need to get on my way."

"I want to help with you findin' Ava."

At Goad's mention of her name, Jeremiah turned fully to face him. "What do you mean?"

"Doc Nuckolls told me about your concerns." He searched

Jeremiah's face. "That girl's had enough hardship in her life, and I know you were hoping to get married tomorrow."

Tomorrow. He bent a little, the reminder hitting him in the chest. "Yes, sir." The admission eked out on a whisper.

"He said you're headin' to your cousin's house to fetch your dog and wagon. I'd like to send a few boys to meet you in the mornin' out there, to help you search."

"What about the hunt for the Allens?"

Goad shook his head and gestured toward the busy street. "We got plenty of help on that front. I feel confident we'll find them soon enough. However, our regular business needs to keep moving forward. Court's opened back up today. Banks too." He pinched his lips tight and stared at Jeremiah. "To tell you the truth, Jeremiah, I don't like the fact that you've heard nothin' from her these past two days, especially with what I know of her and the fact of the wedding. It just doesn't sit right with me."

Jeremiah sighed out his sudden relief. Someone believed him, and from this unlikely source.

"With all that's gone on over the past few days, I don't think you need to take to the brush on your own. Not when we have some men who can help. Besides, if the Allens somehow got a hold of her, they may plan to use her as leverage or protection to escape. *Your* search may lead us exactly where *we* need to go too."

Goad's desire appeared genuine, and his concern? Well, Jeremiah couldn't imagine the Allens resorting to taking anyone hostage, let alone a woman, but times weren't predictable. Five people lay dead, a dozen more wounded, reporters scoured the town, and a posse hunted the county. Maybe a little help wouldn't be such a bad idea.

"I'd appreciate it, Mr. Goad."

The man offered the slightest smile.

"I ought to tell you up front, sir," Jeremiah continued. "I mean no offense, but I ain't interested in searching for the Allens. I just want to find Ava."

Goad hooked his thumbs in the loops of his trousers and leaned back, studying Jeremiah's face. Then, as if he'd made up his mind, he nodded. "Then the more hands helping, the quicker you'll reach your goal. And, maybe, we can get closer to ours too."

Tension fingered the air throughout the day as Keen took off on various runs to scout the area or uncover news. The men kept Ava locked in the bedroom for the better part of the day, allowing her out twice to use the privy, and once to wash their clothes. The way they stomped across the porch or slammed the doors to the house gnawed at her annoyance. This was Jeremiah's house. The one he'd built for *them*.

The window-filled kitchen. The large sitting room with its massive rock fireplace. A small unfinished space which, if she didn't know better, looked like the makings of an indoor privy—far enough away from the kitchen to feel proper for the inside of a house.

She'd never imagined Jeremiah would do something this grand for her. . .for them.

Throughout the day, she'd overheard bits and pieces of the outlaws' conversations.

A posse out on a manhunt for the Allens. The Daniels ransacking Keen's cabin and locating his hidden still. And then there was something about being betrayed by "the Gopher," and Martin suggesting they try to talk to the Daniels so they wouldn't have to leave the state. Keen stopped him short. Staying wasn't a choice.

"We'll need some food, Keen. We ain't got enough here to get us very far." Mooney's words traveled through the door.

"And some money," Martin added. "What I've got won't last me long, and we were supposed to get payment from the Gopher."

"The only thing the Gopher will give us now is a jail sentence," Keen hissed. "Maybe even the chair."

Ava cringed at the thought of anyone dying by that gruesome act. She leaned closer to the door.

"And I saw the posse today," she heard Keen say. "They were at Sid's house and store. Tomorra, some of 'em will come to the brush, and we won't be safe anywhere nearby anymore."

"Old woman Burcham lives close by, don't she?"

Ava's breath closed in her throat. Granny?

"She ain't but a couple miles up the mountain, if that," Martin offered. "I've not been that way in a coon's age, and I'd reckon most folks don't even know where it is."

"Sure enough." The room fell silent and then a chair scraped across the wooden floor. "We'll head her way at first light." Keen's statement brooked no challenge. "I'll scout the way early on and then we'll leave. We can likely stay another night there, and then, if we get what we need from her, we'll head toward the line."

"What about Ava?" This from Mooney.

"We'll keep Miss Burcham with us to make sure her granny gives us everything we want. And then we won't need neither of them anymore."

Ava's skin flushed cold. Her optimism offered false hope that Keen had every intention of leaving her safely in her granny's care, but why would he? She knew too much. Had information to incriminate all three of them. Leaving her alive, even if they planned to cross the state line, only meant he'd end up hunted by the law for a very long time.

She had to escape. And somehow. . .somehow find a way to leave a message for Jeremiah. If Jeremiah had survived the gunshot—she squeezed her eyes closed in silent prayer—he'd come looking for her, and he'd likely return to this house for supplies or to rest. So she had to think of a way to get a message to him that Keen or the other boys wouldn't see.

They'd likely notice anything she left on a fogged window, and there was nothing sharp enough to make a carving. The room held no pencil or paper, and she didn't have either in her satchel. With a groan, she leaned back against the wall and examined the room. How on earth would she get Jeremiah's attention with a message?

Her gaze roamed over the furniture and bare walls for the hundredth time and finally landed on her satchel atop the quilt. She stood straighter then looked to the window. Martin was on watch and nearly asleep. She rushed to her satchel and poured its contents onto the bed, revealing ribbons of various colors, but mostly red, a needle and thread, some lace she'd purchased to add to her wedding dress, and a remaining piece of licorice she kept in case there was nothing left to eat.

She ran a hand over the beautiful quilt spread over Jeremiah's bed. Light fell into late afternoon. Soon she'd be in the darkness of a lanternless room. Martin's shoulders dropped farther forward as he nodded off.

If she could escape toward the creek, then the men would chase her and leave Granny alone for a little longer. Maybe even long enough for the posse to track everyone down.

Because if she couldn't, there was a good chance another Burcham tragedy waited in her future, and *this* time, she might not survive.

Chapter Twenty

Trust, boy, ain't a throwaway. Folks'll always give
clues to their meanness, if you look hard enough.
Granddaddy Sutphin

By the time Jeremiah arrived at Ellis's house, his body ached from the exertion to stay astride and awake. How had he thought he'd make it to his new house in one day with his weakened, healing body? He glanced over at the house the men of the community had helped him build, a sense of pride at the simple and new structure settling through him like a productive day. Ellis and Jennie had moved in and would make their home here, just as Jeremiah's parents had done.

With a few stumbles, he led Sally into a stall, fed and watered her, and then disappeared into the lean-to where a cot welcomed him, Wolf at his side.

Dawn brimmed the skyline when Jeremiah washed up and made it to the house for a late breakfast Jennie had been so kind to keep warm for him. The long ride the day before had taken its toll on his muscles, their resistance screaming with each step he took, but a good meal helped.

Jeremiah had just finished eating his last biscuit when hoofbeats sounded outside.

"Looks like Goad sent three men to help," Ellis said from the window. "I only recognize Pink Samuels."

Jeremiah pulled on his jacket and joined Ellis, his body stiffening at the sight. "Well, the one to the right is Elmer Williams. Good-seemin' man, but a little long in years. Been deputized a few times in the past and even worked with Pa." Jeremiah cleared his throat, studying the other rider. "And next to him is Casper Norris. Another deputy."

"You say that like you're not too keen on him."

Jeremiah forced a smile and shrugged. "Somethin' just don't feel right, is all."

207

Ellis narrowed his eyes, his golden hair bringing out the flecks in his blue eyes. "I don't like the sound of that."

Jeremiah had no proof Casper shot Wolf or was among the men who burned down the cabin. No proof. Just. . .a sense. "It's nothin'. Just antsy, I reckon, from all that's gone on over the past few months."

Ellis didn't say anything, but his brow rose with every bit of doubt.

"What do *you* know?" Jeremiah nudged him with his elbow. "You've been off gettin' an education in Greensboro and findin' a wife." He gestured to Jennie with his chin, inciting her ready smile. "Don't act like you know what I'm thinkin'."

"You think a couple years in the city's gonna take away from decades of knowin' you?"

Jeremiah's throat tightened with sudden emotion, and he looked away. Ellis was all the family he had left, and the idea of having him around again brought a strange mix of gratitude and heart-longing he'd not realized he'd needed. Especially today. When he should have been getting married.

The sound of Wolf barking like a wild dog burst from behind Jeremiah. His furry companion stood at the front door, fur bristling, his nose pressed to the wood as if trying to open the door himself.

"What on earth?" Jennie rushed to his side. "I've never seen him behave in such a way."

Jeremiah sent Ellis a look. Wolf whined at Jennie's touch, lowering his ears for a second before turning back to the door with a low growl.

"Somethin' don't feel right?" Ellis sent Jeremiah a needling stare and then reached for his jacket on the hook by the door.

"What are you doin'?"

Ellis shrugged into his jacket. "I'm goin' with you."

Jeremiah looked from Ellis to Jennie, who smiled like a woman who wasn't surprised at all at her husband's decision. "You got to get prepared for your new job in town, Ellis. I can't have no newly married lawyer scoutin' the hillside with me when he needs to—"

"I'll see you in a few days, Jennie-girl. If not sooner." Ellis gave his wife a quick kiss on the lips, ignoring Jeremiah as if he wasn't standing right beside him arguing a point.

With a roll of his eyes, Jeremiah took hold of Wolf's collar and opened the front door. "Thank you, Jennie. I'll bring him back soon enough." He shot Ellis a grin. "If you want him."

Ellis chuckled and gave Jennie another kiss before joining Jeremiah on the front porch. After a few firm calls, Wolf quieted by Jeremiah's side, an undercurrent of growls his only sign of disagreement.

Ellis marched forward, introducing himself, his smile as welcome as if he didn't have his back up over Casper Norris. "Glad to have the extra hands."

"We've been sent by Dexter Goad to help out today and tomorrow," Pink stated, examining the house and surroundings, his brow and lips tipped low. "But then we gotta get back to town to help with the Allen hunt."

Clearly, they found this task a demotion from the more exciting, and from what Jeremiah had heard, "glamorous" task of finding the Allens. In fact, newspaper reporters kept streaming into the little town from all over.

"We'll appreciate any time you have." Jeremiah kept his eye on Wolf at his side.

"Looks like your dog's healed up nicely." This from Elmer.

"He's almost back to his old self." Jeremiah placed a hand on the dog's head, hoping the action would calm him a little more. Despite his best efforts, Jeremiah's attention moved to Casper. "Just a little jumpy, as you can tell."

"I recommend you keep him here." Casper held Jeremiah's gaze, his expression giving nothing away. "It'd be a shame for something else to set him back."

A tension waved up Jeremiah's back, vertebra by vertebra. Why would Casper want to burn down his house? What did an upstanding deputy have to do with Joe Creed? Did Sheriff Webb's warning have anything to do with a dirty deputy?

"I don't think I could keep him here, even if I tried, Casp." Jeremiah hoped his response kept to a lighter tone. The last thing he needed was for Casper to feel threatened. "He's pretty stubborn on goin' today."

"Well, then, let's get movin'." Casper tipped his chin and turned his horse toward the trail. "Where's our first stop?"

"I ought to go by my house to pick up a few things, and then I reckon one of us can check with Granny Burcham while the rest of us head south."

Pink's frown deepened. Casper's expression took on a humored twist. Elmer nodded with all the solemnity of the situation. What a party!

"I agree. The search has to start somewhere." Ellis started for the barn.

Ellis and Jeremiah readied their horses and led the way down the trail. *Lord, help me find Ava. Please, keep her safe.*

≈

Angry voices bit into Ava's thoughts, rousing her from what little sleep she'd found. She rolled onto her side and squinted toward the window, barely making out the dark silhouettes of Martin and Keen on the porch.

She slid from the bed, tightening the makeshift belt around her waist to secure the trousers in place as she crept through the shadows toward the conversation.

"We need to split up, Keen." Martin's words rose in volume. "The Daniels are after you, not me. And you'll have an easier time hidin' without the likes of me and Mooney along."

"Mooney feel the same way?" Keen's voice growled through the darkness.

"I don't know, but I reckon he'd like to get home to his family, just the same as me."

"And what if the law finds you, Martin? Folks saw us all at the trial."

"Ain't nobody gonna care 'bout what happened to us with all this Allen news. The only ones who want anything to do with us are the Daniels."

"But what if the law questions you, Martin? 'Bout the whiskey? The killin's? The money?" Ava pressed her eyes closed at his list. What all had they done? For how long? "What'll you do then?"

"I'll lie, of course. Besides, how would we get traced back to the killin's? We covered our tracks with all the whiskey fights. Nobody's gonna do nothin' about them mountain fights. And Dunn? Well, how would anybody find out?"

Dunn? Solomon Dunn? They'd killed him too? Ava pressed her

fist against her mouth, stifling a whimper. All because of whiskey and money?

"Well, then, if I have your word you won't mention my name for the rest of your days, then I reckon you ought to get on down the road then."

"I can. . .just leave?"

Ava didn't catch the reply, but within a few minutes, a set of boots clicked against the front porch and down the steps. Keen didn't move from his place by the window, his cigarette blinking orange in the hazy morning light.

The first slits of dawn brightened the shadowy view into a gray scene, the men slightly more distinct, but not much. Ava eased farther down beside the chest of drawers, peering through a slit between the back of the chest and the wall.

A strange quiet slipped through the room, prompting a chill over Ava's skin. Shuffling from the next room announced Mooney's movements and the launch of her plan. She began to move against the wall back to her bed, when a quick flash from the silhouette at the window froze her in place.

Three cracks fired into the shadows.

A scream lodged in Ava's throat. With an easy glide of his arm, Keen returned his gun to its holster at his hip and took another draw from his cigarette. No remorse. No hesitation. Only the calculated response of a broken, black-hearted villain.

She had no choice but to attempt an escape.

Her eyes pressed closed around the fresh warmth of tears. She hadn't liked Martin, but no one should have this end. . .shot down on the road with the taste of freedom on his lips. She could very well die the same way, but at least she'd choose to die trying to escape and her granny wouldn't be involved.

The front door slammed and boots hit the porch again. "What on earth is goin' on out here?" Mooney's breathless whisper sounded harsh in the morning quiet.

"Martin decided to leave us." Keen straightened from his relaxed position against one of the porch posts. "He didn't get far."

Stillness followed.

"I'm gonna get rid of the body." Keen adjusted his hat and gestured with his head toward the window. "Load up our things and ready the girl. We'll leave as soon as I come back."

Ava's breath shuddered from her lips and she fastened her gaze on the room, the furnishings, the bed and quilt. Sunday, March 17. She should be getting ready to marry her best friend, but instead, she was trying to find a way to survive to see him again.

With quick work, Ava slid to the bed, the light growing enough for her to make out the tree line and path down the south way of the house. Away from Granny's. Toward Cana and the state line. She secured her satchel across her body and turned toward the door just as Mooney swung it open.

He scanned the room and finally looked at her, his expression grim. Without a word, he walked the space of the room, peeking behind the furniture, lifting the pillows. "I see you're ready. That's good." His gaze lifted to hers. " 'Cause he's a loose cannon right now, and you don't want him to fire again this mornin'."

Ava shook her head. "No, I don't."

"Well, let's get ready for him. He'll be back shortly."

He grabbed her by the arm and drew out the hideous rope she'd become accustomed to wearing around her wrists. "Mooney, before you go tyin' me up, could I use the privy? I've been cooped up in that room the whole night, and a girl can only last so long."

With a roll of his eyes and an annoyed growl, Mooney tossed the rope on the table and jerked her out the back door, nearly sending her headfirst off the back steps. "Sorry, Ava. This business with Martin. . . well, it's serious. You realize, it's serious."

She kept her face forward, the outhouse within sight. "How'd you get messed up in all this? You had such good marks in school. You could've gone to college or somethin' else."

His jaw tightened with his hold. "A body'll do about anything when they love someone." He flipped his gaze to hers. "I couldn't let Mama die, and the doctor's bills kept pilin' higher and higher. There wasn't a choice."

She refused to break eye contact with him. "There's always a choice."

He didn't answer, only released a rush of air from his nose and pulled open the privy door, shoving her inside. "Be quick."

The new building carried the scent of fresh-cut wood like the furniture in the house. Faint light trickled in from slits Jeremiah had cut in the roof, covered with a clear plastic-like substance, giving her enough illumination to make out the tiny space.

She adjusted her satchel and counted to ten, replaying her plan in calculated detail in her mind. With a deep breath, she grabbed the handle of the outhouse door and held tight. "Mooney?"

"Yeah."

"The door's stuck. I can't get it to budge."

A groan sounded from the other side. "Shoot fire, woman, you're a heap of trouble, ain't ya?"

She held the door as he pulled, keeping the lock in place until the tug of his strength came with the slightest sound of splintering wood.

"I'm sorry, Mooney," she whispered, sending up a quick prayer.

With a flip of her wrist, she released the door and gave it an extra shove to hit him square in the head. He stumbled back into a heap, moaning and cursing on the ground, and without one bit of hesitation, she set out at a dead run toward the forest.

A crack of gunfire echoed toward her. Distant, but close enough for her to know Keen Gentry wasn't too far behind.

Chapter Twenty-One

*You might have to pull strength up from
your boot strings, but you got it in you.*
Granddaddy Sutphin

"What is this place?" Elmer Williams asked as the horses rounded the bend and Jeremiah's house came into view. "Woowee, it's a sight, ain't it?"

Jeremiah almost grinned. He took a lot of pride in his hard work, in the careful way he'd planned out his and Ava's house. The welcome entrance of the front porch from the road, the dark brick, a rock foundation and fireplace. He brought his horse to a stop, examining the house. Wolf's ears perked and his gray fur rose to attention.

Something was wrong.

Why did Jeremiah smell smoke? His attention rose to the chimney. A faint trail of gray wafted into the morning air. He raised a hand to pause the other riders' approach.

"Someone's been here."

He slid from his horse and reached for his Colt, uncomfortably jammed into his waistband. Wolf released a low growl, likely sensing Jeremiah's tension.

"Whoa, boy," he gentled. "Stay close."

Jeremiah squeezed the grip of the Colt, searching the surrounding forest for any sign of trouble. He rarely carried the gun, because most of the time he preferred his hammer or level over the likes of a weapon, but recent circumstances had left him little choice.

"Ellis, you come with me in the front."

"I'll take the others round back," offered Pink.

"I think one deputy ought to go with Jeremiah and Ellis," Casper said from behind.

"Fine." Pink jerked his chin toward the left side of the house and looked behind him at Elmer. "Come on with me, Elmer, and get your gun ready."

Fresh boot prints marked the road, with one set leaving a deep groove behind it as if it dragged something away from the house and into the woods. Jeremiah's pulse ratcheted up a few paces. Something or. . .someone? No! He couldn't think that way. With Ellis directly behind him and Casper bringing up the rear, Jeremiah opened the door, gun at the ready.

The main room sat empty, with morning light filtering through the large windows he'd installed to celebrate the view and usher in the warmth of the sun. Empty bean cans lay scattered across the table. Furniture stood askew in the wrong places. An old shirt splayed in a dirty bundle by the fireplace, but otherwise the room was empty.

The kitchen proved the same way. Plundered, but vacant.

"Ain't been too long since someone was here, 'Miah," came Ellis's voice from across the room. He bent low, hand moving near the ashes. "Maybe an hour?"

Wolf whimpered from the back of the house, followed by a strange scratching sound. Jeremiah looked at Ellis and then rushed to the noise. Wolf stood with his nose down, his paw scratching at Jeremiah's bedroom door. That wasn't warning behavior. Wolf smelled a friend. Jeremiah's pulse jumped into a gallop and he shoved open the door.

Quiet and empty, the room looked exactly as it had when Jeremiah left it a week ago. Dust floated in pale sunrays streaming through the window onto the bed. His breath seized.

The bed.

He'd left the quilt covering the bed, readied for his return with his bride, but someone had rolled up the quilt and tied it with a. . .ribbon? A red ribbon! Ava! She'd been here?

Jeremiah turned back to Ellis. "Would you check the loft and see what damage is done there? See if Casper will go with you."

Ellis looked from Jeremiah to the quilt and nodded, turning to disappear back into the main room. Wolf sniffed the perimeter of the bedroom and found a filthy, soiled dress tucked between the dresser and window.

Jeremiah picked up the clothes, still damp. Sure 'nough. She'd been here. And not too long ago either. He released a sigh and approached the bed. At least she'd been alive then.

His palm slipped over the bumps and bends of the quilt, an unexpected warmth rising into his vision. *Oh God, where is she?* As his fingers moved over the ribbon, something caught his attention. Ridges within the ribbon. A paler red thread. He glanced behind him to the bedroom door and then tugged the ribbon free.

A strange design, in a lighter shade of red, appeared sewn into the silky cloth of the ribbon. What was it?

Words.

He walked to the window to use its light for a better examination of some crude markings within the thread. *South. Creek. Keen. Danger.*

Keen had her? Heat soared through his body, surging every muscle with energy, purpose. He fisted the ribbon and looked down at Wolf. "It's time to find her, boy. Now."

He marched from the room and met Casper and Ellis. "They've traveled south toward the creek."

"How do you know?" Casper took off his bowler and dusted it against his hip. "And who are 'they'?"

"Keen has Ava. I don't know why, but she's headed south, and that's the way I'm going."

"Keen?" Ellis's forehead crinkled.

"Keen Gentry, if I guess right," Casper answered, cramming his hat back on his head and rubbing a palm over his chin. "Are you sure about this, Jeremiah? Why would Keen Gentry take Ava?"

"At the present, I don't care. All I want to do is find her." Jeremiah started for the door, Wolf on his heels. "You don't have to come."

Jeremiah met Elmer and Pink around the corner of the house.

"We found a trail leading southeast through the woods, by the outhouse."

A gunshot interrupted Jeremiah's reply, the sound echoing from a distant place down the trail. A splash of cold shot through his chest. Ava! How far away was the shot? He couldn't tell. Was he too late?

"Found some blood on the bushes near the outhouse," Elmer added. "Someone's wounded."

"What d'ya say we split up?" Casper stepped forward and looked toward the woods. "Elmer and I can go down the forest trail, and you,

Ellis, and Pink can see to the southeasterly one. If you find someone wounded, you'll need the extra hand."

Had Ava meant southeast? Both trails led toward the creek. Had she been wounded?

"I have some rope and extra cloth over by the barn I'm building." Jeremiah walked to the half-built structure, the others following. "And a canteen or two you can fill up with water from the springhouse yonder, if you want."

"'Preciate it, Jeremiah." Elmer took one of the canteens, disappearing with Pink toward the springhouse.

"There's a good rope yonder, Casp." Jeremiah pointed to a hook above their heads. "If you catch Keen, he won't be likely to wiggle out of that one."

"I don't think Keen's gonna go with us without a fight." Casper squinted over at him. "Better to have your gun than some twine."

"I'd think after all the killin' we've been privy to lately, your stomach would be full up of it."

Casper shook his head and sighed, reaching for the rope. As he struggled to unwind the rope from its place, the white skin of his wrist shone between his glove and his sleeve. Jeremiah blinked. What was that? A marking in a strange reddish-brown hue curved into the shape of a hook on his wrist. *A fish hook.*

"Are you all right, 'Miah?" Ellis stepped up beside him. "You look white as a ghost."

The rope came forward, and Casper locked eyes with Jeremiah, some unspoken understanding passing between them. How much did Casper suspect Jeremiah knew? If anything?

"I'm just worried about Ava, so the sooner we get on the trail, the sooner I can get her home."

Casper raised a brow and looped the rope over his shoulder. "Then let's get on with the hunt."

Jeremiah held the man's gaze for a few seconds longer and then led the way up the path to the southeast, glancing back down the hill only long enough to watch Casper and Elmer disappear through the forest trail below. There was no way to know if he was taking the right path or not, but if that blood was Ava's, he couldn't risk waiting another minute to find her.

Jeremiah's throat constricted as he cast one last glance down the hillside. Casper Norris killed Ava's father.

What would he do to someone who knew his secret?

~≈~

She'd stopped to rest too soon.

Barely had Ava tied a red ribbon to the trunk of a tree, then a rifle shot echoed through the forest and the bullet split the bark off a nearby trunk. She slid down to the mossy ground, still damp from all the rain, reprimanding herself. How could she have been so foolish to stop at the edge of a clearing? But the ribbon would be easier to see here, the vibrant color noticeable among the surrounding browns and greens, and Jeremiah needed some clue which direction she'd gone across the creek, assuming he came. She pinched her eyes closed. Surely, he'd understand her clue she left behind. He'd try to find her, if he could.

She searched the forest for Keen. If he was any kind of shot like her daddy, he could be as far as a thousand yards away. Crouching low, she took off again, down the hillside toward the river, slipping between rocky outcroppings as much as possible to avoid being seen. Years of tracking with her father lightened her step, and wearing trousers certainly helped.

Keen may be a good shot, but she had the advantage of youth and speed on him. If she needed to, she could outlast him. She had already been on the run for nigh four hours, if the sun gave any indication, and had rested only a few times within that span of time. She'd fill her canteen at the river and keep moving long enough to get her bearings, find a place to hide, or—she drew in a deep breath—die in the process.

She wasn't sure how long she kept traveling beyond the river. Her body ached with a combination of soreness and scratches, her palms bloodied, her hair loose. She had to be closing in on a road or a house soon, surely.

Dark clouds shadowed the light, giving off the hint of early evening. When she crested the next ridge, she caught sight of a road below, a sizable one from the looks of it. Still a far way off, but if she kept at her pace, she'd likely get there by dusk. A road meant people. And help.

The snap of a twig came from behind.

She froze, alert. The forest whispered with an unnatural silence, an alert stillness. The scent of tobacco drifted over a breeze. She took a few steps forward, her footfall barely more than a murmur against the backdrop of the mossy earth, a skill her father had taught her. Heel to toe. Light step.

Another snap crunched nearby and sounded as if it came from the other side of the rocky cleft behind her. She darted in the opposite direction, turning to look back, only to run directly into a pair of strong, unyielding arms. A scream lodged in her throat.

"Ava Burcham? What on earth are you doin' out here?"

Ava looked up into the face of Sid Allen. As his gaze slid down her, his brows rose. "And in men's trousers?"

Her breath shocked out of her in a sob and she buried her face into his shoulder.

"Good lord, girl." He stood stiff as a board and patted her shoulder. "Come on over to camp and get out of sight before one of those detectives shows up and pretends to know what he's doin'."

He gestured her through the crevice of a rock face, which looked like it came to a dead end, but just before the wall, the rock bent to show a narrow crevice leading to a small, grassy opening surrounded by boulders on all sides.

Wesley Edwards sat by an ash fire, a cast-iron skillet resting on the heat with beef giving off the slightest sizzle. He stood to his feet, pulling his cap off his head as if Ava were a high-class lady instead of a filthy, bloodied runaway in men's clothes.

"Ava Burcham's gonna tell us a story 'bout why she's dressed in trousers." Sid gestured for her to sit down on a rock by the fire, his eyes needling for an answer. "And what sort of trouble's brought her all the way out here with some courthouse outlaws."

<hr>

Jeremiah looked down the hillside path from which they'd come, the roof of his house barely visible now. Wolf continued a steady push forward, sniffing the ground, leading them farther up. He smelled something. . .or someone.

Ellis had kept his comments short, his gaze fixed ahead, his pistol in hand, as he came up last. Pink stayed by Jeremiah's side, glancing back every little while, as if he wasn't too sure of their direction either.

"This all is crazy round here. All this Allen mess," Pink murmured, shaking his head, the birthmark on his face brightening under the exertion of the climb.

"It's changed a lot of lives, for sure," Jeremiah added, studying Wolf as he stopped to sniff the ground.

"And took a few too." Pink pulled off his fedora and rubbed at his red hair before returning the hat.

Wolf started moving again. Jeremiah followed. "I was sorry to hear about Sheriff Webb. He was a good man."

"Sure 'nough. He was."

The last conversation Jeremiah had with Webb came back to mind. "Pink, you mind if I ask you a question about Joe Creed?"

Pink hesitated in his steps then continued on. "Sure can, but I ain't sure I'll know the answer."

"Sheriff Webb said you were on watch the night Joe died—"

"Wait, now." Pink's palms came up. "I already told the sheriff that I didn't leave my post one time the whole night. And that's the truth."

"Of course you didn't." Jeremiah nodded, watching Pink's response. Someone had to have seen or known something. "But did anything odd happen? Did you see anyone else?"

"A few of the boys came by, as usual. We talked a bit, but none of 'em went back to the cell." He chuckled. "One of 'em brought me some of the worst coffee I ever drank in my life. I ain't never askin' Casp to make coffee again."

Jeremiah paused and slid a glance to Ellis, who seemed to catch his concern.

"Casper Norris ain't the coffee makin' kind?" Ellis offered, easing into the conversation to help distract Pink, if Jeremiah knew anything about his cousin.

"No, sirree, and it didn't help to keep me awake a'tall. Most times, a few cups of coffee will get me through the night shift, but not that night."

"No?"

"I reckon I'd worked a few too many late nights in a row." Pink's shoulders slumped. "It was an awful thing, about Creed. If I'd been awake, maybe I'd've heard him tryin' to hurt hisself. That's my regret." His pale gaze came up to Jeremiah. "But I swear, I ain't never been so tired in all my living days."

Jeremiah caught Ellis's look.

"About that coffee, Pink." Ellis moved closer to Pink. Ah, the lawyer at work. "Can you remember what it tasted like?"

"Course, I can. It was awful. Bitter taste. Nothin' like any coffee I'd ever had before. Who knows how old the awful stuff was."

At that moment, Wolf released a yelp and burst into a run. Jeremiah set off after him with Ellis and Pink on his heels. Within about two hundred feet, Wolf pounced on something that looked like a pile of clothes, followed by a man's cry.

"Help! No!"

Pink leveled his pistol with Ellis by his side, but instead of a vicious fugitive, they found Mooney Childers with a bloodstained shoulder, curled up in a ball as Wolf acted like he'd tear him apart. The dog pulled on the man's pants leg, keeping up a fierce growl.

"Down, boy."

As if he'd been playing along the whole time, Wolf looked down at the crouching Mooney and released another yelp for good measure, causing the man to cry out again. Jeremiah grinned. His dog sure knew how to show off.

Pink grabbed Mooney and jerked him up, the wounded man crying out again at the sudden movement.

"What're you doin' out here, Mooney Childers?"

"I'm runnin' away from Keen." Mooney's dirty face streaked with tears. "He's gone crazy. Got the Daniels clan after us. I didn't mean for this to happen. I swear I didn't."

"What to happen?" Pink's voice took on a hardened edge, and he gave Mooney a shake.

"Keen. He. . .he done killed Martin, and I think Zeb Daniels too. It was only supposed to help our business. That's all." He whimpered, his face scrunched into a dozen dirty wrinkles, his hair a matted mess against his head. "It wasn't supposed to be like this."

"Like what?" Jeremiah stepped forward. "It have something to do with Joe Creed's death? And whiskey?"

Mooney's eyes widened into dark saucers and he sniffled. "It was only for the business, see? And Joe was gonna squeal on us. Gopher couldn't let him do that. Not after he'd worked so hard to build it."

"So Keen killed him?"

Mooney nodded and looked over at Pink. "The boys bragged about knockin' you out on duty. Said you snored like a bear and didn't hear a thing."

Pink tightened his hold on the shirt, inciting a wince from Mooney. "What else?"

"Dunn saw Keen and Gopher talkin' outside the jailhouse that night, so. . ." He hesitated, groaning. "So me, Keen, Martin, and Zeb went to find Dunn and quiet him." He looked up. "But I didn't kill him. Martin and Keen did the work. I just drove the buggy."

"What was Joe Creed gonna confess? What did he have on you?" This from Ellis.

"Gopher and the boys were skimmin' off the top from the work we was doin' for the Daniels, and Gopher'd started takin' some of the Daniels' prime customers for himself so he could collect more of the money without the Daniels knowin'." Mooney sniffled again. "If Creed told about it, we wouldn't have to worry about the law finding us. The Daniels would have got to us first. But then Keen killed Zeb, and that sent the Daniels after us anyhow, 'cept they think Keen's the one who did all of it."

"But he's not." Ellis looked to Jeremiah and back to Mooney. "It's this Gopher fella?"

Mooney's eyes widened as if he'd realized his mistake.

"Who is he, Mooney?" Jeremiah closed in, his voice tinged with enough anger that Wolf responded with a much more sinister growl than he'd used a few minutes before. "Who is Gopher?"

Mooney pinched his lips closed, his chin blotched from the effort, his face reddening.

Jeremiah's stomach tightened. The mark on his wrist. The odd warnings about the Creeds. The deputy that brought Pink the coffee.

"My dog will be happy to loosen your tongue, Mooney." Jeremiah gestured with his chin toward Wolf. "And this time, he won't be as nice."

Mooney looked from Wolf to Jeremiah and back, then whimpered out the confession Jeremiah already knew. "Casper Norris. He's Gopher. He's the one who started it all."

Jeremiah locked eyes with Ellis. Casper Norris. The manipulator who'd murdered several men, betrayed a clan of mountain bootleggers, and covered his tracks with a badge. And now, Jeremiah had just sent the man who killed Ava's father in Ava's likely direction with a half hour lead.

"Go!" Ellis waved toward the slope leading back the way they'd come. "I'll help Pink get Mooney to your house. We gotta keep him alive as a witness. Take Wolf and go!"

Without hesitation, Jeremiah set off down the hillside, Wolf at his side.

"Find Ava, Wolf." Wolf's ears perked, and Jeremiah leaned down to him, drawing the red ribbon that had been wrapped around his quilt out of his pocket. He scratched the dog's head and offered the ribbon for Wolf to smell. Wolf licked the cloth and whimpered. "That's right, boy. Find Ava before it's too late."

Chapter Twenty-Two

Don't underestimate coincidences.
I've found a way to live my life off of 'em.
Granddaddy Sutphin

"That's all we need to do, then?" Wesley stood after Ava finished telling them everything she'd heard and all that had happened from the time she'd awakened in Keen's buggy after the courthouse shooting. "Get Keen to confess that he started the ruckus at the courthouse and then we can go back home."

Sid sighed and rested his elbows on his knees. "He never said he started it, Wes. And there's no way to prove it unless someone saw him fire that shot." Sid sighed again. "No, the law's out for us. They've already found us guilty. Until things calm down, we can't go back home."

Wesley threw his cap against the ground and paced away from the fire.

He was about the same age as Ava. Lost his daddy early on too.

"Have you had a hard time out here?"

"Naw, this is the first night we've slept outside. Every other night one friend or other's offered to keep us, despite the threat of the law. They know we aren't guilty of the charges against us. Though I'm no fan of being idle." Sid's smile crooked and he reached into a nearby bag. "I've found that runnin' from the law makes a man about as idle as they come. We've seen the detectives a few times, watched 'em walk right past us in their manhunt." He chuckled and pinned her with a look. "Could've shot a few without 'em even knowin' what hit 'em, if I wanted to."

She looked away from him, fingering the strap of her satchel.

"But I ain't that kind of man, Ava." He pulled an apple from his bag and passed it to her. "There're plenty of things I'm guilty of. Plenty of things I'll be accountable for in the hereafter. But starting a massacre at the courthouse? That's not one of 'em. Not for any of the Allens, I'd say."

"It won't matter, will it? Uncle Floyd had a fixed jury from the outset." Wesley slumped down on the rock again. "They'll make sure he has a fixed jury again, I'd wager. They'll see him in the electric chair for every last dead man in that courthouse, if they have their way."

"The papers say we conspired to shoot up the courthouse all along. Do you believe that?" Sid's gaze rose to hers, but he didn't wait for an answer. "If that was the case, do you think we woulda done such a sorry job of it?"

Her grin twitched. "No."

The thought of the results of the Allen clan actually *planning* a massacre sent a chill up her spine. She'd already heard rumors of what happened to a man who'd killed one of the Allens in cold blood years ago. A mob murder without one person being tried for the death. No, if they'd planned to shoot up the courthouse, they'd have come much more prepared.

She took a bite of the apple, her empty stomach growling with gratitude. With a slight hesitation, she turned back to Sid. "You didn't shoot anyone in the courthouse?"

He studied her a moment, his piercing blue eyes measuring her. "Truth be told, if I could have killed Dexter Goad, I would have. I tried, but I didn't want to see no one else harmed. Judge Massie was a friend to the Allens, and we had no cause against Sheriff Webb. We weren't too keen on Foster but wouldn't have wasted time to shoot at him without a reason."

"I only shot at the men who was shootin' at me or my kin," Wesley interrupted, snatching his cap from the ground and shoving it back on his head. "That's called self-defense."

"Shh." Sid raised a palm to his nephew and tilted his head toward their rock-fortress entrance. "I think we got company, and I've been thinkin' up a plan for catchin' us a fox."

❧

Ava stood just behind the broad shoulders of Sid Allen as a shadow moved from the crevice in the rock. Keen Gentry emerged, his hat low and his Colt up. No doubt, he hadn't expected to come face-to-face with Sid Allen and a pistol, but Keen only gave his surprise away for a second before his expression flashed back to neutral except for a slight curve of his lips.

"Well, well, looks like I've found one of our local outlaws."

"Sounds like I could say the same about you." Sid's cadence failed to match the tension in his stance.

"I wouldn't believe everything Ava Burcham has to say." Keen's dark gaze moved over Sid's shoulder to Ava. "You know where she came from."

Ava fisted the strap of her satchel, her muscles flinching at the implication.

"I do. In fact, I considered her daddy a friend."

"It isn't takin' after her daddy that bothers me." Keen shifted a step to the right, pistol directed toward pistol.

"Well, she's got enough of her daddy in her to survive three days of your hospitality and outrun you for a good five miles."

Keen grunted and stopped his approach, tilted his head in examination. "Why don't you give her on over to me, Sid? Then we can be on our way, and you on yourn. 'Cause you don't want to die over some unwanted girl with half a mind."

"I don't plan on dyin' over anybody, today, if I can help it."

With those words, Wesley rushed from behind Keen and gripped him in a hold while Sid moved forward and disarmed him. Ava ran forward with a rope Sid had given her, and though Keen fought to free himself, he was soon crouched against a rock, arms tied behind him and looking much less vicious than he had a few moments before.

"What do you say we restock our armory, Wesley?" Sid handed Keen's pistol to Wes, who tucked it in his belt and proceeded to sift through Keen's jacket.

Sid slid Keen's other pistol into the pocket of his jacket and then examined an envelope with cash money inside. "Well, lookie here. Wonder what you've done to get such a healthy pay."

"Ain't none of your business," Keen spat out.

Ava rounded Sid to stare down into the face of her captor. "You told Martin and Mooney that you didn't have no money to pay them."

His grin turned ruthless. "What they don't know. . ."

"And what about this?" Sid pulled a gold pocket watch from another hidden place in Keen's jacket and examined the item. He whistled. "This is somethin' fine, 'cept for the little chip here in the corner." The shopkeeper emerged as he examined the piece, holding it up to catch some of the late afternoon light. "Mechanical. Tourbillon, even. Don't see many of these types in our parts." He narrowed his eyes at Keen. "Doesn't quite seem your style, Keen."

Ava peered over at the strangely familiar watch as Sid lowered it, her gaze catching on the tiny dent in the otherwise perfect circle. Her pulse skipped up a beat or two. Sid popped the watch open. The inside revealed roman numerals surrounding a center open to the mechanics of the watch and a tiny crescent moon marking the side near the roman numeral III. She knew this watch.

"Looks like this belonged to someone else, unless you're goin' by a false name." Sid ran his thumb over the back of the watch. "Steal this from a gent in town? 'Cause these initials ain't yours."

Ava couldn't take her attention from the watch, the truth rising like a clearing fog, closing off the air in her throat.

Sid squinted at the watch. "A.B.?"

Abraham Burcham. A whimper slipped between her pressed lips. Her daddy.

A sudden fire coursed through her chest and into her limbs. Her thoughts blurred, whirred with memories. She jerked the pistol from Sid's pocket and pointed it directly at Keen's face, the shiny end of the pistol shaking like the rest of Ava's body.

"You. . .you killed my daddy."

Keen merely shook his head, a sneer twisting his lips. "I didn't even know your daddy."

"Ava, honey." She barely heard Sid's voice brewing beneath the rush in her ears.

"Not only have you dragged me through the woods, half starving me for three days, planning on killin' me, but you killed my daddy." She leveled the gun on him, closer.

"I've killed a lot of people." Keen's expression barely flickered with her accusation. "Can name 'em all. Your daddy ain't one of 'em."

A darkness hovered in her mind, a fury taking hold. One man's choice initiated a destruction of her family. Stealing her daddy's life, then causing an avalanche that took her brother and mother away. *This* man. This vile, horrible, murderous man. The heat fell away. Her body cooled, steadied. . .numbed. He deserved to die.

"Ava, put down the gun—"

Her thumb reached for the hammer, slowly clicking it back. "Why do you have his watch if you ain't the one who shot him dead?"

Keen's eyes widened. "I got it as part of payment for a job I done." His voice had lost some of its steadiness. "That's all. Payment. I don't know nothin' else about it."

"Payment from who?" He was lying. He'd murdered others. Why not her father?

"Knowing who it was ain't gonna change—"

She hit him across the face with the pistol, pain slicing up her hand. "Who?"

"I think she's serious, Keen." Sid's words came through the roaring in her ears. "And if she was smart, she'd shoot you in the stomach so you'd die slow and painful-like."

Ava lowered the pistol a few inches at Sid's suggestion.

"All right. Fine." Keen growled, shoulders dropping in accession. "I got it from Casper Norris."

Casper Norris?

"As payment for killin' Joe Creed."

The admission knocked breath from her in a gasp.

Casper Norris? Ava blinked against the contradiction. The deputy? He'd paid Keen to kill Joe? Casper Norris? *He'd* killed her daddy?

"Ava, put the gun down." Sid's voice emerged into her thoughts. "There ain't no goin' back once you pull that trigger."

The visions of her daddy's dyin' face, her brother's gasping breaths, blended into a dizzying fury through her. Keen deserved to die. He'd hurt so many. She'd carried the cost of his actions, the scars, for years.

Her fingers wrapped more tightly around the gun, the trigger cool beneath her skin.

"You are not your mother." The phrase whispered through the murky madness in her mind. *"You belong to Me."* She blinked as tears invaded

her vision. *"I give you a future and a hope."*

Hope. The word anchored her spinning thoughts. Jeremiah's face came into view among the dark memories. The brick house he'd built for them. Her granny's words of. . .hope. Ava released a shaky breath and lowered the pistol. No, she wasn't her mother.

"Good girl." Sid reached over and plucked the gun from her hand, his gaze intent upon her face. "Good girl." He returned the gun to his pocket. "I think it's time you find your way back home." He turned to Wesley. "Let's pack up. You know where we're stayin' tonight."

Wesley moved to collect their supplies.

"You plan to turn me in?" Keen directed his question toward Sid, his pallor returning to normal, along with his smirk. "Because I'd like to see one outlaw turnin' in another."

"If the Daniels are huntin' you, Keen, there's nothin' else I need to do." Sid slung his pack on his shoulder and shrugged. " 'Cause you can be sure they won't show the mercy Miss Burcham gave you."

Sid nudged Ava toward the crevice in the rock, Wesley following.

"Wait. You gonna just leave me here?" Keen called, struggling to stand. "With my hands tied and no way to protect myself?"

Sid looked back at Ava, as if waiting for her response. She almost smiled at the irony. Arms tied with rope? No weapon? Captive in the forest? Yes, it sounded familiar.

She cast a look at him before disappearing through the crevice. "Don't worry, Keen, you won't be alone too long. When I get to Hillsville, I'll make sure to let the law know what you've done and where to find you."

≈

The sound of the river reached him long before he saw the whitecaps swelled from the recent rain. He followed the tracks toward the water, the rocky shoreline coming into view, and then he stopped. Wolf slowed his pace, doubling back to check on Jeremiah, but Jeremiah's focus landed on a motionless shape lying among the rocks at the river's edge. Water covered the lower half of the body, but from the man's torso up, he lay on dry ground.

Jeremiah closed his eyes for half a second, knowing who he'd find before he even reached the man. Wolf edged closer along with Jeremiah, his nose raised, sniffing the air. Elmer Williams lay still and pale, a bloodstain down the right side of his shirt disappearing beneath his jacket. He lay on his side, no sign of life, and Jeremiah leaned closer, pulling the jacket back enough to see the extent of the blood.

At the slight jostle of his jacket, the man grunted.

Air burst from Jeremiah's lungs. "Elmer?" He gave the man's jacket another little tug. "You're alive?"

"The rascal shot me in the back," Elmer muttered as he opened his eyes. "I knew I didn't like him for a reason, and this proves it."

Jeremiah grabbed Elmer and pulled him out of the water to a sitting position. "He has a track record long enough to impress my granddaddy Sutphin."

Elmer released a weak chuckle. "That's sayin' somethin' for sure."

"I think he's on Ava's trail too. Hold on, Elmer, let's get you farther away from the river." Jeremiah placed his arms around the man's chest from behind and pulled him back toward the woods, propping him against a tree. "I think we're about a mile from the main road, east. I can get help there."

"You need to find Ava first, boy." Elmer reached into his jacket pocket and pulled out a small flask, raising it with a grin. "I'll just wait here till you get back."

"Elmer—"

"No, son." His voice softened. "You need to get that girl before somethin' worse happens. I already thought I was left for dead." He adjusted his body against the tree and winced. "I've made my peace."

"Stay alive, Elmer. I'm coming back for you." Jeremiah shook off his jacket and wrapped it over the man's chest, holding his gaze. "I promise."

Elmer's eyes crinkled into deeper ridges at the corners. "You're a good boy, Jeremiah Sutphin. Good boy." He gave Jeremiah a weak shove. "Now go get your gal. Norris ain't got more than a half hour lead on you, but you can cut the distance if you hurry."

He gave Elmer's shoulder a pat and scanned the area, trying to hold the landmarks in his mind for later. Wolf looked up at him, as if waiting for direction. If Ava crossed the creek, then her scent would be lost in the water. The closing dusk dimmed his clarity, but then he saw it. A red ribbon, dangling over the creek near a narrow forest path by a rock outcropping on the other side. Jeremiah almost laughed. He loved a clever woman. Not that he doubted her cleverness before, but this proved it all the more. Jeremiah looked down at the creek, then to Wolf, and marched forward into the icy water.

Elmer had said Casper was a half hour ahead. He had to move fast. With Casper's track record, every second mattered.

Chapter Twenty-Three

*Life might come with a heap o' sour, but it only takes
a teaspoon of love to sweeten up the bitterest taste.*
Granny Burcham

The main road's half a mile thata way." Sid gestured with his hat in the direction of a more well-trodden path through the woods. "This is as far as we ought to go if we don't want to see some trouble."

Ava turned and gave the man a hug. "Thank you so much, Mr. Allen."

He stiffened but gave her a little pat before nudging her back a step. "I'd want someone to take care of my girls if they were in trouble. Just doin' the same, especially since your daddy can't be here."

She swiped her hand over her eyes to dry the tears and nodded. "He'd have been much obliged."

"Luke and Laura Spence live 'bout a half mile up the main road once you get to it." He held her gaze. "Tell 'em I sent you. They'll be happy to help you out."

"Thank you again. So much." She moved back a few steps, glancing over at the darkening path.

"Hey, don't I get a hug too?" Wesley wiggled his brows, cocking his head in playful camaraderie.

"Act like you got some sense, boy. Look what happened the last time you went sparkin' on the wrong girl." Sid turned his gaze back to Ava. "This one's a mighty fine pick, but I have a notion her heart's already called for."

Ava's vision blurred with her smile. *And today should have been my wedding day.* "It is."

His entire expression softened into a smile. "Well, get on your way then, Ava Burcham."

She took a few steps. "Wait, Ava."

She pivoted back around, and Sid walked forward. "Folks like

Keen and Casper Norris ain't the only ones to watch out for round here at night." He placed a pistol in her palm. "For your protection." He winked. "You gotta get home to that boy of yours."

She looked from him to Wesley, put the pistol in her satchel, and nodded. "Thank you again. I hope. . .I hope y'all can find your way home again soon too."

He hesitated, as if he was going to say something, but then touched the brim of his hat in silent salute, and the two of them disappeared into the forest. Ava stared at their shrinking frames until the darkening forest took them from view. She only had, at most, an hour of fading daylight left, and even its faint glow failed to give sufficient light to the path ahead.

Katydids and crickets competed for volume, as if they'd missed making their music all winter and were finally free to perform a full serenade. She quickened her pace through the shadowy wood. In only a few hours, she could see Jeremiah again. Her pulse skittered. If he was alive. *Oh Lord, please let him be alive.*

Wouldn't she know down deep in her heart somewhere if he'd died? Wouldn't she feel the loss to her core? He'd gotten shot trying to save her, putting her safety before his own. Then there was the whole kidnapping scheme and Martin's death and. . . She sighed. Trouble truly seemed to follow her.

She was lost in thought when someone gripped her from behind, his arms like bands across her chest, squeezing until she could barely breathe.

"Did you really think I hadn't cut my way out of ropes before?" His whiskey-laced words breathed a putrid odor against her cheek. "And you can be sure I checked to make sure your Allen friends are nowhere to be seen."

Keen.

She reached for her satchel, but he grabbed her hand and twisted it up behind her until she cried out.

"You've shamed me for the last time." He slammed her against the nearest tree, the sudden impact stealing her breath and reigniting the ache in her head.

A blast of fury shot energy through her and she thrust her knee upward with as much force as she could muster. He grunted and bent forward, but just as she began to twist loose of him, his hold tightened again, thrusting her back with added force against the tree. The impact stunned her long enough for him to tighten a rope around her chest, arms trapped at her side, her satchel hitting her at the hip. She attempted to slip her hand into the folds of her bag, but Keen hit her across the face, blurring her vision.

"I've been waiting for this moment," he murmured as he rounded the tree, likely to knot the ends of the rope together. Ava wiggled the slightest bit, her fingers barely making their way over the lip of her satchel and into its folds without him noticing. "I'd contemplated just shootin' you outright." He returned to face her, his spit splattering her face as he spoke and his dark eyes gleaming like two sinister orbs. "But you deserve a little more personal treatment for all the trouble you've caused."

Her fingers slipped around the metal of the pistol, but with her arms pinned at her sides, she wasn't sure how to aim to make an impact. He'd knotted the ropes so tightly, she could barely catch her breath. She pressed her back as far against the tree as possible in an attempt to draw air into her lungs. *Lord, are You here? Even here?*

"A little something your friends didn't find." He slipped his hand down into his boot and drew out a knife. "And in honor of all the trouble you've caused me, I've decided to take killin' you nice and slow." The knife flashed in his hand, and he slid the blade down her cheek. "One slice at a time."

She stared back at him, holding her expression immobile. She would not give him the satisfaction of seeing her fear, of knowing he had power over her. "You think killin' me is gonna make you feel better?"

"Sure is." And without warning, he jabbed the knife blade into her shoulder.

She cried out and nearly dropped her hold on the pistol.

"Hmm. . .that seemed to make a point, didn't it?" He chuckled at his pun and brought the knife back to her cheek, smearing her own blood against her skin. "What should I hit next? A finger? An ear?"

He lifted the blade toward her face, and with a little turn of her wrist upward, she pulled the trigger. The gun fired and shook from her hand. Keen howled and stumbled back, reaching for his knee. Ava took the distraction to struggle against the ropes, a slight give offering a little hope that Keen's handiwork came with more speed than skill.

A string of curses rose from him and he rebrandished the knife. "So, I reckon you want me to remove your shootin' hand then, don't ya?"

Ava struggled against the loosening ropes when another gunshot cracked the darkness. Keen paused in midstep, his gaze wide, and reached for his side. Had the Allens returned to help her?

A figure sauntered forward from the dusk-hewn path, slowly.

Keen raised his knife toward the man, but another shot rang out, buckling Keen to the ground. Then the figure emerged into recognition, fedora at a fashionable tilt, and a grin to chill Ava to the core.

Casper Norris. What. . .what was happening?

"You. . .you've killed me," Keen gasped, grasping for the pistol that had fallen to the ground a few feet away.

Casper shot at Keen's hand, the ground near his fingers bulging from the impact of the bullet. Keen curled his fingers back. "Why?"

"I said no loose ends." Casper kept his face forward, his profile unreadable. "No trace."

"I'll disappear." Even as he spoke, Keen slipped closer to the ground. "She's our only witness."

"Is she?" Casper's attention flipped to Ava, and without moving his gaze from hers, he shot two last bullets into Keen until his body slumped lifeless to the ground.

Casper stepped closer to her, searching her face. "*Now*, you're our only witness." He released a sigh and tipped the brim of his hat up slightly as he closed in. "It's a shame we've come to this, Ava. A real shame."

"Is it?" Her mind whirled, searching for a plan. She'd loosened the ropes enough that they'd slid slightly down her arms. The pistol she'd dropped lay at her feet. Not that reaching it would help her much, with a sharpshooter like Casper around.

"Sure is. I like you and Jeremiah, but you're both too meddlesome for my good."

How could she keep the man talking? Distracted? Buy time?

"After all this time. You're the one who killed my daddy?"

It only took a second for his expression to recover from surprise. "I didn't figure Keen's tongue was so loose."

"I saw Daddy's watch."

He eased his way toward her, head tilted in study. "You're a clever one, ain't ya. Seems you're followin' in your daddy's footsteps in more ways than one." He slowly shook his head, edging nearer in the fading light. "Wrong place. Wrong time."

"That's what happened with Daddy? He came up on a deal gone bad?"

Casper shook his head in mock disappointment. "Puts me in an awful predicament for making tough choices."

"If you hadn't killed people, you wouldn't have to make this choice."

He grinned and wiped the back of his palm across his smile. "Point made, but it's too late now." He shrugged a shoulder and raised his gun. "I have to kill you. Blame it all on Keen—or the Allens, if I want—and then get back to my work without anyone knowing otherwise."

"The truth always comes out."

He raised a brow. "Maybe, but not soon enough for you, Ava."

She closed her eyes, bracing for the impact. *The Lord is a mighty one to save. He will quiet me with His love. Oh Lord, help me.*

But instead of a gunshot, the sound of a growl swelled from down the dark trail like an echoing round of thunder. The crooked deputy turned toward the eerie noise. A flash of white and gray rushed forward at high speed. Furry. Large. A coyote? Ava squinted, her breath shaking out on a sob. *Wolf?*

Casper aimed his gun at the approaching form.

No! Taking advantage of Casper's distraction and her loosening bonds, Ava kicked forward, sending Casper off-balance just as his gun went off. He stumbled and nearly fell, but within seconds Wolf attacked him.

He screamed, raising his hands to struggle against the dog. Out of her periphery another movement came into view. A gait and silhouette she knew as well as her own name.

"Jeremiah!"

He rushed forward, jerking Casper's gun from his hand and

assisting Wolf in pinning the villain to the ground. Ava shook free of the rope and brought it with her to join Jeremiah.

"Use this." She pushed the rope forward, locking eyes with him for a second. He was alive. Whole. Here.

His gaze roamed over her face, as if his thoughts weren't too different from her own.

With a nod, he took the rope, and between the two of them, they secured Casper, who looked much the worse for wear after Wolf's thorough defense. Ava dropped to her knees, and the dog whined against her, licking her face as if he thought she might have been a goner too.

"Good boy." She buried her face in his fur.

Lantern light shone ahead, revealing a large group of men approaching on horseback. Ava reached down for the discarded pistol, keeping it by her side this time instead of making the mistake as she'd done before by putting it in her satchel.

Wolf released a warning growl.

"It's okay, Wolf." Jeremiah met Ava's gaze as he tightened his hold on Casper. "It's the posse."

"The posse?"

He nodded. "The detectives out to catch the Allens, but tonight?" He looked up at them and nodded. "Tonight, we'll give them a different outlaw to talk about with their newspaper buddies."

It took several minutes to share the story of what had transpired over the past few days, Ava conveniently leaving out her encounter with Sid Allen and Wesley Edwards.

They learned from the posse leader that they'd come into contact with Pink and Ellis on the main road with Mooney. Pink sent them in this general direction, in hopes of catching Casper or Keen along the way.

The gunshots had alerted the posse to their location.

Jeremiah gladly gave Casper over to the posse's authority and turned to Ava. She buried her head in his chest, ignoring the pain in her shoulder, needing Jeremiah's warmth and presence, embracing the feel of him whole and alive.

He rested his head against hers, allowing the silence and their embrace a moment's comfort.

"Casper killed my daddy." Her admission shook from her.

Jeremiah's hold tightened. "I learnt that too." He pulled back. "I'm sorry you had to find it out on your own."

The tension in her face relaxed. "I wasn't alone. Not really."

He raised a brow but didn't ask her to elaborate. She'd tell him about Sid and Wesley later, when other ears weren't close enough to eavesdrop. "We need to get you some doct'rin' for your shoulder." He tugged her toward the posse. "And after we do that, I've got to go find Elmer Williams."

She stopped him with a hand to his arm. "Find Elmer Williams?"

"Casper left him for dead by the river."

She tightened her grip on his arm, searching his face. "Go find Elmer, Jeremiah. The posse can see me home."

"Ava." He shook his head. "I can't leave you after all this."

"There's been enough death." Her voice broke and she searched his familiar face. "If you can save one?"

He brushed his thumb against her cheek, shaking his head in response.

She held his gaze, gripping the sliver of courage, of awareness growing in her mind. "I'll be all right. You and Wolf have the best chance at findin' Elmer the fastest, and you know it."

He studied her, searching her eyes, touching her cheek, and finally sighed, as if in resignation. "I'll ask a couple of the detectives to come with me."

She blinked from the tears in her vision and buried her face in his shoulder again, reveling in the feel of him.

"Oh Jeremiah, I bring so much trouble with me. How on earth could you want to marry me?"

He pulled back and took her chin in his hand. "I knew you were trouble the first time you looked over at me in school and said, 'Ain't you never learnt to spell?'"

She winced at his words, but he slid his hand down her arm, holding her close. "I knew right then I wanted to be a part of any trouble, as long as it was with you." He searched her face, so tenderly, so loving. How could he look at her that way? She shook her head, dislodging a few tears.

"You havin' second thoughts?"

"Second thoughts?" A soft laugh burst out of her. "Why on earth would *I* ever have second thoughts of marryin' *you*? Look what you've done. You've survived bein' shot, scoured the woods in search of me, risked your life to find me. I—"

"Ava, I don't want you to marry me because you think I rescued you, 'cause from what I see, you were doin' a fine job of takin' care of yourself for most of the time." His brows crinkled, his frown deepening. "I want you to marry me because nobody else in the whole world will do for you."

Oh, how she loved him. His kindness and quiet strength. His humor and tenderness. His protectiveness and country charm. Her smile quivered ever so slightly and she stepped closer to him. "Jeremiah Sutphin, nobody else in the whole world will do for me but you."

His grin split wide and he brushed her hair back from her face. "That's good to hear, Ava Burcham."

The posse's voices invaded their conversation, and Jeremiah stepped back, holding her gaze as he did. "Go on with them, Ava. They'll get you home."

As one of the men helped her onto a horse, her wounded arm throbbing from the effort, Ava overheard Jeremiah discuss his plans with one of the detectives. A few separated from the group and started following Jeremiah back down the trail, Wolf trotting at his side. "I'll be at Granny's," she called. "I'll be waiting at Granny's."

His grin crooked and he doffed his cap before disappearing into the shadows of the forest path.

"We're going to need to get your testimony, Miss Burcham." A detective tapped his hat in her direction. "And I'd imagine the newspapers will be hungry for the details." He looked back down the trail where Jeremiah had disappeared. "Sounds like quite a story."

"Yes, sir." She followed the detective's gaze and allowed a sigh to relax her weary body. "It *is* quite a story."

Chapter Twenty-Four

*Ain't nothin' quite like a happy ending to make you feel like spring
and Christmas is happenin' at the same time.*
Granny Burcham

After arriving at the Temples' long after dark, having her shoulder wound treated, and enjoying a warmed-up meal of beef and potatoes, Ava barely kept her eyes open to wash the filth from her skin before she slipped into bed.

By the time she came down to the alterations shop the next morning, midday light shone through the windows and a crowd had gathered awaiting Ava's arrival. Folks from all over Fancy Gap piled into the little shop, bombarding Ava with questions about the shooting, her kidnapping, and what became of Keen Gentry. Mrs. Temple finally ushered out the last curious neighbor late in the evening, and Ava disappeared back to her room, her mind whirring with the events of the past few days, her exhausted body still recovering.

Settling down in her desk chair, she loaded a piece of paper into her typewriter and closed her eyes. Whispers of a prayer moved across her mind, weaving in and out through the scenes of her life. Everything converged in the past few days. Her past and her present. A tie to the loose end of her father's death. Jeremiah's presence and pursuit of her. The resilience God had forged within her through years of rising above her past. How had she ever believed that He'd abandoned her?

She smiled down at the blank sheet of paper waiting to be filled with a story. *Her* story.

God had been with her in every moment. Calming her mind as she was held captive, giving her ways to leave clues behind for help, bringing rescuers her way in the most unlikely ways...and now, allowing her an opportunity to express all that had happened to her in the way she loved best. Through words.

The story moved from her thoughts through her fingers to the paper, slowly, as she sorted out the keys. The fresh details poured from her, running from the courthouse, the blurry moments after she awakened in the wagon, fragment by fragment emerging into an accounting of what she'd experienced, only leaving out her encounter with Sid and Wesley.

When she typed the last sentence, tears dampened her face. A weight somehow transferred from her heart to those words, and she realized *this* was her gift. Her calling. Finding truth and hope in the middle of real-life stories.

With a little note, she sent the papers via Mrs. Temple to town the next day and then rode her mule over the familiar trail to her granny's. She paused in her ride when she came to the fork in the road which led to Jeremiah's house. A shiver slipped up her arms at the memories of her time there.

No, she wasn't ready to travel there on her own.

Granny welcomed her with open arms, slowly pulling from her the entire tale and carefully applying some of her homemade ointments to Ava's wounds. As Ava shared the worst of her memories of the events, and Granny asked gentle questions to clarify, they finished beading Ava's wedding dress. Somehow, the simple action in the presence of her granny's tender care coated the traumatic events with a sense of hope. She'd survived. Remained strong.

God had been with her all the while.

Two days of quiet togetherness followed, without a word from Jeremiah. She knew he had a great deal to work through with Casper's arrest, but she wouldn't have minded one of them newfangled telephones, just to hear from his own lips that he was all right.

But the past two days had been good. Healing. Having the opportunity to bathe in Granny's comfort and common sense, not to mention a few of her own stories for comparison, soothed the edges of the memories with a bigger reminder of God's love. The same message He'd been sending her since she'd written out the events of the kidnapping. . .the same message He'd been showing her for much longer than that.

Except for the one interruption of their solitude, when the

Baldwin-Felts agents searched Granny's house and property without cause and without a warrant, Ava relished the rest afforded by the solitude in Granny's location. The hills brought a bud-scented breeze to fill her lungs and usher in the new day.

She'd finished up her dress hours ago, even worked a little on a story from Granny's childhood she'd wanted to write, but her thoughts kept traveling back to the window. He'd come soon. Orange hues from the late afternoon sun warmed the small room with a happy light, and birdsong ushered in the waning of the day.

As if drawn by some invisible thread, she walked to the window and glanced out over the forest, golden treetops leading to a blue-mountain horizon. She'd not seen Jeremiah since they parted in the forest. She missed him. A few minutes of talking in the forest had not been enough to make up for the hours of wondering if he was alive.

She leaned her forehead against the windowpane, closing her eyes and embracing the beautiful memories. Life always afforded a choice. Jeremiah had shown her that. She could focus on the losses and pain, allowing those dark thoughts to color the filter of every other scene in her life, or she could choose thankfulness, gratitude, and the belief that God touched it all with hope—held it all—and never took His attention away from her.

She chose hope.

The sound of hoofbeats drew her attention to the mountain trail. Between the pink frame of newly budding redbuds, a lone rider came into view, a gray dog leading the way. Her breath weakened and she gripped the window frame, squinting into the sun's glow.

Without another hesitation, she rushed out the front door to the porch railing, watching his steady approach. He raised his head, his grin brimming beneath the shadow of his fedora, welcome gaze holding hers as he closed in. Oh, how she loved that man.

"It's about time you decided to show up, Mr. Sutphin."

He slid from his horse and stared up at her in such a way her heart tripped into a gallop. "You're awful bossy, you know that?"

Her attention never strayed from his as he took his time climbing the porch steps and breaching the space between them. "Don't you try to distract me with your sweet talk."

He stepped forward, one hand removing his hat, the other slipping around her waist and stealing her breath. "Then what if we don't talk at all?" He captured her lips with his, slow, careful, wordlessly saying all the things they'd missed over the past few days apart.

Her fingers twisted into the folds of his jacket, every lingering touch a reminder that they survived, together. They'd been granted a precious opportunity to savor. His mouth gentled against hers, tender as his words, and she slipped her right hand up around his neck, sliding her fingers into his hair. Her left arm still ached from the wound, but she didn't really feel it at the moment. Every particle of her focus found a wonderful reprieve in his kiss.

He lowered his forehead to hers, slipping his hand down her braid. "How are you feeling?"

"Better now." She caressed his cheek where tiny scratches marked his journey through the forest to find her. "Much better now."

He leaned down and claimed her lips again. "Yep, me too."

"What all's happened? What's the news about Casper?"

He braided his fingers through hers and sighed back against the porch railing, his smile slipping from his face. "Trial is next week, but he don't have much of a chance. With Mooney and Elmer's testimonies, plus mine, yours, Ellis's, and Pink's, the truth is stacked against him."

"And Elmer?"

"We got him back to town." His palm smoothed down her arm. "We almost lost him on the trip, but the Doc said Elmer's too ornery to die."

She chuckled, slipping close enough to rest her cheek against his chest. He draped his arm around her, wrapping her in his leather scent, and everything slowed into a wonderful sense of belonging, of safety. Home. "Maybe this'll take some of the attention away from the whole Allen mess."

He offered a humorless chuckle and reached into his jacket to pull out a newspaper. "I don't think anyone's gonna pay attention to our little trouble with Casper Norris when the whole world's focused on the Allen outlaws and their attack on the court."

"What are you talkin' about?"

He handed her the newspaper, shaking his head. "There are reprints in here from all over the nation. Richmond, Chicago. Even New York City."

She opened the paper to the front page and stared at the headline. MANHUNT FOR THE MOUNTAIN OUTLAWS OF COURTHOUSE MASSACRE. "Chicago? New York City?"

"And the town is nearly spillin' over with outsiders from all over, mostly reporters, tryin' to get their next big story about the lawless mountain men and their uneducated ways."

"Uneducated? Half the Allens went to Fairview Academy. Sid's been all over the world, and Claude studied business in Greensboro." She reread the headline and first few sentences of the article, espousing the rugged and savage ways of the mountain people. "Why on earth would people from New York City care about what happened down here in our little town?"

"I don't know, but I think it may have a little somethin' to do with those detectives and their pleasure in getting their pictures made for the papers." He rolled his eyes. "And some of the stories they've told." He tapped the page. "Near catches of the Allen clan? Wild shoot-outs in the woods? Never happened."

She'd tell him about her little encounter with the Allens later. When they had a long evening of being together and time to unravel the full story of the last few days. Not now. Not when finding each other brought its own sweet reward. "Well, I've learned my lesson about writing truth over sensationalism, and I've decided I'm going to take the advice of a very wonderful friend of mine."

"Zat so?" He tugged her back toward him, his eyes lighting with an unleashed smile. "And what did this wonderful friend advise?"

"Write the truth through story." She slipped her good arm around his waist. "Bring hope."

"Smart friend." He winked. "Speakin' of writin' hope." He tugged an envelope from the pocket of his shirt and offered it to her.

"You're just full of gifts today, ain'tcha?"

"Special people and all that."

Warmth zoomed into her cheeks and she rose on tiptoe to kiss him. He didn't seem to mind, because he kissed her right back. . .and then some.

"And what would this be?" She slipped open the flap of the envelope to reveal a ten-dollar note. "Ten dollars?"

"Seems the newspaper liked your article and wants to publish it as a three-part serial."

"Are you joshin' me?"

He shook his head, grin brimming. "Not one bit, Miss Burcham."

"But I just wrote the story of what happened and tried to share some of the good from it. Some of the hope."

"Maybe that's what people need most." He tugged on her braid again, and she tapped him with the newspaper.

"So, they're going to publish it under my own name?"

"Well, that all depends." He raised a brow, leaning close to her, his pale eyes glimmering with mischief. "About the whole name thing."

"The name thing?"

"I have a preference for Ava Sutphin, personally."

She leaned back into him, snuggling close. "Well, that does have a mighty fine ring to it, but at present it sounds a little like sensationalism, and I've promised my friend to write the truth."

"Well, we definitely want you writin' the truth. So that brings me to an idea." He narrowed his eyes and examined her face. "What do you say we take some of that mighty fine trouble of yours and find a preacher?"

"Tonight?" Her question burst out on a laugh.

"Mmhmm." He nuzzled a kiss against her neck, and her body nearly melted onto the aged oak floor. "We're already three days past due, and I ain't interested in holdin' off anymore."

"He's sure to be in bed by the time we get there." Her breath shuddered at the tingles he left down the side of her neck.

Jeremiah raised his head. "Come on now, Ava. I think we've earned a little rebel-rousin' for a good cause, don't you?"

Her grin split wide in answer, and he grabbed her hand. "Now, let's see if your granny's buggy is still in workin' order, because I'm sure she's not gonna want to miss this."

"Wait just one second." Ava stopped him with a palm to his chest.

"I have a dress I aim to wear, and I'd rather you not see me in it all the way to the preacher's house."

"All right." His shoulders slumped forward and he sighed. "We can wait till tomorrow, then."

"Or. . ." She squeezed his hand, an idea forming that would not only give her the chance to arrive as a bride but also recreate new memories at Jeremiah's house. Memories to overshadow the ones from the past few days. "You can hitch up your horse to the buggy and ride my mule on to the preacher's, then. . .Granny and I will meet you at your house, 'cause I think havin' a wedding on that porch at sunset might be one of the best things ever."

His laugh grew loud enough to bring Granny from the kitchen. "What kind o' party are we havin' out here, you two?"

Jeremiah ran to Granny and pulled her into his arms. "Why, Granny Burcham, we're gonna have a wedding party!"

"You crazy young'un." She swatted at him, her chuckle joining in with theirs. "Well, it's about time, and I have a stack cake just waitin' for some festivity like this."

⤨

Jeremiah thought he'd never seen anything as beautiful as Ava Burcham stepping out on the sunset-lit porch dressed in a white lace gown, her hair twisted up into dozens of white ribbons like a halo against her wavy, walnut-colored hair. He was glad he'd stopped in to alert Ellis and Jennie of his last-minute nuptials, because having family witness this moment, even if he didn't have much family left, made the simple ceremony even sweeter.

Reverend Marshall hadn't been too disgruntled by the request. After the harrowing events of the past few days, the reverend extended some good-natured long-suffering and hitched up his horse to follow Jeremiah without much complaint.

The wedding didn't last long. Granny Burcham recommended singing the hymn "How Firm a Foundation," accompanied by Ellis on his fiddle. The evening breeze turned cold but brought with it the scent of redbud and the song of the katydids, as the world moved on beyond the dark memories of recent days.

Jeremiah looked down at his hands entwined with his bride's, her wrists still raw from rope burns, and as he spoke the same vows couples for generations before had spoken, he slid the simple pearl ring onto Ava's finger.

Her bottom lip dropped and those marble-like eyes swam with a glossy glow. Haloed in sunset hues, he'd never seen anything as lovely in all his days.

"You are blood of my blood, and bone of my bone. I give you my body, that we two might be one. I give you my heart to beat for you alone. I give you my spirit, till our life shall be done. Before God and this company I pledge you my troth."

Tears streamed down her cheeks as she spoke the vows with the preacher's guidance, her fingers squeezing his as she finished each sentence, as if to add punctuation to her promise. He tried to memorize every feature—each fleck of gold in her eyes, each hue of rose in her cheeks. It seemed he'd loved her his whole life.

And then, the reverend announced them husband and wife.

The little party applauded and moved inside the house to enjoy their simple celebration of fiddle music and stack cake. Jeremiah had delivered a few provisions before visiting Granny Burcham's earlier in the day, hoping Ava might agree to his plan to wed straightaway, and it had given him time to remove any remnants of her captivity in the house. The broken furniture. The empty cans. Even the scent of tobacco, he'd replaced with a few store-bought flowers.

They enjoyed some delicious cider provided by the reverend and some dancing accompanied by Ellis, with Wolf trying to join in on a few occasions. It may not have been what either he or Ava originally planned, but something about finding her after almost losing her. . . after all they'd experienced. . .made the simplicity and tenderness of the evening spill over him with gentle, hopeful peace. They belonged to each other.

Before too late, each guest found their way to the door, bidding their blessings and goodnights. Ellis and Jennie offered to take Granny Burcham home, and the good reverend procured the signature of all the witnesses, took an extra piece of stack cake, and went on his way just as the moon rose to its highest perch in the night sky.

The scent of stack cake and cider lingered on the air in the quiet.

As Jeremiah turned from bolting the door, he caught sight of Ava standing by the window, looking down at her ring, her profile bathed in moonlight. His chest squeezed with a fierce love, an irrepressible happiness. With slow steps, he came up behind her and wrapped his arms around her, the soft scent of rosemary mingled with mint in his senses.

"I'm glad you like that ring."

"I do." She sniffled. "It's the most beautiful thing I've ever owned."

He grinned and pressed his face into her ribbon-wreathed hair. "The pearl was my mama's. She would have wanted you to have it."

Ava leaned back against his chest. "I like knowing such a sweet mama's gift belongs to me. Both the ring. . ." She turned and looked up at him. "And her boy."

He lowered his mouth to hers, offering a lingering kiss more intimate than the ones he'd given before. She turned into his arms, allowing him easier access. When he pulled back, she stared up at him in a beautiful and smiling daze.

"I'm quite fond of kissing you, Jeremiah Sutphin."

"That's mighty convenient, Ava Sutphin, 'cause I feel the same way about kissing you." He slid his palm down her arm to link his fingers through hers and gave her a little tug. "I want to show you somethin'."

She squinted up at him but didn't respond, merely let him lead her up the stairs where the rooms weren't complete, except one. With a turn of the door latch, he drew her inside a small, freshly finished room. Bookshelves lined one wall, and a large window took up most of another wall. A delicate, hand-carved desk stood in front of the window with a matching chair fitted beneath.

"What is this?"

"It's for you." He waved toward the space. "To write. To read." He gestured toward the bookshelves. "When I have enough saved to buy a cushioned chair, I'll place it right—"

She rushed into his arms. "Oh Jeremiah, I love it." She stepped back and looked around the room, her palm going to her chest. "It's more than I could have ever dreamed."

She proceeded to show her gratitude till the situation became serious and more comfortable surroundings necessary. If she rewarded him in kisses on a regular basis, he'd make sure to find a way to keep building all sorts of things.

He guided her down the steps and down the hallway to their room, turning down the lanterns as he went. When they reached the bedroom, he nudged Wolf out into the hall with a gesture toward the fireplace rug. The dog tilted his head to one side and yawned, evidently too tired from the events of the day to argue.

Jeremiah still had way too much on his mind for sleep.

He stepped toward his bride as she stood in the middle of their room, looking a little like she wasn't sure what to do next. He grinned. Well, he knew exactly what he wanted to do next. He'd been waiting for this moment for years. In fact, he'd been working up a whole list for weeks, and he felt pretty certain Ava wouldn't mind a bit.

"Ava, may I . . ." He skimmed his fingers along her temples, searching her eyes, her face—overwhelmed. "May I take down your hair?"

Her brows rose, she hesitated, and then she guided his hand to a braided ribbon by her temple, turning to give him ready access to her wealth of hair. With gentle motions, he untwisted each white ribbon, slowly released strand after strand until her hair tumbled over her shoulders in waves of silky brown. Her chest pulsed with her breaths at the same rhythm as his, the intimate act adding a thick warmth to the room.

"You're beautiful."

She lowered her gaze, a lovely blush deepening her cheeks. He took her hands in his and raised them to his lips. Turning over each wrist, he grazed his lips across the raw skin. Her gasp encouraged his tender continuance up her arm to where her sleeve stopped at the elbow.

Her shallow breaths brushed against his face as he straightened and cradled her cheeks with his palms.

"You are blood of my blood and bone of my bone," he whispered, pressing a kiss to her waiting lips. "I give you my heart to beat for you alone."

"I give you my body that we two may be one," she whispered,

looking up at him, haloed by her hair, her eyes searching his. "I love you, Jeremiah." Her breath hitched ever so slightly and she pressed closer to him. "We are my favorite story, and I'm so glad I can keep living it, troubles and joys, with you."

Historical Note

This story was particularly special to me because it takes place in my hometown of Carroll County, Virginia. From the time I was a little girl and our family would drive past an old, Queen Anne style house sitting in disrepair on the side of the road in Fancy Gap, I heard the story of "The Courthouse Tragedy" or "The Courthouse Massacre." The true events, which took place in 1912, brought the little town of Hillsville to national prominence and, to this day, is the largest manhunt the state has on record.

It's tricky writing about something that takes place in the same community in which one lived *and* about a topic that still holds a great deal of controversy over a hundred years later. Many of the descendants of people involved in The Courthouse Tragedy still live in the county. . .and still care about how their "side" is understood. Within the true story, it's difficult to find any one hero or villain. Too many mixed narratives passed down through the years have muddled the already murky details of the story. Loyalty and human pride likely discolored the memories and testimonies of many in order to spin their own version or to protect their kin. To this day, *no one* knows who fired the first shot in the courthouse, so I wanted to keep that part vague as well. There has been lots of speculation, but nothing for certain.

It was my hope to invite the reader into the world of Appalachia and to tell a fiction story inspired by true events and shaped by a love for my culture and the history of Carroll County. Unlike my fictional couple, Jeremiah and Ava, the true story of The Courthouse Tragedy ended as a tragedy.

First off, let's talk about the characters in this story who were created from my wild imagination just for the purpose of *The Red Ribbon*. Jeremiah Sutphin and Ava Burcham took center stage, but they were joined by Granny Burcham, Elmer Williams, Ellis and Jennie, the Combs family, the Creeds, Casper Norris, Keen Gentry, Mooney, Martin, the Daniels, and Mr. and Mrs. Temple, plus some minor roles.

Here is a list of the historical characters and a little about their fates after The Courthouse Tragedy:

Dexter Goad became a loud voice in the murder and conspiracy case against the Allen family. (There were forty-eight indictments against the various Allen folks.) He remained an active member of Carroll County politics and passed his love for his position and his town down to his family. His great-grandnephew was sworn in as Carroll County's clerk of circuit court in 2015, carrying on the family tradition. Dexter Goad's celebrity status after the shoot-out garnered him a great deal of newspaper presence. He died of a heart attack in 1939.

Pink Samuels left Carroll County shortly after the courthouse shoot-out and moved to the Richmond, Virginia, area. He died some time around the World War II era.

Sidna Edwards got tired of hiding out and turned himself in to the detectives on March 22nd. Some say his mother convinced him to surrender. He decided to accept a plea bargain and was found guilty of second-degree murder and given eighteen years in prison. He was pardoned in 1923 and went to live with his mother, who had moved to Richmond to be near her boys who were both in the prison there. He reportedly married and lived in Norfolk until his death some time before 1937.

Wesley Edwards (along with his uncle Sid Allen) remained in the woods around Carroll County in hiding for over a week before leaving the state and heading to Des Moines, Iowa. There, they took assumed names and began working jobs. It was only after Wesley went back home to Carroll to visit his sweetheart, Maude Iroler, and ensure she'd marry him that one of the few detectives still on the hunt befriended her and learned about the planned elopement. The detectives went with Maude on the train to Des Moines and there found Wesley and Sid, who both went with the detectives without a struggle. Wesley refused a plea bargain and was given twenty-seven years in prison. He was remembered as a "model prisoner" and was pardoned in 1926, at which time he went to live with his mother and brother in Richmond. Last records of him were that he had married, operated a filling station in Henrico County, and died of influenza in 1939.

Victor Allen was tried and found not guilty. His quiet, gentle demeanor appeared to win over folks from all over the country and may have helped with a shift in public opinion about the Allens as "lawless, murderous outlaws." While he was in jail for four months awaiting trial, his wife gave birth to his fourth child, a little girl, that his wife named Claudia. . .likely in honor of Victor's brother who'd been found guilty of first-degree murder. In 1921, Victor and his family and his mother moved to New Jersey to escape the memories of all that had happened during and after the courthouse shoot-out.

After the manhunt detailed above in Wesley Edwards's description, **Sid Allen** was found guilty of murder and sentenced to thirty-five years. He lost all his property and the beautiful house he'd only lived in for about a year. He was a model prisoner and began making intricate woodcrafts while in prison. He was pardoned in 1926, after fourteen years in prison, and moved with his wife to Eden, North Carolina. He died in 1941 and was described as many to have been a mild-mannered, polite, and soft-spoken man. It is the belief of some researchers that while in prison, Sid gave his life over to Christ.

Claude Allen hid near his home (mostly around Sugarloaf Mountain) for seven days, receiving food from relatives and friends. He was captured about 3½ miles from his house with two guns, eighty-four dollars, cigarettes, plenty of rations, and two quilts. He was tried three times for the murder of three different people in the shoot-out. In the first two cases he received second-degree murder charges, but in the third he finally received the death blow of a first degree. It seemed as if the prosecution wouldn't rest until they'd found the young man guilty of first-degree murder. Claude stated that he only tried to protect his father after the shooting started. Claude's sweetheart, Nellie Wisler, was a local teacher and determined advocate for him. She wrote eloquent letters (along with thousands of letters from people all over the county) requesting clemency be granted to Claude, in light of new evidence which would have benefited both Claude and Floyd Allen's fates. Unfortunately, none of this came in time to save him, and Claude Allen was executed in the Richmond Penitentiary by electric chair on March 28, 1913. The account of his last few months of life is heartbreaking, but he met his fate like a gentleman and someone sure of his eternal future.

Floyd Allen pled self-defense and was found guilty of first-degree murder. Both his and Claude's final statements before execution are poignant and interesting peeks into the last moments of a person's life. It was clear that Floyd felt deeply the injustice he perceived happened to him and agonized that his son Claude had to bear the brunt of the conviction as well. He died in the electric chair on March 28, 1913.

When reading about these types of events, it is easy to feel a sense of hopelessness and cry out at the injustices in the world, but as Christians, we are not people without hope and truth. In a fallen world, broken things happen, but Christ came to mend the brokenhearted and raise up those who have fallen. Thankfully, there is no tragedy too great for His love to surpass, heal, and restore. . .even in stories that reveal the most base and heartless in the world. As Christians, we live for another world and embrace the knowledge that God is still working in all things—and we look forward to a time when every story will have a happy ending because of the beautiful work of Christ and the hope of heaven.